How had she ended up in a place like this?

When he'd moved back to England after his uncle's death, the first thing he'd done was look for her. That had to be some five years ago. His sources had said she was still married to that lowly baron with an estate up north. Perhaps Griffin had given up his search too easily.

Griffin turned away from the scene and looked for the man who had escorted them up to this section of the palace. Griffin had made his selection. He'd had to pull himself through a long path of self-destruction to make it to this point. Was this some sick ironic award for moral behavior? It didn't matter. It was what it was. After all these years, she was finally going to be his.

The
Surrender
of a Lady

TIFFANY CLARE

St. Martin's Paperbacks

This is a work of fiction. All of the characters, organizations, and events portrayed in this novel are either products of the author's imagination or are used fictitiously.

THE SURRENDER OF A LADY

Copyright © 2010 by Tiffany Clare.
Excerpt from *The Seduction of His Wife* copyright © 2010 by Tiffany Clare.

For information address St. Martin's Press, 175 Fifth Avenue, New York, NY 10010.

ISBN: 978-0-312-37211-8

Printed in the United States of America

St. Martin's Paperbacks edition / October 2010

St. Martin's Paperbacks are published by St. Martin's Press, 175 Fifth Avenue, New York, NY 10010.

10 9 8 7 6 5 4 3 2 1

This book is dedicated to Ely, my dearest friend
and sister in all things but blood.

ACKNOWLEDGMENTS

Without the love and support of my husband and children, I never would have found the time to write this book. "I love you" doesn't even cover it.

A heartfelt thank you to my critique partners, Elyssa Papa, Kristina Coi and Maggie Robinson, who have cheered me on since the crazy idea of a sad, heart-torn slave woman with her jangling kuchi bells first appeared in my mind's eye.

Anna Campbell, you pushed me to the next step and your words of wisdom will always stay with me. There is no pussyfooting around between us! Trisha Catton, Marnee, Seton, Tessa—you all offered me great insight and were part of the shaping of this book; never forget I couldn't have done it without you.

Helen, I can't thank you enough for taking a chance on the unknown and for believing in me. Thank you to my editor, Monique, for stating up front that you are my biggest fan, and Holly for answering my million-and-one questions. A very special thank you goes to the art department for the most beautiful cover I have ever laid eyes upon!

PART ONE

CHAPTER ONE

Slave Trader

1841
Constantinople

"What do you mean, you'll work this out? You've gambled me away! I'm your wife, for heaven's sake!"

"Elena, please. Calm yourself. I'll think of something."

Did he really think to placate her after such a proclamation? She was entitled to more than a fit of rage right now. She was livid. "It's a little late for alternatives."

With her hand clutched over her chest, Elena felt the frantic beating of her heart beneath her thin nightgown. She was desperate to calm it and her nerves; otherwise she'd never think this through rationally. What he said couldn't be true. It was outrageous and too despicable to contemplate. A sickening sense of fear had her itching to crawl through the floor.

Two eunuchs flanked her husband. One was pure ebony, with a wide, firm frame common to the palace eunuchs, and a severe, menacing posture that terrified the wits out of her. The bitter fear made her want to retreat to the other side of the room. Out of his reach. The other was shorter and fatter, with a round, pockmarked face and a red sash about his waist that accentuated his girth. Whenever he spoke to her husband, she caught a glimpse of gold teeth behind his anger-thinned lips. The sight made her quiver in disgust.

Both projected an air of command. They wore traditional caftans, and their forearms bore large gold cuffs, their fists were loose at their sides. One couldn't mistake their intent. Nor did their poised outward appearance fool her; they would not be stopped from collecting payment. It was just a matter of sorting out *what* that payment was.

"Tell them to leave, Robert. We will think of something." They would leave Constantinople to escape what her husband had done. Start afresh, just as they'd done last year. This place was supposed to have been their refuge. A place where their son could grow up without being looked down upon by society because of his father's recklessness.

Foolish of her to think Robert had changed. He never did the decent thing by his family. How had she been duped into believing he'd mend his bad habits after all these years?

"I'm afraid it's not so easy as that."

She knew he played at being calm with those men hovering around. They were almost enough to frighten her into silence. But she knew her husband wouldn't defend her, he never had. Not from the first moment he'd set his sights on her.

She swallowed back the fear closing in around her and stilled her shaking hands by clasping them together. She needed to remain strong, to remember that Robert was a betraying swine. If she focused on that thought, she might be able to talk her way out of this.

She would not be the bargaining chip for his gambling debts.

Tilting her chin up, she looked down her nose at her husband. "I refuse to go."

Yet she knew in her heart that payment had been made in the form of one young, nubile wife, not yet six months from the birthing bed. She began to believe these men wouldn't leave without her, but what did they plan to do with her, a woman still showing the signs of childbearing? Did they fancy such sport as she? She was no pale-skinned odalisque.

There had to be a solution, something to stall them. She just didn't know what would work.

The back of her knees hit the worn damask settee. She sat with a thump, fingers worrying a small tear on the edge of the seat. If one looked around the room it was more than obvious money was not abundant in this household. The floral printed paper on the walls was peeling in many places, the carpets underfoot pitiable, threadbare. The furniture, scratched and dented over the years, looked as worn out as she felt. Even the china didn't match. Anyone who came into their home knew immediately the impoverished state they lived in.

It was unlikely the eunuchs could be convinced with promise for payment. But there must be a way to bribe them.

The maidservant had heard the commotion and came in looking askance at her. Elena knew she wasn't here for her sake, though. Everyone in the household would want to know if their wages would be paid, as her husband kept promising. Now they would all know Robert had gambled away what little money remained. It was no secret that the servants had been collecting bets on the span of her husband's life. Robert played a dangerous game. He was a foreigner here and easily swindled out of their pittance. This wasn't calm and proper England but a hostile land with hostile natives.

The smaller man said something in Turkish to her husband. She wasn't used to the language and only recognized smatterings. None of what they said made sense. Robert ran a hand through his hair, his words careful as he asked them in his most authoritative voice—sorely lacking a tone of command since the devolution of their old life—to leave his home.

The one who had spoken shook his head and placed his hand on his hip, perilously close to the bloodred handle of his scimitar. An ominous sign.

Elena swallowed what little saliva she had and watched her husband's Adam's apple bob. The eunuchs weren't moving. Robert's only reaction was to clench his jaw and take a step away from them—clearly done arguing on her behalf. Giving up on her so easily.

It shouldn't surprise her. Still, she fought tears of sadness for how little she meant to the man who had shared the last five years with her. It didn't matter any longer that he'd secured their marriage through deception, cornering her in Lady Aberney's study, approaching her with a wicked gleam in his eye. She had been won, so fun in the chase was lost after that night.

The silent guard looked to her. Elena stared him in the eye, unwilling to cower before eunuchs who on further assessment could only be slave traders, not palace guards.

She was safe in her own home. She had to be. She would *not* leave. She made that resolve clear as she looked at him. But it was lost. The eunuch's eyes held no expression. No pity, no sympathy for what her husband had done. Those were the empty, soulless eyes of a man who had seen and lived a hard mercenary life in a world with too many cruelties to keep a compassionate heart for those less fortunate—she being the less fortunate.

She was a noblewoman. They couldn't possibly mean to take her! How could they take her away from her baby?

Forcing her gaze away from the eunuch, she glared at her husband. "What of the silver, Robert?" There were candlesticks that could be melted down, some cutlery, too. Was that enough to send these ruffians on their way?

Robert stepped toward her. Looking to the maidservant, he jerked his head in a violent fashion that had the woman leaving the room posthaste. Elena could imagine the maid's whispered words to the rest of the serving staff. Would they stay on after this? She really didn't care. She needed to sort all this nonsense out so she could hold her son. She would fix this. She always fixed her husband's blunders.

He stood before her, looking down but not meeting her gaze. One hand grasped her shoulder; he gave it the smallest squeeze in reassurance. It was lost in the gravity of the situation. "Listen to me, Elena. I've had a bad turn of luck—"

She snapped her head to the side as though struck by his words and glowered. He found some courage to look her in the eye when she let out a hiss of air between her teeth.

"You've always had a bad turn, Robert! You promised me you wouldn't fall into old habits!" She pounded her palm against the seat. "You promised me a new life when our son was born." Her fingers clutched the edge of the settee, grasping for any sort of balance to her lopsided, unfair life.

"I know. And I did keep that promise, Elena. I restricted my outings to a gentleman's establishment. Ali Admen came in for a round of loo with a mutual friend, so I agreed to sit for a hand. I was doing well and stayed on at the table. A little blunt would have not been remiss." He shook his head as though recalling the exact moment of his downfall. "Before I knew it, luck wasn't about me."

She took a deep breath. She must remain calm. Even though the voice in her mind screamed for her to get out of here. As fast as possible. A dread was building in her blood that she would be taken away from her son. God knew what else they'd do to her. Bile rose in her throat. She closed her eyes, breathed in deeply through her nose and out through her mouth. She clenched her hands so tightly into the seat she thought she'd tear right through the material.

"You *always* lose," she said between gritted teeth. "I will *not* go with them."

I will take my son and head back to England the moment you turn your back, you swine.

"Elena . . ."

"I mean it, Robert. They'll have to drag me out of here." Her voice caught on those words, and she had to force out the next, "I *refuse* to go anywhere."

Eyes flooding with angry tears, she *really* looked at the man who was supposed to be her husband. How could he do this and without so much as a shrug? Was she so worthless?

"Please, Elena." Again his hand swept through his hair, never a good sign when his agitation got the better of him. "I'll talk to Ali Admen's man of affairs tomorrow. We'll work out another arrangement. We cannot afford—"

"No! You disgust me, Robert. What made you think you made a morally sound judgment wagering your own wife for a hand of cards? How dare you! I will not leave. This is my home. In case you've forgotten, our son needs us. He needs *me*." She pressed her clenched fist to her heart, voice breaking on a sob. "You would take away his mother?"

Elena trained her eyes on the larger and quieter of the eunuchs. His expression held nothing useful for her. She stared into those mud-brown eyes and wondered how to mend this before falling into the snare of those deep wells.

The sound of the baby crying had her on her feet and at the door in a trice.

This was her chance. She'd leave Constantinople and never look back.

"Elena—"

She glanced sidelong at Robert, hand already around the door latch, her heart tripping faster than ever as she looked at her husband for the last time. She had to leave here as quickly as her feet could carry her.

"If you think for one moment I'll let Jonathan cry through your good-for-nothing *negotiations*, you're mistaken. You can take my place in their slave quarters until you fix this! I'll be with the baby, should you come to your senses and wish to make amends."

One of the eunuchs grasped the base of her neck, and spun her painfully around. As he pushed her to the closed door, all the air whooshed from her lungs. Her shoulder ached from its impact against the molding. She refused to cry out her pain and bit her lip till she thought it would bleed.

Realization dawned as she tried to dislodge his hand unsuccessfully; he could snap her just like this. Hopefully, she was worth more alive than dead. His hand was unrelenting, and with his weight behind it, it proved almost impossible to drag any air into her lungs.

She tried to squirm out of his grasp. She brought her hands up to his chest to push him away but his grip tightened, his body pressing hard and heavily into her, rendering her powerless to move. Deep down, she knew there was never a hope for escape. Why she attempted it, she didn't know. Foolish bravery, perhaps.

No. She attempted it for her son. *Her son. God, what would happen to her son?*

A thin knife rasped against her flesh and jabbed into the vein that beat a furious tempo above the eunuch's thumb. It was the only thing to stop her from pushing at him again. Nothing more than the threat of the sharp tip held her down, the still weight of an ox standing behind that deadly pinprick. Her hands dropped to her side in defeat.

If she were dead, she wouldn't be able to help her son.

The eunuch loosened his grip. From her peripheral vision she saw his other hand swoop down toward her temple. She ducked the blow too late.

"She'll fetch a pretty price. She has nice form. Skin's tight and free of blemish."

The tall, thin Englishman was the one who spoke, his spectacles resting on the end of his nose as he pinched various parts of her flesh in his inspection. His touch was light but no less invasive than some of the crueler handlings she'd had over the days. It angered her that he talked as though she were a fine piece of horseflesh and not a human being.

This was the same man who'd looked her over three days ago. The first Englishman she'd seen in this pit worse than any hell imaginable. She'd begged his help then, tried pleading that her being here was a grave misunderstanding. Told him that the life of her baby rested on his goodwill.

He hadn't listened. So Elena said nothing, just bit her lip to still her shaking. She wanted to cry when he prodded at her naked breasts and touched her bare stomach through the tear in her chemise. No sense in crying out. That would earn her another beating. She'd given up begging for help days ago—or was it a week? Time was irrelevant; days leached into night then back into day. No one cared about her here. She was just another slave in their dark, cold gazes.

When she had awoken in this dilapidated warehouse the first thing she noticed was the dingy faded ashen walls. When her head had stopped throbbing she was nauseatingly assaulted with the smell of unwashed human bodies. The stench of excrement and urine so thick in the air it was as though it had sunk into the very foundation of the building. When she breathed through her mouth she tasted that awful, stale reek of dirty human bodies. Better to smell that rotten stench.

Heavy muslin over the large windows stopped the light from reaching its warm rays out to her and blocked fresh air from cleaning out her aching lungs. The slave handlers bound her with thick rope, looping it through a rusted metal collar that tethered her to the wall. She'd been treated like an animal since her arrival. Poked, jabbed, humiliated with their scrutiny and quibbling of a price over her.

She should be happy they hadn't completely forgotten her like some of the other slaves huddled in their own reek and filth. They gave her a grayish sludge they called food once a day. Sometimes there was rice or pilaf, which she'd refused at first. But after a couple days of dire hunger, she'd learned to close her eyes and eat around the cockroaches infesting the food. She pretended the wriggling of their bodies was merely a product of her overactive imagination.

Every man who looked her over had torn more of the meager clothes she wore, all in an effort to see her in the flesh. She tried to cover the exposed parts, but it did her no good. Most of her nightclothes were shredded or gone. All that remained was her undershirt and drawers, soiled from the grime crusted on every surface. They'd even taken her slippers and stockings. Her left heel had blistered something fierce on the first day, when she'd tripped over the chain nailed into the floor.

At first, she'd begged and cried that they spare her some privacy. All to no avail. Having had enough of her antics, the guard had hit her so hard in the stomach she'd fallen over gasping for air. The pain still bothered her, a low persistent ache, but it lessened as the purplish bruises faded to an unsightly green. She had learned her lesson that night. Now she only cried out her misery when the slaves bedded down on the hard earth at night. She didn't beg to be released after that, realizing they might do worse next time. If they did treat her any worse, she might never escape. Not that she knew *how* she would escape.

"Yes, but she's used goods. They don't like their women in *this* state in the high court."

The other man said this and then grasped one of her engorged breasts, squeezing the areola and nipple until milk flowed down her torso. She let out a cry of distress and pain with the release of built-up fluid. Mostly it was a cry against the abject humiliation of being handled in such a fashion. That milk was for her child. Her child that she might never see again.

God, she did not belong here. She could not survive here much longer.

Her whimpers had the slave guard yanking the rope around her neck, forcing her to silence as she was pulled back a step. She wedged her fingers beneath the collar so she could breathe. Her neck probably sported the same bruising displayed on her abdomen. It ached and itched so much from the incessant tugging and sweating through the hot days.

She stood as tall and straight as she could and stared defiantly at the two men. Could they see the hatred in her eyes? The English one looked at her thoughtfully. Assessingly. She didn't like the flicker in his gaze; it looked too much like desire. It repulsed her to be looked upon so lecherously. What did they think to do with her?

Then their words registered. High court. Did they mean to purchase her for the Sultan? She wouldn't co-operate with any of them; she was English, not some slave they could do whatever they pleased with. Though if one were to look upon her now for the first time, they'd see nothing but a dirty, half-naked woman taking on the stink of a chamber pot. Her skin was crusted with dirt. She couldn't even scrape the soil out from under her nails, as much as she tried. Even the beautiful curls of her hair hung limp, greasy and tangled around her like a banshee's wild mane.

She'd been forced into something less honorable than her worth. Made worse because any attempt to stand up for herself would earn her another beating. She didn't think they cared whether she lived or died. It made her want to fight, to scream, to hurt these men who treated a human so low. These men kept her away from her child. She despised them.

The Englishman called over the slave trader, whom she now knew was Ali Admen, the devil her husband had wagered all but his soul to. He sat at a great wooden table conducting a transaction with a Turk. When he rose, he strode toward them on light, silent steps. A trained warrior would walk in this manner, as if on the very air. Silly thought that, but her mind had taken some unusual turns these few days. Bound to happen, being deprived food, water, and any privacy to spare a scrap of her modesty, or her sanity for that matter.

The older man said something in Turkish. She only caught a few words: *private* and *goods*. And those two words were enough to frighten her. She shrank back a small step. The slave handler didn't notice this time, so did not reprimand her with another tug.

She didn't want to be under their scrutiny anymore.

The buyer wanted to look her over. In private. Others had left the main area under force and were taken to the door at the far end of the room—she heard their whimpering, crying, and sometimes their screams. All from no more than a dozen feet away. She didn't want to know what happened in there.

Why didn't one of her servants come and find her? Had her husband still not paid them? Surely one of them would be kind enough to spare her this evil, this life she didn't belong to. Wouldn't they help her for her child's sake? Her husband wasn't coming for her; it would be a servant. Otherwise, Robert would have been here days ago. He was probably lost in his cups watching the horse races, losing more money they didn't have.

What was left to barter? Another human being? Their son? He wouldn't dare.

She closed her eyes and made the slave handler drag her to the room. If she could have done it unscathed, she would have dropped to the ground and clawed her hands into the packed earth in pure defiance. But she didn't. The guard would have no compunctions about strangling her to prove his supremacy, her worthlessness.

Once inside, a cursory glance told her the room was empty. Was this a good or a bad sign? She didn't know. There were no windows to escape through should they leave her alone, just four stark walls with lit oil lamps set into them. The guard led her to a wooden bench and

motioned her to sit with a jab of his finger. She did as
ordered. The guard came around to her side and looped
the rope through a metal ring at the end of the bench.

Was that to prevent her from defending herself? She
wasn't fool enough to think she could escape this place.
She wasn't strong enough. She saw other slaves held
down and beaten for disobedience in their desperate
attempts to flee.

There had to be another way to escape, someone she
could bribe into releasing her. She was desperate. She'd
been away from her baby too long. But she had nothing
of value to offer for her freedom.

The Englishman stepped into the room, saying
something commanding to the guard in Turkish. Then
he looked her directly in the eye. "I've asked him to
leave us in private. Will you behave if you're left un-
chained?" He spoke English.

Elena swallowed hard and stared up at the Englishman's unforgiving stance. She gave a small nod in
agreement. She couldn't run, but she would defend herself with her free hands if he took advantage of her
vulnerability.

The guard turned and left. The Englishman came
forward with no readable emotion on his face.

Fingers prodding into her neck, he looked over the
blisters and scrapes made by the collar. Instinctually,
she jerked away, not wanting to be touched. He moved
gently. She guessed he didn't want to hurt her more
than necessary. Tilting her this way and that, he inspected her cuts and bruises with care. He had her open
her mouth so he could check her teeth, his fingers pushing them to see if they were loose or rotted. Nothing
was left untouched except the private area between
her legs, a small thing to be thankful for. He palmed
her dispassionately, kneading around her aching, heavy

breasts, under her arms, over her stomach, looking closely at the bruising there and pressing into it. She couldn't help but cry out in pain and hunched forward, protecting her belly.

"Bleeding seems to be on the surface," he said. "That's good."

He lifted her bare feet next, almost toppling her from the bench, to examine them toe by toe. Then he stood to inspect her hair, picking through the knots, looking for lice. She held herself inert and closed her eyes against the degradation. She wanted to remain strong. If she fell apart now, what good was she to her son? But her body was sore, stiff, and hurt worse than anything she'd ever experienced.

Her tears fell anyhow.

When he finished, he shuffled back a step and tilted his head to the side in question. "How old are you?"

She didn't answer. Just gave him her most incredulous look through flooded eyes. He had no right to question her, not after she'd begged for his help and made a fool of herself in the process. He had reduced her to an abject slave, throwing herself down at his feet. Begging for the safety of her son, only to be ignored and then punched in the stomach by the guards—who laughed as she cried out for them to stop.

"There are a number of ways we can go about this. So either answer my question, or I'll have you chained to the wall in the slave quarters, where I will inspect you in the public room."

She turned so she could look him in the eye; he was level with her face, one fist planted on the bench beside her thigh. "Four and twenty."

"Old enough"—he pushed off the bench with his fist and walked away from her—"but not too old that this business will grow tiresome and wear your body down."

He said it so bluntly she almost didn't believe the words she heard. *This business.* She had a good estimation what *this business* entailed. And *this business* was not a safe place for her son, nor a place she wanted to be. "Why are you doing this to me? Why won't you help me?"

"I'm not doing anything, dear child. I've looked into your claims. You are who you say. A surprise, really. It's not the first time I've heard such a tale."

"Then why am I still chained here like a wild dog?"

"Because you belong to the slave master of this establishment. And now, I wish to purchase you for my employer."

"I belong to no one."

Oh God, what had happened to her family? Her baby? Please, please let Jonathan be safe.

His lip lifted in an arrogant smirk. What wasn't he telling her? The blood pounded in her ears so loudly she almost didn't hear his next words . . .

"I'm sorry to inform you, madam, but your husband is dead, his properties seized."

She gasped. Though she had never professed to love Robert, he *was* her husband. Helpless to stop fresh tears from flowing, she bowed her head into her hands, her tears washing away the dirt crusted there. *Dead?* How was that possible? He was part of the embassy here; how ludicrous that someone would harm him. No matter his flaws, he was an English gentleman.

But this wasn't England.

He only mentioned her husband. Could her son still live? Every time she opened her mouth to ask, her voice caught on another sob. She swiped the tears away without success.

He went on. "It seems he didn't make it through his negotiations. I know naught of all the gruesome details, nor do I care to. What I do know is his properties, including you, now belong to Ali Admen. You're to be sold to pay off your late husband's vowels."

Was such a thing possible? Would this country trade in the enslavement of English women? She sucked in a breath and put a hand to her chest as she tried to calm herself. The air was hot and thin in this room, making it difficult to breathe. She needed to know about her child. "What of my son?" She was almost afraid to hear the answer.

"Let us discuss our business before the welfare of your babe."

"How can you be so cruel!" She made to stand but the collar caught and jerked her back down to the bench. She clenched her fists in her lap to still the shaking from the rage and fear building throughout her body.

Was her son well? Was he hurt? She needed to know. She needed to be with him. She took a deep breath; it did nothing to calm her tattered nerves.

He ignored her questions. "I'm here to make you an offer. One which will not only better your future, but also save you from a fate far worse than the one you've lived this past week. I should hate to think what *will* happen should you choose to be difficult."

"How could all this come to pass? How dare you do this!"

"Madam, I dare do nothing. Your husband is the sole person responsible for your current circumstance."

Feeling more bravado than she ought, she said, "And why should I take your offer?"

"I daresay mine comes at a prettier and much more advantageous price than you're likely to find in the bowels of this hovel. I can also offer you the safety of your child." His lip tilted upward the minutest amount in a satisfied sneer.

So that was his bargaining chip. Her cooperation might guarantee her son's safety. Could he really help her son? Did he even know the whereabouts of her child? She clenched her jaw and her fists as she stared up at her nemesis or her savior—one and the same at this point. Could she trust him? She was at a grave disadvantage. How was she to know if her son was even alive?

"How can I trust you?" Or anyone for that matter. Her own husband, sworn to protect her, had sold her to this fate.

This might be her last chance to see her son while they both lived. If she stayed here much longer, she wouldn't survive the handling some of the other slaves endured. Not in the long run. It was only a matter of time before they treated her like a mongrel, good to no one but for beating out their frustrations.

"You can't trust my words. Nor do I expect you to. I'll make you a generous offer."

"Feeling charitable to a white slave, are you?"

The heavy weight of despair constricted her—suffocated her. He didn't even flinch at her words. She didn't care. It was hard to hold her tongue when death stared her in the eye daily. Eventually, she knew she'd beg for the end staying here.

"I'm employed by a wealthy man, madam. His sole indulgence is his harem. I would ask you to become one of his harem girls . . . in exchange for the safety of your son."

She stopped breathing alltogether and repeated the words in her head. Could she really be hearing this right? A harem girl? A harlot? Is this what her husband had managed to reduce her life to—to become the plaything of some strange man in the hopes of saving *their* child?

She dropped her head into her hands and cried from

the hopelessness of the situation. For the life she once knew, knowing it was no longer for her. She cried for her son, who would grow up with a whore for a mother if she agreed to this madness.

Should she agree to this? How could she not? There was no other option. Her tears came harder and faster with every despairing thought.

The Englishman waited quietly for her to compose herself.

She was to find her way alone. To sell her body for her son's safety.

No one would even note her absence from society. Now her only escape from this slave trade was in sexual servitude. She'd be doing nothing more but trading one form of slavery for another. Rubbing the last of the tears away, she looked up to the only salvation left to her and Jonathan. His arms were braced, his expression blank as he leaned on the far wall, standing calmly as he awaited her decision.

She bowed her head and stared at her lap. "Will your employer be kind to my son?" Her voice was so faint she almost didn't recognize it as her own.

It was her son's welfare that mattered now. She would sacrifice her comfort a hundred times over for her child. Without Jonathan, there was nothing left to live for.

"If *you* obey him, he'll have no reason to cause harm to either of you. He takes great pride in his harem and business. You've no need to fear him. He does not abuse his women, nor do I imagine he would abuse a child. He doesn't have any so I cannot say for sure."

Could she ask for more assurance than that? She could take this offer and what may come, may come. Or she could rot in this hell on earth and never see her son again. She licked at her dry, cracked lips. "Why me?"

"Ah, there are many reasons for that, madam."

"Am I to guess your reasoning, then?"

"My employer has a certain fondness for English women with dark skin. Imagine my surprise when I happened upon you speaking the Queen's English in your dulcet, educated tone in this place. You'll also fetch a fair price from the other lords who visit his pleasure island. But only after he's trained you to do your duties as one of his harem girls."

Her stomach flipped. Elena raised her hand to her head to massage her temple, hoping it would help her find balance in a suddenly spinning room. She was to be a sex slave. Not just the whore for one amoral man but the sex slave for a plethora of men.

She looked up and focused on the Englishman. "If I agree to your offer . . . will you take me out of this place and reunite me with my child?"

He nodded. "Are you agreed?"

She couldn't swallow past the lump in her throat to ease the tension tightening her body, threatening to hyperventilate her. She nodded her yes. With that nod she threw away any hope of comfort. There was no other choice. She did this to protect her son.

She felt so helpless and despondent that the last bit of spirit in her heart—once so strong and determined to make something of the unfair life she'd been given—withered away. She was the wounded deer looking into the predatory eyes of a wolf, knowing this was it. This was all that was left. Do or die—what choice was there in that? What fairness lay in this world? None.

He pushed himself from the wall, still expressionless. "Then, my dear, I'm off to haggle a decent price for you."

Elena hung her head in shame. What had she agreed to? God save her if this was the wrong decision for her son.

CHAPTER TWO

Initiation into the Harem

The Isle of Corfu

Large hands spanned the whole of her waist and lifted her from the skiff to carry her ashore. Set down on solid earth, she sighed in relief to be on land. After a few steps her legs gave out. No one caught her as she sank to the sand as easily and gracefully as she could. Her legs were unsteady and shaky after being in the boat for so many days.

Sand flowed between her fingers, smooth siltlike grains filled with flat, small pebbles. What beach was this? Where had they brought her?

Elena bowed forward to rest her head against the ground and clawed her hands deep into the sand surrounding her. All she cared about was the stillness. Complete and utter stillness.

And her son. How much longer before she saw his chubby, smiling face?

How many more days would they continue onward? This breakneck pace in travel was taking its toll on her body. She was tired and needed to regain her strength.

A warm wind blew in from the water and pushed her hair forward. Despite the warmth, she shivered. This was the first place she had been allowed to sit alone since leaving Constantinople.

Repulsion had goose bumps forming on her arms at the thought of the slave market. Tightness clenched the nerves throughout her body, creating a nausea she could do without. She never wanted to experience the degradation of the slave markets again.

She took in another deep breath, cleaning out the putrid scent left in her nostrils from her sickness on the boat. She'd been dreadfully ill the whole trip over the sea as the boat tipped her one way then the next.

She raised her forehead from the ground and swiped away the sand stuck there. Still kneeling, she raised her head to the sky. Hot sun beat down on her, warming every part of her body that was thrust upward to the rays of light. She could sit just like this for the remainder of the day, absorbing the air around her.

The sunshine penetrated the thick cloth over her eyes. The citrus smell of the Englishman's cologne, like fresh peeled oranges, told her of his proximity.

Was he letting her savor the last moments of her freedom? Not that she was free. Freedom had long ago been stripped away.

When the silence grew unbearable, she asked, "Do you only allow me a small bit of fresh air to restore my constitution?"

"No, no. We've arrived."

She didn't say anything, just raised her hands to the back of her head. Elation filled her. She could take away the cloth that seemed to bind what was left of her free will. Was she allowed to remove the cloth now that they'd untied her hands?

His hands covered hers to stall her progress. "Leave

it until we are within the safety of the palace walls. No woman who enters this place is permitted to see the way."

Her hands dropped away. She pushed herself up from the ground and at once toppled to the side; her legs were still a trifle wobbly. The Englishman was quick to put a steadying hand around her arm before she teetered to the ground.

She smoothed her skirts in embarrassment, then stood firm. "Will I see my son soon?"

"Soon." He took her elbow to lead her to their destination.

It had been the same answer since her purchase. Why she expected to hear differently, she wasn't sure. But she hoped the solid knot lodged in the pit of her stomach wasn't a warning that this man lied. No, she needed to keep her thoughts positive. There had to be some good to come from this disastrous turn in her life. Besides, why would he lie? With Robert dead, this was the last option available to her. Now this Englishman held all the cards.

Robert's death had been a hard truth to swallow. Five years she'd given that swine. Five years of her youth, and he'd wasted what could have been a good, mutually respectful union. Never did she imagine she'd be sold into slavery—sold to be some man's harlot. It was ludicrous, unheard of, but it was the truth of her existence.

A *whore*.

There was no pretty way to label it.

In a twist of fate—or terrible luck, really all the same thing at this point—not only had she married the man who ruined her reputation in one eager embrace she hadn't even encouraged, she'd also signed away the security she thought to gain in marriage. Husbands were supposed to honor and protect. Robert had done neither.

Then there was her son, an innocent child not yet exposed to the cruelties of the world. For years she'd thought herself barren and been thankful for it. She hadn't wanted to bring a child into the impoverished life her husband forced them to live because of his penchant toward gambling.

She stumbled on the path when her foot caught in a hole. She landed hard against the Englishman. He grunted and stood her upright. "Take your steps slowly. The terrain is rocky here. We're almost inside the palace."

The blindfold was becoming tedious. Truth be told, it had become tiresome after a few hours of wearing it—days ago. She was helpless to do anything for herself. Did they really expect her to remember the way to this place? To remember the roads they had ridden and then the waterways they had sailed to reach this unknown destination?

The loss of sight certainly impeded any escape she might have planned. Where did they think she would escape to with a baby in tow? There were no relatives who could help her. What distant relations she did have would shun her for the trials she been through these last weeks. No self-respecting *lady* would ever allow such a thing to happen.

As if she could have stopped her husband from betting at the races or staying on at the gaming table when he knew he ought to leave. Stopped him from selling her into this life.

Her captor stilled, his hand yanking her elbow back when she kept walking. "Slow down, there are some steps here. I'll count them out for you. We'll be there momentarily."

She followed silently at his side. Finally, they stepped into shade. She guessed they were indoors when a shroud of darkness immediately enveloped her. At least she got a break from the unbearable heat of the sun; she was baking in her clothes. Their steps echoed around them. How much farther could it be? After a few minutes of slow walking, they ascended more stairs, then went down some more. They turned about so many ways she would never have a hope of finding her way back outside.

Doors opened or closed around her, she couldn't tell which. A cool draft brushed over her the deeper they walked. The hair at her nape rose in sudden trepidation. The cool stone walls under her fingertips must keep the heat of day at bay in this long corridor, but not her fears.

Darkness soon made way for light. There was quiet and stillness everywhere. Then they stepped into full-blown daylight. Elena turned her head to the side, straining to hear her surroundings. Songbirds chirped close by, and the sound of the sea was a soft din farther off.

Would she be forced to meet her owner now? Would she have the opportunity to see her son? So many questions, but she was afraid to ask anything. Afraid to know if she stood before her owner she was to address as Amir—a word that meant "prince." She wasn't sure if he was a real prince, or if his name was a way of placing himself on a pedestal above his slaves.

Fingers tugged at the knot behind her head. The cloth fell away. She didn't open her eyes. Not yet. She wasn't quite ready for the final outcome of this journey.

"There's no one here, Elena. You can open your eyes."

"No one here?"

"No one."

She cracked her eyes open slowly, afraid to see the new world around her.

The room she stood in was simple but pretty. A rose-colored divan with throws and pillows of many colors occupied the open-windowed wall. Fresh, hot air blew inward. Green and blue strips of silk floated toward her on the breeze, brushing around her toward the arched door at the opposite end of the room, presumably where they had entered. There was a bold red rug underfoot. A small table topped with a porcelain washing bowl at the entryway. Was this to be her room? If so, where was her son?

"You have time to refresh yourself after the journey. I'll send in Laila to help you with your bath. She'll also assign a slave to you in the next week or so."

"Slave. You mean I'm to have my own slave?"

A slave owning a slave? What a most peculiar concept, and a most disgusting concept—for a well-bred lady to have charge of a slave.

"Of course." His narrowed gaze said he thought she understood these things before arriving. "You are to be at Amir's call at all times—day or night. Someone must guide and instruct you in this life. There is much for you to learn over the next few weeks."

She nodded her understanding. "When am I to meet my new master? And—and my son? I want to see my son."

Her voice came out anxious, threaded with too many conflicting emotions. How would a man who kept a harem treat her? Why wasn't her son waiting for her arrival?

"You won't see Amir until you are properly prepared." His gaze slid down the length of her body. Slouching her shoulders forward, she hoped to stop his lewd assessment. He raised his eyes back to hers. "I know not when you'll be ready for Amir. Much depends on your cooperation. And your son has been here for some days. You'll see him later. Laila has much to do with you first. By the by, my name is Harry Chisholm."

She looked down to where her hands were clasped, suddenly shy, afraid he'd give her another once-over. She didn't want to witness such looks from anyone. Was this commonplace in a harem? For men to look at the women and see one thing . . . a creature of ill repute at their disposal? She swallowed the bile rising in her throat. She knew this was to be her life. It was too late to balk.

"I'll send in Laila." He cleared his throat. "She knows her way around better than anyone. She'll assign all the duties to the slaves until you can take on the task yourself. She'll see to your bath and teach you some of the . . . *customs* you'll have to adhere to."

Again, she nodded, not understanding what he hinted at. She had nothing else to ask Mr. Chisholm. As she continued to stare down at her hands, a woman's naked feet came into view. Her skin was smooth and youthful, her ankles painted with vines and flowers wrapped around her bared skin all the way up her calves till it disappeared beneath her dress.

Elena looked up into the beautiful face of a pale-skinned woman—her skin as white as freshly fallen snow and free of blemish. She wore a piece of amber cloth wrapped about her body and tied in a knot between her breasts. Her shoulders and arms were bare. Filigreed bracelets of every width adorned her wrists. Long, dark brown hair fell over her back with golden thread woven through it. Big brown almond-shaped eyes stared back at her, a smile evident in them.

With that warm gaze, Elena gave a small sigh of relief. This woman could be a friend.

A quick glance told her Mr. Chisholm was nowhere to be seen. She stood alone with this strange woman looking her over, from the top of her head down to her heeled shoes.

She motioned with her hand as she spoke. "We will get you washed." To Elena's surprise the woman spoke English. "Off with all of it."

Elena's smile slipped. "What do you mean, off with it?"

"You'll not be wearing these clothes anymore."

"What will I wear?" She looked around the room for clean linens.

"A lot less," Laila said with a grin. "You need to take these off. They are travel-worn and frayed. Most importantly, Amir does not like English clothes. The only English he likes is your prim voice whispered in passion."

Her cheeks flamed with the insinuation. It wouldn't do to start on the wrong foot, so Elena swallowed her retort. "If you'll provide me with clean clothes, I will change."

"Not here. You have to go to the baths. You'll have a bath every day now; it is important we have cleanliness. You English are dirty."

She would not part with her clothes. Elena wrapped her arms around her middle, wondering why this woman disdained the English so much. Perhaps she was mistaken to assume this woman a possible ally.

"If you don't remove them, I'll call in the eunuchs. You have to go down to the baths and be prepared should Amir want to see you in his chambers tonight."

All the air left her lungs. Tonight? Was she serious? "Mr. Chisholm said a few days—"

"A few days before you occupy his bed." Laila nodded her head and clucked her tongue in annoyance.

"You will still have to see him before then." Her fingers snapped and two men filled the entryway. The men came forward. Elena took a step away, the back of her knees hitting the divan.

Laila continued, "You must undress, the baths will take some hours."

"Please send them away." That step back didn't give her any distance from the guards as they continued their advance.

"I think it will take you a long while to get used to this place if you play so shy. These are not men but eunuchs and our harem guards, as well. They are here to assist me."

"I can't walk around without any clothes in front of them. *Please*."

The woman's eyes narrowed. The stern look did not bode well for further argument.

Elena knew with sudden clarity that Laila would not be swayed. She hugged into her middle tighter, trying to shrink inward to hide from what they were going to do. Would they hurt her as they had in the slave market? Was she in for another beating at the slightest show of disobedience?

"Could you—" She licked her dry lips, suddenly more nervous than when she'd been in the slave market. What if she angered this woman and they wouldn't let her see her son? "When will I see my son?"

"Make your questions quick." Laila crossed her arms over her bosom, foot tapping in impatience.

It was useless to play a simpering, scared woman. She stood up straight and looked Laila directly in the eye, trying to ignore the fact that the two men still approached her. "I want to see my son." Her voice broke, giving away the fear she tried to hide. She needed more bravado than this and yanked out her shirtwaist to undo the buttons, showing her willingness to obey. The guards came forward regardless of her obedience.

"After you are prepared." Laila smiled, her expression softening. "Your son is in the private harem quarters. The other girls are watching him. There are no children here, so we are well pleased to look after such a fine beautiful babe. A wet nurse was brought to the island with him, too. So you can let your milk go." Laila's eyes dropped to the swell of Elena's breasts above the corset. "If it hasn't already dried."

To her dismay, her milk had stopped flowing a week ago. She thought it a sign that her life as a mother had shriveled away with the nourishment and sustenance drying up. The truth in the woman's words filled her heart to overflowing, and a few tears leaked out the sides of her eyes. She swiped them away and returned Laila's smile. "Thank you for telling me."

She squealed in surprise as she was jerked clear off her feet when one guard pulled her corset away from her back and slashed a dagger through the ties. Would she seem unworthy and weak if she cried? The boned contraption fell away, and she stood there helplessly, crossing her arms over her bosom—only the thin material of her chemise still in place.

"The sooner you take off this fine English wear, the faster you can see the child. It is not so bad." Laila pointed to her skirts, and the guards stripped them from her with a deft flick of their daggers. "There, you see, I believe that was much faster."

Elena kneeled to a hunch, still covering her chest, and untied her shoes as quickly as possible, then pulled them off. She ducked her face as tears swelled. Rolling her stockings down, she chanced a look at Laila. The

woman raised one eyebrow at the short chemise and
pantalets. After a deep calming breath, Elena stood with
every last scrap of dignity she could muster.

Laila shook her head and held aside the material
hanging in the doorway. Elena slipped underneath
and hid her rear against the wall, one arm firm across
her bosom as she hurried after Laila. The sound of the
guards' slippered feet followed them.

This was a far worse humiliation than what she'd
been subjected to at the slave market. To be paraded
around all but naked. It was too much to bear. It made
her want to scream her fury. This was a new low. How
could she live this new life? What had she been thinking when she'd agreed to such a fate? Was it true that
her husband was dead? Or was this some ploy so her
husband didn't have to look out for her welfare?

"Oh, now, now, little beauty. No need to look forlorn. Come." Laila pushed her with a gentle, coaxing
hand down the length of the hall.

Elena paid no attention to her surroundings. Her mind
was too scattered, imagining every possible course her
new life might take. What if she couldn't live up to the
expectations of her owner? Already she balked at the
idea of something so simple as a bath. Admittedly, it
was the presence of the men that made her uneasy, filling her body with barely tempered rage. She wanted to
lash out with clawed hands and rake her nails down
their faces. Blind them from her humiliation.

She was at odds with herself. She'd never felt this
kind of anger before. Not even when she was in the slave
market. There, fear had drowned the anger that now
boiled over in her blood. She closed her eyes for only a
moment and took a calming breath.

Laila stopped when they reached a narrow passageway. The door in front of them was arched at the top in an elegant Turkish-style point. Small green mosaic tiles were inlaid around the stone, giving this part of the palace a less sterile feel with its warm, earthy colors.

Elena stepped into the room and hit a wall of steam.

"This is part of the private hamam." Laila motioned to the clouds of steam rushing out to swallow them both. "There are also public baths, which you will use daily."

"Hamam," Elena repeated, puzzled. She could barely breathe, the air was so thick. How could anyone bathe here? Steam rose all around her, tightening her chest and wetting her skin. Her chemise clung to her, and she felt as though she'd been doused with a boiling bucket of water.

"This is where I will remove your hair. Then we go to the public bath."

A gasp escaped Elena's lips with the pronouncement. Laila turned to look at her with a skeptical eye. Elena retreated, her shoulder blade hitting the corner of the entrance, stopping her escape.

"Remove my hair, you can't possibly mean . . ."

"You will see." Laila pushed wooden clogs into her hands without further illumination, nodding toward the swirls of misty air that rose from deep within the room. "These are called *nalin*. They're for your feet. You must wear these whenever you are in the bath. The tiles below are hot enough to scald your feet. And it is better than walking in the filth below us and harder for *djinn* to kidnap you when you are out of their reach."

Fitting her feet into the strange contraptions, Elena stood up and made a tentative step forward. They were heavy, maybe so the person wearing them didn't slip on the wet floor.

"I will walk slowly. You needn't worry about falling"—Laila held her arm out in an offer of support—"it is a few steps to the benches."

She took Laila's arm and made her steps slowly. She slid her feet more than walked, unwilling to risk a fall. Soon enough they were situated on one of the stone benches. It warmed her bottom. Tilting her head to look over the edge of the seat, she saw mother-of-pearl inlaid into the whole length of stone that was embedded into the floor. There was so much steam swirling around them she couldn't make out the pattern of the tiles beneath.

"You must take off your undergarments now."

"I can't possibly."

Laila shook her head, clucking her tongue. The guards made their presence known again. Elena crossed her arms over her bosom, her reddened flesh beneath the chemise surely visible in this humidity. Her anger had simmered away, and in its place, fear rose again. The stress of the last few weeks must have taken its toll on her mind.

"You must cooperate while you are bathed. You have to be prepared properly before Amir receives you." The words held more meaning than a simple bath.

"Then why should there be men present?"

"They will pay you no heed." Laila stood, pulling up Elena's chemise.

When Elena refused to raise her arm from her breasts, one guard stepped forward and pried her fingers from her middle and held her arm straight up. She cast her gaze to the floor when the material was removed, staring at the humid air hovering around her ankles. Laila pasted a thick substance onto the hair at her armpit with a flat wooden spoon. It was hot and Elena felt a slight tingling burn. Time ticked by—it felt like a moment trapped in an eternity of disgrace—before

Laila scraped it off. It burned more when she did that, made the skin feel raw, like spilling hot tea on the back of your hand.

"This is what we do the first time; it is easiest to remove hair with the *rusma,* but it discolors your skin and hurts if you use it too much or leave it on too long."

Elena cried silently as she was forced to raise her other arm for the same treatment. She looked to no one, not that she saw much of her surroundings through her tears of shame. She could only imagine what they would do with her more private area. Sweat and steam beaded all over her body, dripping into her eyes, stinging them.

Laila carried on. "After this, Maram, another sister here, will thread what hairs grow back. It is quick. Not as quick as the paste, but safer." Laila placed a hand on her shoulder and gave it a light squeeze. "Stop crying, my sister." Her voice held new warmth. "You will get used to this."

"I won't. I can't possibly live this way." Her words came out a blubbering wail. She clamped her mouth shut and bit her lip to still the tremor.

"But you have no choice. You can never leave. The only way to find yourself in the land beyond is with your dying breath. Think of your child. He is the only child you will know. We are not permitted motherhood here. You are blessed in life. Never take that for granted."

Elena choked on a final sob and looked up with a nod. "How can you not have children if you are slaves of a . . . a bawdy nature?" She tripped over the last few words and looked away from the woman, swiping away the wetness on her cheek, though it did no good when the whole of her was sticky from the steam.

"Ah, I see how little you understand. There are ways. When we go to the bathing room I will show you how to use the sponge. It collects a man's milk, so it cannot plant within your womb. If his seed is persistent, we use strong herbs to purge our body of the union."

Laila took Elena's arm in her grasp, lifting it level to her eye, and inspected it closely.

"You have no hair on your arms, this is good. It always hurts to take it from the body here." The warm hand of the man holding her tilted her head back. "No hair in your nostrils, either. That hurts the most. It will sting a little to remove from your legs, though. I ask you now, will you cooperate to have the hair of your woman's mound removed?"

Elena took a deep breath and answered with as steady a voice as she could muster. "I—I will. If you'll send away the men." She gave a pointed glare toward the dark-skinned, fat one who stood in front of them. He looked uninterested in the task at hand and paid her no mind.

"They will stay in the room, but I will send them to the farthest wall. They are not men. You must remember this. All in the harem quarters are either woman or eunuch. The only man permitted in our living quarters is Amir."

"Will I truly be expected to keep Amir company tonight?"

"Maybe tonight, maybe in a few days. Much depends on his business outside the harem. You have no need to fear him. Perhaps that is something you can only understand with time. But remember, he brought your child here."

Elena nodded her agreement with that. "How many women live here?"

Distracting herself with conversation was easier than paying scrupulous attention to Laila's ministrations. The hair being scraped off her lower legs burned a great deal. It felt as if a layer of skin had been torn from her.

"Thirty-six. His harem is not so big as the one I grew up in. Of course this is different, since other men may purchase us. But only from time to time."

"I'm afraid I don't understand the inner workings of a harem."

"I will explain it all in due time. I can tell you that this is a kinder existence than being forgotten, should you have one man for a thousand women. That life is much more lonely."

Elena gasped. She seemed to be doing that too much. *A thousand*? How was it possible that one man could have so many women at his disposal? How could any woman tolerate living that way? She'd only ever wanted to spend her life with one man—Griffin. She remembered him fondly, but when he'd left England for whatever reason, she'd been forced into marriage with an altogether different kind of man. Both those men were now gone from her life and in their place was another person wanting to force her hand to his own advantage.

"Stand, my sister." Laila's words pulled her back to the present. "You must take your pantalets down. Do not blush so. This is not something I haven't seen before. It will be done before you know it."

Elena looked wearily around her. The *men* had retreated, and she wondered if that was the reason her fear had abated slightly. How could she ever get used to the eunuchs' presence during ablutions, if one could call it such? Laila started to pull her pantalets down when Elena stalled mid-thought. She lowered one hand to cover herself and looked about nervously.

"Lie on the bench." Laila tapped the seat beside her and Elena sat. "You don't need to be shy. Put one leg on either side and lie back."

"Might I have a moment to collect myself?"

Laila gave a sultry chuckle. Elena did as directed, one arm across her breasts and the other clenched in a tight fist as she spread her legs to rest on either side of the stone slab. Laila didn't give her a moment to change her mind, smearing the paste over the hairs at her center.

"Spread your legs farther. You do not want this on your inner pink skin."

Since she did not obey quickly enough, her legs were pressed wider, small fingers covering the hair lower down, even around her rear entrance. Elena was shocked into stillness, her breath frozen in her lungs. Then the scrape of a shell pressed against her skin, leaving another burning patch of tender flesh in its wake. Warm water was poured between the folds of her sex while impersonal fingers washed away remnants of *rusma*.

"You see . . . we are done."

Elena lowered her hand to touch her center. She kept her eyes squeezed shut. The skin was bare, sensitive. She was like a prepubescent girl with no hair to identify her as a woman. What kind of perversity was this? She spread her fingers out to cover her nakedness. She opened her eyes. Laila stared down at her.

When she found her voice, she said, "My name is Elena . . ."

"Pretty name. But you will want to change it. A new identity will free you from your old life. Now come, we have to go to the bathhouse. The water will soothe the afterburn."

CHAPTER THREE

Griffin Summerfield,
Marquess of Rothburn

Spring 1846
Isle of Corfu

Griffin watched the women through a gauzy-white silk screen. All the patrons were situated in a wraparound balcony that faced the baths below. The harem girls lounged, played music, and braided each other's hair. They were posed so strategically, it was almost enough to fill any man's fantasy seeing them this way.

And wholly unrealistic. This had so obviously been staged for the benefactors of the auction. Not that he cared it was staged.

"What do you think, my good man?" Asbury asked.

Griffin leaned back in his chair and crossed his arms. "I see no difference in the women here from the beauties found at any established bawdy house."

"True. But you don't get quite this variety in Europe unless you go to one of the opium dens."

Griffin turned and gave his friend a look that said otherwise.

"Fine, you've probably had your fair share of Orientals traveling China. And I'm not likely to forget how I found you."

"I wouldn't expect you to forget, merely thought you shouldn't be one to judge. I think you've supplied all those opium houses back home."

"When did you become such a priggish maid? Good God, Rothburn. You'll recall who supplied me with opiates to sell in the beginning."

"I have come to my senses since. You will eventually, too."

"Well, if the variety of women here isn't as pleasing, just know they are a sight bit cleaner than where you were playing. They're also willing to do anything you fancy."

"I can imagine."

He looked away from Asbury and back to the voluptuous harem girls on display. Asbury had brought him here in hopes of lifting Griffin's ennui, and annoyance with society in general. He wouldn't disappoint his friend. He'd indulge in whatever the island had to offer. Better that than slipping back into that dark, welcoming well of excess dissipation again.

A distinctive laugh caught his attention and had his gaze narrowing on the scene below.

He searched out the source; it came from the veiled bronze beauty. That sound took him back in time. There weren't many women who expressed a free exuberance like that. He remembered the husky deepness of a laugh like that on another night—from another woman—some ten years ago. It was one of those contagious laughs that had everyone in a room turning, and every man rising in salute.

He leaned forward with his elbows planted on his knees and studied her.

There was the shy tilt of her head when she listened to another talk, the soft but clear timbre of her voice as she spoke Persian—which seemed the common language in the palace. The inborn grace with which she sat poised so ladylike made her seem as delicate as an orchid in bloom, so easily destroyed if not properly cared for. There was something about the way she brushed her hair from her brow, as though it were done up in some other fancy style society women liked. The motion stilled his breathing altogether.

It occurred to Griffin that his imagination had finally gotten the better of him. After dreaming about Elena Ravenscliffe for what felt like a lifetime, he found it hard to identify the tangible reality from what could only be an illusion in front of him.

He stood, edged around the other men in order to see her from another angle.

She laughed again, halting his steps. He put his hand out on the rail to steady himself and leaned in close to the screen. There was no mistaking what he knew for the truth.

He knew her as well as he knew himself. His memory was like that of a bloody elephant. There were some things he wished he could forget. He might have fared better had he been able to forget *her* in the first place. He shook off the thought.

How had she ended up in a place like this?

When he'd moved back to England after his uncle's death, the first thing he'd done was look for her. That had to be some five years ago. His sources had said she was still married to that lowly baron with an estate up north. Perhaps Griffin had given up his search too easily.

Lady Elena had proved impossible to find once she and her husband moved abroad. Her husband had sold his properties in York and left for Constantinople hastily.

Griffin had been disinclined to ferret out any other information. Really, he'd recognized it as a hopeless venture to pursue a married woman.

What could have happened between then and now to bring her to a place like this?

How had such a fine young English lady come to sell herself into such a degenerate life? He supposed she wouldn't be the first to find herself in such a situation. Well, now he'd know all of her sordid tale. Once he talked to the owner of this fine establishment.

Griffin turned away from the screen and looked for the man who had escorted them up to this section of the palace. Griffin had made his selection. Now it was time to see what his little lady friend was worth. For the first time in years he felt like smiling; he had reason to express himself happily. He'd had to pull himself through a long path of self-destruction to make it to this point. Was this some sick ironic award for moral behavior? It didn't matter. It was what it was. After all these years, she was finally going to be his.

Asbury slapped him on the back. "I see I've brought you to the right place, my friend. Hope you aren't taking up too many old habits." There was censure in his friend's voice. He didn't want to hear it but the reminder was for the best. He had a feeling old habits were going to be hard to ignore.

"There's not much else to do." Griffin folded his hand. Standing from the card table, he bowed and took his leave. He was done gambling for the night. "I've found a beauty to occupy my time. I'll bid on her tomorrow night, when she's on auction."

"Which one's caught your eye?"

"That's for me to know." Griffin gave a slow smile. Asbury's only response was to laugh.

That secret was his for now. The beauty could be none other than Elena, his fiancée for all of a day before he foolishly left her side, and she became vulnerable, unable to protect herself from the greedy clutches of the Baron of Shepley.

They walked toward some empty chairs off to the side of the room, and away from any ears. It was decorated like any Englishman's establishment back home. Leather furniture—mostly chairs—a billiards table, gaming tables, Turkish carpets underfoot, heavy smoke from pipes and cigars that filled the dimly lit chamber. The walls were paneled with dark wood, and the room had been fitted with bookshelves. Though not many came here to read. Only a dozen gentlemen were there now, most of them trying their luck at cards.

Earlier, when he'd gone to inquire about the bronze beauty, the owner, Amir, had asked Griffin not to say anything about paying in advance. It didn't matter either way to Griffin, so he'd readily agreed so long as he could have her history. Amir had given Griffin some cock-and-bull story of her being part of his brother's harem in Turkey before she was sent to this island. There was a great deal of assurance as to her abilities in the arts of seduction, like so many of the women brought up in these settings. It made him want to snort in disbelief.

Griffin didn't believe the concocted story for one second. He wasn't sure if he'd ever heard a cleverer spouting of lies. She was no more a harem girl than he was an impoverished lord.

For now, he'd comply with house rules. And tomorrow, he'd finally know if he'd gone mad with his obsession for Elena, or if he'd been handed a second chance to court her. It would be a very different sort of courting they did this time around. He should be ashamed of his ungentlemanly thoughts. What he should be doing was attempting to remove her from this place. He might in the end, but not before he heard her version of the tale of how she came to be here.

"You always were a devil, Rothburn. It'll be interesting to see which girls stand on auction tomorrow. I've my eye on a few. One I've yet to win, she's damnably expensive. The others . . . well, we'll see about the others."

A slave brought over a tray with brandy.

Asbury waved her away, knowing how Griffin felt about the stuff. He rarely touched it—hadn't for some years now—and for good reason.

He'd traded one addiction for another since he'd built up his empire in the silk trade. He had been schoolmates with Asbury; they'd attended Eton together. Griffin had disassociated himself from his old life when he'd left England, including all his friends. He'd wanted to bury the past when he couldn't have the one woman who had had a stronger effect on him than any opium he'd tried.

When he'd heard of her nuptials, through his uncle, he'd headed to the East: trading, whoring, luxuriating in depravity for some years. Then along came Asbury, his long-ago friend, who pulled him from the swarm of naked Asian beauties he'd been tasting in the opium den. Asbury had cleared away the fog clouding Griffin's mind. Told him to pull it together or he'd beat the snot out of him. There was no doubting Asbury, always a man of his word. If Griffin had slipped over the years, and there were a few occasions he had done just that, he thought of the trouble Asbury had gone to and forced himself out of the grasp of obsession.

If Griffin were a weaker man, he'd blame his fall on

his uncle. But he knew better; he was his own man, the type of man who relied on one constant or another, be it in the form of a healthy addiction or not. He had pulled himself out of every overindulging vice he'd relied on over the years, all of them pursued in the hope of erasing the one woman haunting his mind. Strange that she'd had such a strong pull on him, like the talons of a falcon with a bleeding rabbit in its sharp clasp.

And now here she was. Causing new wounds to open, while old ones tried to heal beneath.

"She's really got you interested, this ladybird."

Griffin snapped his head up, and pinched the flesh at the bridge of his nose.

"You surprise me, Rothburn. You rarely take such a quick liking to any woman."

Griffin raised a brow at that. "And what if I have?"

"Well, for one, it's a good change. You were losing interest in the world around you. I've known you too long not to know you were on another downward slope."

"I'm fine, Asbury. Just tired of late. You sound more like a worried mother than a friend."

"Yes, well, be less tired and less sullen and I'll stop fussing like Mother Goose."

Asbury leaned back in his chair, crossing his ankle over one knee as he got comfortable for what looked like some business talk. Griffin really wasn't in the mood for business, but he supposed there wasn't any way to avoid it. It was a better topic than Jinan the Turkish princess or his current state of ennui.

"I've got some big shipments coming in I want to discuss."

"So, you had ulterior motives in bringing me here, Asbury."

"Of course. How did you not realize that?"

"I realized you were softening me up for one reason or another. Where are your goods shipping through?"

Asbury smiled, more than eager to get business dealt with before their fun began tomorrow evening.

Griffin had been correct in his assessment last night. There was no mistaking those eyes lined with dark kohl. This was the right choice. He couldn't be more positive of her identity.

She stood perfectly poised, ignored the majority of men milling around her with varying degrees of lechery in their pointed, suggestive stares. She was by far the most delectable creature in the room.

Asbury walked toward the podium Jinan stood upon. His friend had told him a moment ago that he saw a girl he was interested in. So it was Jinan who always went out of his price range. He would have laughed if his nerves weren't on edge.

Jinan gave Asbury a cursory glance, her eyes lighting with what he could only describe as a smile—hard to tell with that damned veil in place. She leaned down to say something to him. The girl standing beside the podium laughed. He couldn't hear anything with the drummers and singers screeching in every cranny of the room, and patrons grunting, talking, and laughing all around.

Pushing off the pillar where his foot was perched, he walked toward her. Was it possible she would even remember him? Not likely. Though he hadn't forgotten a single thing about her. Ten years was a long time so there was no harm in showing himself to her before the bidding started.

He'd already arranged the price with Amir. The man was a shrewd businessman. Had he known the extent of Griffin's interest, he might have negotiated a higher amount for the few months they'd agreed on. Griffin was fool enough that he would have paid the moon and stars if that was the only way to have her.

He passed a young count buried in his ladybird. Griffin had never been one for public displays of passion, but he wouldn't begrudge the man his pleasure. So far, though, he was the only one openly displaying his . . . abilities. The girl was young and exotically beautiful. The count was probably helpless to stop from testing the girl's finer talents.

Hell, Griffin had no idea if he'd be able to keep from publicly touching the beautiful princess displayed before the minions ogling her.

He almost believed her a figment of his imagination; perhaps his memories had fabricated some chimera from what the opium had done to his mind.

Her eyes widened when he came into her line of vision. A flicker of fear lit within them and then it was gone before he could ascertain any deeper, lurking emotion.

Regardless, it was a telling reaction.

The poor creature wore nothing but her bared skin with a curtain of hair loose behind her. A great number of baubles dangled around her wrists and ankles and that veil hung defensively about her face. A clever disguise, that. Amir had been adamant that she remain veiled at all times. If Griffin had any problems with that part of the contract, he had been advised to choose one of the other women.

How many men had she recognized over the years to have to don a cloth shield?

He still found it hard to believe that he was looking at her after all these years. He should never have given up his search for her. He might have even saved her from this life. She was above selling her favors. Why he had put her upon a pedestal in his mind was anyone's guess. But that was where she'd always stand for him.

She had filled out nicely over the years. Time had turned her into a well-rounded woman; her hips were generous, her thighs lush, her breasts heavy and more than his hands would hold. She was perfection and not far from the creature he'd been dreaming of whenever he fantasized about her. Her skin was darker than he remembered; it used to be a light bronze, now it was a darkened copper, probably stimulated by sitting in the sun.

He looked only to her deep brown eyes. If he focused on any other part of her exposed body, he would not be able to continue with the proceedings. It was tempting to haul her down from the podium and carry her off like some barbarian warlord. He shook off the thought. She'd be his soon enough. And this time, he wasn't so inclined to let her get away.

She met his bold stare with one of her own.

Remember me, Elena . . . show me some sort of recognition.

Surely their time together had been mutually enjoyed. She'd laughed and danced freely with him, all without putting on the simpering airs other young chits displayed. With her free spirit, she'd been the embodiment of everything his uncle despised. The quintessence of everything Griffin had wanted to obtain for himself. He was sure his obsession stemmed from the fact that she was forbidden. Though it was hard to recall which exact trait had reeled him in, sinking those sharp claws deep into his flesh, mind, and heart.

Movement in his peripheral sight had him dropping his gaze to where her hand curved around her hip. Was it her intention to draw his attention to her more fleshly attributes?

He raised his brow and thought of giving her some

mock insulted look but decided now was not the time. He'd give her the rest of the auction to compose herself . . . that was, if she recognized him. Surely once she heard his name she'd show recognition. For God's sake, they'd been engaged, even if only secretly.

Without further ado, Griffin walked to the outskirts of the room. Amir had been insistent about having the auction go forward so others didn't think to take advantage of bidding in advance. It was bad for business, Amir said. It stopped the patrons from spending more money than they were willing to part with.

So be it. No one but he would warm Jinan's bedside.

No one but he would have the privilege of touching her, and revealing all her secrets.

"Eight and a half," came the pinched, angered voice of Asbury.

So his friend had reached his limit in bidding. The man had as much money as Griffin. Why he came to a place like this and refused to spend a pretty penny on these beauties puzzled him.

"Ten." That came from the young count. The man had quite an appetite. At least he'd pulled himself back together and tucked everything decently away before voicing his bid.

Frenchmen.

A hush came over the room. So that was as high as they'd go for *his* Jinan.

They'd think him a fool once he voiced his price. He waited with an unnatural calm for the auctioneer to chime in. The middle-aged man had been informed about the rigged bidding before Jinan had even stood upon the dais.

"Excellent. Well, then, gentle—"

"Twenty thousand." His voice seemed to boom around

the palace walls even though one wall opened to the outside, welcoming the gardens into the fold of the harem quarters.

It seemed as though every head turned his way.

Griffin stepped forward. Asbury looked disgusted until he saw Griffin, then his expression changed considerably, to one of bemusement. Griffin tried for calm, hoping he pulled it off, as his gaze slid to the prize. No one else mattered as he focused on Jinan.

She was his.

And there was nothing to stop him from touching her . . . taking her . . .

Now.

Would she tell him the truth? Or would she hide behind her silks and veil, and her fictitious story?

Griffin didn't hear what Mr. Chisholm said. In fact, he wasn't sure the man had said anything at all. His hand clasped around the princess's hand, and he would have let her walk down on her own, but once he felt the warmth of her fingers infuse his own, he stepped forward and caught her up in his arms without so much as a backward glance.

His cock was rock hard the moment she slid her arms around his shoulders. Dammit, he was no better than the count, displaying his shamelessness.

He'd explored the grounds of the Pleasure Gardens when he'd arrived a few days ago and he knew exactly which alcoves were unoccupied tonight. He walked to an empty cove, without releasing his prize, without glancing at anyone else in the great room.

Let them think what they will.

When he was inside the lamp-lit room, he released Jinan's legs to slide down his body. The motion only inflamed his desire to taste the delectable creature, without delay.

Motionless, she stood next to him, her nipples puckered so tightly he felt them through the cambric of his shirt. She was a tiny morsel standing next to him like this. He stood a full head above her. It shouldn't surprise him that she didn't shy away from his bulk. She was far from her days of being an innocent miss.

Her hands came around his face as though she wanted to see him with the touch of her hand. Her thumbs pressed lightly against his lips as her fingers explored his face. Shutting his eyes, he let her have her fill. There would be a breaking point to his control once he touched her. It was only fair to allow her to become acquainted with him. Or reacquainted, if she remembered him—as he hoped.

He took a deep breath and enjoyed every sweep of her measured touch. How many nights had he dreamed of having her explore him this way?

Why couldn't he strip her of that damnable cloth shield and force her to admit the truth of their past? He wanted so badly to take her away from this place, this life. He wanted to be the only man taking care of her. The last man to ever touch her.

This burst of feeling he had for her was almost as alien to him as was backing down when he wanted to pursue something. A strange notion for him since he'd fought the institution of marriage for so long. Not that he'd avoided the prospect of marriage with her. In fact, he'd been willing to dive in headlong without a second thought.

Once, so long ago, he'd wanted to sweep her off her feet and whisk her to the altar. Had his uncle not intervened and arranged her marriage to that idiot— something his uncle had gloated about after the fact—she would be his wife now.

While she molded his features, he raised his hands

to the back of her head. He was sure there was a clip threaded through her hair, holding the wisps of silk in place. She leaned away from him.

Her voice was husky, her words came in Persian. "Amir would have been explicit in this. My veil stays for the duration of the contract."

It had still been worth the try. Would she ever allow him this privilege? Time would tell, he supposed. She had perfected this disguise, this persona, if she planned only to speak Persian. He'd not get the truth of how she had ended up in this place—not when she hid behind the façade of a Turkish princess.

When she looked as though she'd speak again, he cut in. "Shh . . . no words between us this night. I want you silent, no matter what I say to you. Your owner will discuss the contract we've agreed upon when I leave. Just give me all of your true self this night." There was deeper meaning in those words.

He loosened his necktie to pull it off. He'd use it to blindfold her while he took her. The tether on his control would not last much longer; the silken threads were liable to snap if he let her do what she was trained for. He needed her in so many ways, but his physical desire was winning out. Control seemed lost to him in her presence.

Turning her around, he tied the stiff material over her eyes. He squeezed her arms before releasing her. How much would she be willing to do with him? The contract negotiations had been a blur. He'd only been thinking about *her* the whole while her owner had prattled on.

His emotions ran rampant, hot as an angry wildfire roaring through his body.

He would force the truth from her later. Right now all he wanted was to feel her wrapped around his body to further imprint her upon his mind. Too many fantasies about her had haunted him over the years for him to temper his lust. She stood proudly naked before him without fear and without any indication that she *knew* him.

The sensual little creature arched her breasts forward. His reaction was immediate. He wanted to touch every part of her, to learn what pleased her, to know what would make her scream out. To make her scream his name.

Would his dream woman come to life in his arms? Would she surrender her desires to him?

He pulled her in tight to his chest, her rear pressed against his groin lightly, teasingly. The temptation was there to grind into her, but he couldn't—not yet. Turning her head to the side, he grazed his mouth over the tip of her ear.

How easy, in the height of passion, it would be to whisper the truth to her. Tell her that he knew who the real woman was beneath the veil. But it was too soon to reveal the depth of his feelings. The depth of his insanity over the years in thinking about her. He closed his eyes, inhaling deeply. A faint smell of rose water filled his nostrils . . . and the scent of woman beneath that. She did not wear the cloying perfumes of an English lady.

This was the pure, clean scent of a woman. Reaching around to her front, he ran his hand over her heated flesh and stopped before reaching her mound. There were so many things he'd dreamed of doing that he didn't know where to start. The breath coming from his lungs rasped, panted. Too many sensations fired his blood to a boil.

God, he'd needed this woman too long.

He had been thinking about her most of his life. The Marquess of Rothburn had been brought to his knees after a few weeks in her company. Did she remember his boldness when he'd sequestered her in the Duchess of Glenmoore's gardens? They'd laughed most of the night away. He thought they'd been friends after their shared horror stories of society balls. Thought they'd had a deeper connection after his confessions of feelings for her, after their heated kisses when he'd proposed to her under the stars.

Or had she forgotten? Had it all meant so little to her? Or had she doubted him after his hasty departure from England?

He held her close as he remembered the past. The last night he'd seen her had ended on a high note. What had she thought when he hadn't danced attendance upon her thereafter? Instead he'd hightailed it to his villa in Italy after his uncle arranged for him to marry some thoroughbred chit. As soon as he left, his uncle had sent the indebted baron panting after Elena. Both men had made sure to ruin her socially, arranging for her to be caught in a forbidden embrace. Not that Griffin believed for one minute she'd welcomed the baron's advances. Although the blackening of her name had forced her to marry the scoundrel while Griffin had been abroad licking his wounds.

So stupid of him to leave her behind when they could have eloped and lived abroad.

So very, very stupid.

Bending at the knee, he scooped her up into his arms again. She was lighter than her figure suggested. Maybe because she didn't have the cumbersome skirts of English fashion to bulk her up and weigh her down.

He tossed the blankets aside as he laid her on the wide divan. His mind was lost when his body needed her touch so badly, needed to be in her, on her, around her lush form soaking up her very essence. Setting her legs so they bent at the knees, he spread them apart and knelt between them. It shouldn't have surprised him when she displayed her flexibility with an aptness that would make most bawds blush.

The folds of her sex glistened with moisture in the moonlight that reached its faint white fingers through the open window. He didn't hold back the appreciative groan that came from deep in his lungs, robbing him of air. He swallowed against the sudden dryness in his throat.

What was she thinking? He wished he could see her expression, but he wouldn't give back her sight just yet. Not until he had lived out this one fantasy. He held his hands slightly above her waist, not ready to touch her. Once he did that, he would lose himself in what she so willingly displayed without shame. Lose himself in the long obsession he'd had with this particular woman.

Finally, he grasped onto her hips and lifted her, placing her open, wet core against his cloth-covered erection. With a thrust of her hips her sex came in tighter against him. He just needed to touch her, to hear her scream in release. He wanted his fantasy woman on fire with passion beneath him.

He felt her holding back as her hips stopped moving. She wanted to feel him. She wanted to be closer to him. She wanted him, at least in a carnal sense, which he could live with for now. It was beyond him to deny her such a simple thing.

Leaning over her, he rubbed his face against the underside of her breast. If only it were so easy to mark her as his own in this primal fashion. He caressed her delicate flesh, indulged with his lips and tongue the taste of her sweet female musk. There would be rapture this evening. Complete abandon to indulge both their bodies and senses.

What did she think of him rubbing over her as if he were some great predatory cat tamed by her mere presence? When she lowered her hand, sliding it between their bodies, he had a feeling she wanted to aid him in release. But this wasn't about the gratification of sex. This was about reacquainting his mind with his dreams, his fantasies. This was about holding on to the one thing that had kept passion and reason flowing in his veins over the years.

He stopped her hand from reaching its destination. "Do not touch me this eve, unless I give leave to do so." He didn't mean for his voice to sound so harsh.

When he released his hold, her arms fell loose to either side of her. His teeth grasped her crested nipple; he wanted to test her limits—Amir had promised a woman willing to explore the darker nature a man had.

When her back arched higher off the divan, her desire seemed to get the better of her. Both her hands shot out above her head to push against the wall. There was no need to guide her hips over his desire-ridden body. She moved to fulfill her own need. The thrust of her pelvis was jerky and it took everything in Griffin to hold out until she peaked.

"Thread your hands together, above your head." Better to have her not touch him when his release was so close.

It didn't matter that he'd purchased this right. He would purchase her a thousand and one nights more, if it were the only way he could spend more time in her company.

He tasted her freely now everywhere his mouth and tongue landed with each one of her thrusts. He couldn't seem to pull her in tight enough to appease either of them. Biting at her breast with as much gentleness as his sex-crazed body could deliver in this current state of excitement, he heard her let out a deep moan. He ground harder into her, his control gradually slipping as he rode out both their pleasure.

Her body slid with ease over his clothes. He could feel her wetness penetrating the material of his smalls when her body let out a gush of feminine fluid and her legs dropped farther open. There was no reining in his desires at that point. His cock swelled and there was no hope of stopping the release so close to overtaking him. They jerked together in the abandon of their congress.

"By all that is holy . . ." Her words came in Persian as she arched farther off the divan, bringing her ribs right up to his chest as she came to her crisis.

Another rush of fluids aided the slide of their bodies. He rocked his hips a few more times as the last of his seed pumped out painfully in the constriction of his trousers. With a slight collapse onto her, he released the tight grasp he had on her hips and breathed heavily against her for a moment. He needed to catch his breath.

Had they really just done that?

There was no thinking straight with her sensual body wrapped around his.

It didn't matter what they'd just done. They'd both been consenting adults in this. It was obvious they had both needed this release. She wouldn't have taken her own pleasure so fiercely if she hadn't needed it.

The bigger question remained, though. Did she play this game with everyone or did she remember him and find comfort in losing herself to his touch? After tonight he'd have answers, or at least he hoped to. It was obvious she would continue with this charade of hers.

But would she keep denying the truth after a few months spent in his company?

CHAPTER FOUR

Reunion and Reconciliation

1841
Five Years Earlier

They walked down long corridors, the next indistinguishable from the last. They turned about so many ways she was lost within a few minutes. Elena wasn't sure if she'd been to this section of the palace yet or not. Color started to slowly invade the sterile white walls, bronzes and rusts, greens in the tiled floors, then they took another turn and deep red carpet cushioned her bare feet.

She looked up from her curled toes. Doors were spaced out evenly in this hall. At the end she spied an open sitting area and could hear the laughter and chatter of other women. She was ushered into one of the rooms with Laila before she could explore farther on.

"When will I see my son?" she asked.

"Very soon. I'll just show you your sleeping quarters. All the harem girls' rooms line this hall and the hall on the other side of the garden." Laila pointed out the large open window to a courtyard beyond her room. There was a square of similar windows lined with burgundy shutters, surrounding the greenery outside. Songbirds sang loudly and cheerfully, mixing with the talk and activities of the women walking or lounging in the garden.

Pulling her eyes from the outdoors, Elena focused on the room. Lush textiles of silks, velvets, beads, and brocades covered the furniture in an array of bold colors. A zebra-striped animal fur stretched out in front of the divan. It was a handsome room that nearly left her breathless, but her mind couldn't take in material things.

She turned to Laila. "I thank you for showing me this, but I want to see my son. I've missed him so very much. I have done everything you asked of me, please let me see him," she said in a small voice. She really couldn't bear being refused again to see Jonathan. Her hands shook in nervousness and anxiety.

"I understand. He is a beauty, and we've all enjoyed looking after him. Come then." Laila took her hand, leading her to the main sitting area she'd wanted to go toward moments ago.

There was a crowd of richly dressed harem girls. At the center of their chattering and cooing came the sounds of a happy gurgling baby.

"Oh, Jonathan!" Elena screeched her excitement and rushed forward. Dropping to her knees, she picked her son up.

She held him fiercely to her bosom and didn't realize she was squeezing him so tightly until he cried out in complaint. She loosened her grasp enough to rain kisses on his plump face and tasted her own tears as they fell unashamedly. The happiness she felt in seeing him lifted her heart and her hopes.

"Oh, my sweet baby," she cried out again.

Tears continued to blur her vision as she looked him over. She had to keep swiping the dampness away with the bottom edge of her dress. She'd never cried so much in all her life. But then, she'd never had such a happy moment as this. To have this joyful reunion after the despair that had ridden heavy on her shoulders these past few weeks was more than a blessing.

Jonathan had grown in the short time they'd been separated. His hair had filled in on his head and a cowlick in front stood up on end. She brushed her fingers through the dark, baby softness. She noticed in his smile the beginning of a tooth. Goodness, she'd missed so much while they were separated. She vowed then and there, she'd never be parted from her son again.

He wore white muslin designed like the caftan robes, and she felt extra padding on his bottom under the outfit. His arms were still chubby and his tiny fists clenched through the locks of her loose hair. He cooed back at her, giving her a wide, mostly gummy smile. Thank God he hadn't forgotten her in their time apart— that would have been too heartbreaking to bear.

Elena sat heavily on the carpeted floor and pulled him into her lap, rocking and hugging him intermittently. She kissed his cheek. "I have missed you, my little boy. Do you know that?"

Content that he was comfortable in her arms, she looked up to the smiling faces around her. There were at least a dozen women. She smiled at them. Jonathan tugged again at her loose hair, and she looked down to unravel it from his small, insistent fingers.

"You see . . . your boy is nice and fat. We have kept him fed and very happy."

Elena turned and faced the woman who spoke.

The girl was young, maybe seventeen, and a swarthy beauty. Her round eyes were large and bright, the color of amber. Her nose was narrow and well suited to her oval face. She had a red dot between her eyes, painted in place—Elena couldn't remember what that was called, but she knew this woman must be Hindi to wear the mark. Her hair was worn in two thick braids on either side of her face and hung clear down to her hips, dancing on the floor where she knelt. The young woman had a beautiful smile, her teeth a bit big for her mouth but very white.

"I am Maram," she said. "Your boy is very beautiful. He's been such a delight to us."

Her English was slow and slightly disjointed, as though she weren't sure she used the right words. It almost surprised Elena to hear her native English tongue in a place where there didn't look to be any other of her background. She wondered if everyone here spoke English.

"Where did you learn English?" Elena asked.

Maram gave a sweet laugh and ducked her head in shyness. "I grew up in a big house where my parents served an English lord and his family. His children taught me. This is how you find me here speaking your tongue not so well, but it helps that most of the men who come to the Pleasure Gardens speak English. They laugh and pinch at us when we say words wrong. They like us to do that." She shrugged. "I do not mind it so much."

"You wouldn't," another woman said from the divan, then went back to talking to the girl beside her.

Elena smiled at Maram and looked around her. Most of the women who had played with her son had more or less wandered off although a few stayed close, watching her little boy with rapt attention but giving her enough space to enjoy the reunion. It was so wonderful to have him in her arms and to feel his warmth; she'd been so cold and lifeless without him.

She squeezed him to her breast and buried her nose in his hair, breathing in his scent.

Sitting in front of Jonathan, Laila dangled one of her golden bracelets. Jonathan swatted at it, gurgling and laughing at the bright object swinging before him. Maram chimed in and tickled one of her son's feet, making him wriggle in her lap.

"This one will be spoiled with all of us to mother him." Laila leaned in and blew raspberries on Jonathan's cheek. He laughed and tried to grab at the golden hoops hanging from her ear. "Won't you, little love?"

"Will Amir . . ." Elena started. There were so many questions she wanted to ask, but most importantly, she needed to know how her son was received. "Will Amir be kind to my son?"

"He adores your son."

"Oh"—she chewed on her lip nervously, unsure how to respond—"he's met Jonathan?"

"How else would the boy be here? He brought him into the harem. Amir said it was a matter of days before you joined us." Maram snorted her laughter. "Even going so far as to say we shouldn't get too attached. Men do not understand women's business."

Laila laughed and added, "You don't mind that we all want to help raise him, do you? We will never be mothers. It is a blessing to have Jonathan here."

Maram leaned forward and put her hand against Elena's cheek—a comforting, accepting gesture. "You are welcome here, too. We will get to know each other later, but for now I must go," she announced and stood to leave. She winked and left them.

Elena turned to Laila. "I was worried about how Amir would treat him. Mr. Chisholm told me Amir had no children of his own, so I wasn't sure whether or not he was fond of little ones." She shook her head, at a loss for words. "Thank you for the reassurance."

What she didn't voice was that she had thought her

son wouldn't be here when she arrived. How many days before coming here had she spent fretful and distraught that motherhood was but a distant memory? If her little angel hadn't been here, she didn't think she could continue to live. How could a mother let her child go when it was a forced, unnatural separation?

She ran her fingers through the soft, fine hair on Jonathan's head—she couldn't stop touching him, savoring every single moment. His hair had grown so much and was a shade darker than she remembered, a rich brown so much like her own. The only thing he had of his father's were his green eyes.

She leaned in close and gave him another kiss on top of his head, then turned her cheek, resting it there as she rubbed her hand over his back. He still smelled the same, that calming baby smell she could never get enough of.

Not an hour after all the excitement, Jonathan grew agitated and cried out his frustration, as babies are wont to do. She hitched him up on her shoulder, singing a lullaby as she patted his back and bottom waiting for him to fall asleep in her arms. Rocking him as he quieted, she lowered him to sleep more comfortably on her bosom.

Laila still sat with her on the carpeted floor. A slave came forward as if to take Jonathan. Elena shook her head up at the woman, not ready to release her sleeping bundle. The only thing she needed was to hold him, to know without doubt he wasn't lost.

Laila sent the woman off after a few soft words spoken in Persian. Then she got up to retrieve a few bolsters to make it more comfortable for them on the floor. She also carried a small green blanket, obviously made for her son. Fresh tears stung at her eyes.

"Thank you," was all she could mutter to Laila.

Slaves came in with silver trays laden with dried and fresh fruit, nuts, olives, and sesame flatbread. Her stomach growled as the tantalizing aroma hit her. She hadn't been hungry until she saw the food spread out before her. Her mouth watered as she reached for the first tray and took some almonds. After eating a few she picked up a quartered chunk of pomegranate and let the bittersweet juice wash over her parched tongue. She'd only ever had pomegranate once before and she wasn't sure it had tasted this good. She sucked at the seeds then chewed them. Laila ate with her in companionable silence, picking the seeds of her pomegranate from the skin, and popping them into her mouth individually.

"They want to give you time with your son." Laila motioned with her head to indicate the other women in the room. "We are all friends here. There is no place for resentments. Don't think they are ignoring you."

"I didn't think they were," Elena replied, and picked up a slice of orange.

They were her favorite, but costly. When was the last time she'd had this particular fruit? At her last soiree. Before she'd been forced into marriage with Robert. There'd been a platter of sliced oranges at that party. She put the whole slice in her mouth and savored the first sweet bursting taste as it sluiced over her tongue.

They ate their fill in silence. Elena kept rubbing her hand soothingly over her son's back, willing him to sleep the rest of the day. There was no better feeling than holding him again; to know they were both well and alive. When she had eaten as much as she could and drunk a strange yogurt concoction to wash it all down, she leaned back against the bolsters and closed her eyes.

She and Jonathan snuggled up together at long last.

Never again would she be separated from him. They were safe here. And she prayed that it would stay that way.

Her neck was wet where Jonathan drooled, and she was uncomfortably sweaty as he slept sprawled across her chest. She yawned but couldn't find it in her to sit up and move him. He belonged next to her like this.

On opening her eyes, the first thing she noticed was how dark it was around her. A flickering of light danced around the walls from the oil lamps. It seemed as though everyone had gone to bed for the evening. Everything was still.

The air had cooled and a gentle breeze touched her periodically. Unwilling to wake Jonathan, she stayed on her side tucked against the pillows. It took her a while to focus her eyes. The crickets chirped their night song so loudly out of doors that the sound echoed all around the sitting room. She perched up on one elbow. Her hip was sore where it pressed against the hard floor. A more comfortable spot to sleep was in order.

There were divans against most of the walls, full of lush pillows, calling to her. That would be as good a place as any to sleep if she could get the feeling in her side to come back to life.

The only other wall she could see in this position had a series of windows facing the garden. All the shutters were open to let the fresh air filter through the room, carrying with it a rich floral scent. Night-blooming jasmine prickled at her nose, as did other unfamiliar but pleasant scents.

Her son's fist shot out and he let loose one muffled cry before settling back down when she sat up to reposition him. Her whole heart almost pounded right out of her chest at the sight of a man sitting a few feet from her.

He sat reposed, one leg bent with his arm casually stretched over it. The other leg was flat on the ground, a bowl resting upon his thigh. He leaned back against a divan, and his head perched against a loose fist. His feet were bare where his white linen trousers ended. The shirt he wore was unrestricting and exposed the whole of his chest where the vee of his shirt shot down through the center. She noticed a gold band flashed at his wrist whenever the material fluttered around his moving arm.

His complexion was a dark olive in this lighting. His hair looked almost black and was not tied back but fell in gentle waves to his shoulders. He had a close-cut beard. Black eyes fringed with thick lashes stared back at her. She guessed he was around thirty or thirty-five. He was handsome.

Was it a terrible thing for her to take notice of that?

This man planned to turn her into a whore, yet he looked so kind, calm. Gentle. Where had that thought come from? How could she know he was any of those things? This was her tired mind playing tricks on her yet again.

He popped a fig into his mouth and chewed it slowly. His eyes didn't leave hers once, not even when he reached into the bowl for another piece of the dried fruit. Elena looked around the room again. There was no one else here, not another harem girl, slave, eunuch, or even a wet nurse.

Elena couldn't find it in her to say anything, so she watched him with weariness, and to her self-disgust, a tinge of curiosity. He studied her in kind. Her hair must be a mess from sleeping on it while it was damp. But her dark curls draped around her in a protective curtain, hiding what the strip of silk knotted about her failed to cover. Her feet, ankles, and shin were bare for his scrutiny. She tried to tuck the skirt over them, but Jonathan fussed at the movement and she refused to wake him, so she stopped.

"I am Amir." It was simply said in a deep accented voice. He spoke English, his voice clear and strong in the big room, but not so loud as to wake her baby. Moving the bowl from his lap, he crawled over to her in a swift, stealthy motion, like a tiger playing with his prey. His finger came under her chin and he lifted her head closer to his.

"Harry's description did you little justice. You are far more beautiful than I imagined."

Her eyes widened as she waited for him to do something, although what that something was she didn't know. Her son sleeping against her should have acted as a shield, and it was terrible of her to think of her baby that way, but she didn't know what this man expected of her.

Would he take her with her son right here?

She licked her lips without meaning to, and closed her eyes to hide the embarrassment that would be evident in their depths.

Amir only chuckled at her reaction and released her chin. "I'm no barbarian to take you while you hold your sleeping child."

Elena opened her eyes and stared back at him. His smile seemed genuine as he inspected her. Pulling the knot of her robe loose, he parted the silk and exposed her from breast to belly; not once did his hand graze her skin. He could only inspect one side since Jonathan still slept soundly over her other breast. She tried not to flinch, but with her skin exposed to the air and her nerves running rampant, her nipple puckered and gooseflesh rose wherever his eyes caressed her. She couldn't help but tremble in fear.

The wail of her son had never been a more welcome sound. But that relief died in the next moment.

Amir snapped his fingers sharply, and a round squat woman came forward from the shadows. She held her arms out for the baby. Elena was afraid to let him go but more afraid of what Amir would do to her if she defied him so soon into their arrangement. When she made no move to give Jonathan up, the woman bent over her and swaddled her son close to her bosom. Jonathan's mouth latched onto the woman's plump bosom, obviously hungry.

Elena felt immediate remorse for not being able to feed her own son. That joy and closeness had been taken away from her.

"Please . . ." she said in a small voice. She didn't know how to deny this man his rights to her body. At least till she was better acquainted with this place and her role here.

Her son was safe and healthy. She shouldn't want for more than that. But would he remain safe if she refused this man?

Elena clenched her fists, staring after her son. The gurgle and suck of her son feeding grew quieter as the woman walked out of the great room. She had a fleeting moment of fear, wondering if she'd see her son again. Were they to sleep in different parts of the palace? She wanted him close and couldn't bear for him to be taken. Not after she'd just gotten him back.

"I only want to see what I've purchased. You need never fear me."

The voice might be reassuring, but she still couldn't face him. Half her body remained uncovered for his perusal. The other half of her dress slid from her front, and it took everything in her not to cover herself again. She was desperate enough to want to huddle beneath the meager shield the silk afforded.

"You will be more comfortable if you lean back against the pillows."

His voice was soothing and meant to calm her panic, but it did no such thing. A slight whimper escaped her lips before she bit it to hold the trembling at bay. She was losing control of her emotions and was close to blubbering all over Amir.

The Lord's Prayer went through her head in a perverse parody, but it would not protect her from him taking what he wanted. She bit her trembling lip tighter. She couldn't still her shaking as she leaned back against the pillows exposed to a man she didn't know, a man who was not her husband and never would be.

"Shh . . . you are so frightened and for no reason."

She flinched at his touch even though it was light, tender. Those freely wandering fingers of his caressed the curve of her breast, over her rib cage, and farther down to the slight roundness of her belly. His hands grazed the skin above her mound, exploring but never touching her with full strength, the heat of his hand more predominant than his touch.

"Are you sore, here?" His fingers pressed more firmly into her womanhood before easing off.

She nodded, tears leaking out the side of her eyes. Would he leave her be if she were sore? What if she complained of the pain? He seemed a reasonable person since he hadn't forced himself upon her—in her—yet.

A strong hand wrapped about her ankle and he pulled her leg down so there was no hope of shielding any part of her body. She was laid flat out on the floor for his view, his hand molded over her leg caressing her up to her hip.

Did he not feel the tremble of her body? Fear in a woman should repel so gentle a man, not attract further advances.

"You see, this isn't so terrible."

It was so simple for a man to say such things, but it wasn't the case for her. She felt sweat trickle under her breasts and roll off her rib cage, the small of her back felt wet and hot against the rug, and even her palms started to perspire in nervousness.

"I have no protection against a child." Her words were hissed so low and fast she barely heard them. She bit her lip to stop from saying more.

Amir only leaned close to her face. "I'm not so cruel as to subject you to more. It is not my goal to frighten you out of your wits, little bird. You are safe from my advances tonight."

Those words were said with such conviction that she wanted to believe him, but his hand still caressed her leg. She had no reason to trust him yet—no reason not to. It'd be foolish to balk at his touch.

"You will have to prepare yourself for me. I assume Harry told you I'd let you spend time with your son and become more acquainted with life here?"

"Yes," she whispered.

His hand fell more firmly on her, lifting the weight of one breast, then the next. His fingers clasped around her nipple, his mouth came close to the taut peak, hot breath fanned out over her skin.

She shivered in revulsion, itching to shrink away, to put any small distance between them. There was nowhere left to escape. Instead, she grasped the silk of her robe that had fallen to her sides and squeezed it so tight her nails cut into her palm right through the material.

A moment later a blanket fell over her, and she heard the soft padding of his feet walking away. She curled into herself on the floor, clutching the blanket close. She didn't want to find her way in the dark to her own room. No strength remained in her body, and she wanted to feel miserable for herself. Was it fair for her to pity the path she'd chosen even if it was just for a moment?

No, it wasn't fair to her son.

She'd agreed to be this man's slave to protect her son from harm, to save herself from probable death. This was about giving Jonathan the chance to live his life out from under the shadows of his misbegotten father. She would endure whatever her owner doled out. Jonathan was all that mattered. Nothing else.

She was not so weak as to lose advantage in her predicament. It certainly wasn't beneath her to take what she could from the arrangement. One thing Amir had proved about his character was that he was generous— perhaps *manipulative* was a more apt word—when he wanted something. If he was cruel, he would have purchased her and forgotten her son. Yet, he hadn't.

Whatever Amir asked of her, she would do, but she would also benefit from it. She'd been a beggar too long under the feeble hand of her husband. Life had dealt her a strange twist of fate. It would be foolish not to take the fullest advantage of her situation.

Someone tapped her arm. She peeped her head over her shoulder. Maram kneeled next to her, a smile lighting her face.

"You've met Amir."

Elena nodded. What was she supposed to say? That he'd been so disgusted by her behavior he'd left? Hardly a way to make peace with these women she was to live with for the rest of her days.

"You don't want to sleep in here," the girl continued, "it gets cool in the evenings. I'll take you to your room."

There was no reason to argue, so she followed the

girl out of the main sitting area back to her private quarters. She sat in a dazed state on her divan and said nothing as the girl took the edge of her dress and retied it, knotting it between her breasts.

"Do you want me to stay in your room, sleep here with you? Amir won't come back. He is a patient man, more patient than any I've ever known."

"I'm well enough to sleep alone." She grasped the girl's arm before she left. "Thank you for the offer."

"I like you. You are kind—a little broken, but I think you'll be fine in time. The rules are different here, but no one will cause you any harm."

"I don't think I ever will find my way."

"You will. Give it time"—Maram chuckled and gave a shrug of her shoulder—"we have an abundance of *that* here."

There was no doubting the truth of the girl's words, she thought as she watched Maram leave.

With the affirmation that this was to be her life, Elena came to a series of conclusions. If she were adamant about doing this for her son, she would not be a martyr. That would make her miserable and kill a big piece of her spirit. How could she ever give her son a good, fulfilling childhood if she destroyed what spark of life was left within her?

Accepting this fate meant taking what comforts this life might offer. Otherwise she'd spend the rest of her days shelled in a miserable husk. Her son deserved more. To grow up without bitterness, even here, in the life they'd landed haphazardly in.

If she wanted her son to be happy, she'd make this situation work. She'd embrace this to the best of her abilities. No matter what she endured, she'd stay strong for Jonathan.

CHAPTER FIVE

The Way of Life

"It's time to wake."

Her shoulder was nudged gently.

"We have to go to the baths."

Elena rolled over on the divan and faced Laila. Covering a wide yawn, she rubbed at her tired eyes. "What do you mean, we go to the baths? We were in the baths last night, and for some hours."

"It does not matter. It is necessary here to follow all the customs."

She could probably argue with this woman until she was blue in the face. Besides that, she was too tired to squabble about anything. Sitting up, she gathered her hair on top her head and twisted it in a knot as best she could. What she'd give to get hold of some hairpins. "Where does Jonathan sleep?"

Laila's face lit up at the mention of her son.

"He's only across the courtyard." Laila pointed out the open window. "In the room with the shutters blocked off. The air at night is not good for the baby."

"Will you take me to see him? I'd like to know the way."

"Of course." Laila seemed surprised by the questions. "You can see your son whenever you are in the harem quarters. No one will keep you from him. Except when you are with Amir, or another lord. Those times will be spent in another part of the palace, which we call the 'Pleasure Gardens.' Your son will not be permitted in that section. Probably never."

Elena couldn't agree more with such good sense. The fewer people who knew of her son the better; his reputation would stay intact.

She'd almost forgotten about that part of the bargain. Not that it had been much of a bargain. It was a matter of choosing the lesser evil: accept the life of a harlot or stay in the slave quarters. She'd agreed to this place, this life.

She followed her new friend through the corridors. Indeed, this was a new life.

The man who had purchased her was not cruel. There was a whole harem of women who welcomed her as a sister. Above all, she'd been given her son when she'd thought him lost. But here she was, her spirit mending in the kindness offered by the other women, and open arms all around her.

This time when they walked through the corridors Elena took in the surroundings to better remember her way around. Most of the walls were whitewashed. The floors afoot were great blocks of gray and tan stone. The way was simple to the baths. She attributed her earlier confusion to her fear when she'd arrived. So much had happened between her arrival yesterday and now. The weight that had constricted her spirit in the slave market seemed to have been chipped away overnight. Though she wouldn't easily accept her owner, she would try as best she could to adjust to this place.

That familiar choking wall of heat greeted her at the

public bath, and then clutched around her as they stepped inside. There were women everywhere, unlike yesterday when it had been just her and Laila. Now slaves and mistresses milled about and lounged in groups around the pool; the stone fountains were built into the wall where a steady stream of water poured into the wide, low bases. All the women were in various states of dress and undress.

Some lazed by the great pool in the center of the room or sat on upturned wooden baskets close to the walls. Slaves walked around with trays of food ranging from fruits to nuts to sweet pastries. Others carried linens and towels or pitchers, which must contain something to drink to stave off the heat in this insufferable place.

Elena couldn't imagine eating in here; she could barely swallow the saliva in her throat the air was so thick. Though something cool to drink would be welcome if she had to stay in here for any length of time. She turned to Laila, who had already stripped out of her robe and waited for Elena to do the same.

Looking to the eunuchs and other nude women around the bath, Elena swallowed any argument she thought to make, and slipped out of the material that did little to hide her figure beneath anyway. A slave stood by and whisked her garments away. Elena crossed her arms over her bosom.

"How will I end up in other lords' company, Laila?" she asked as she stepped down into the pool, and hunkered beneath the water to better hide her nakedness.

"You will not be expected to share relations with other men for your first year. Amir will train you in your duties first." Laila leaned back, her elbows on the stairs of the pool. "And I will teach you some tricks he cannot."

"A year," she parroted. She didn't know what to think of that. She didn't know what to think of any of this.

"Sometimes he keeps us longer but usually not. He will parade you in front of the rich lords, in the Pleasure Gardens. Draw their interest to drive up your first bidding price."

"Bidding? So we are auctioned? No better than the slaves sold at market?"

Laila chuckled. "Not like a slave market."

"Everything is so different here. So unlike anything I've ever known." Elena shook her head, pulling the heavy mass of her hair over each shoulder. "There seems to be a lot of adjustments I must make. So much to accept when I've never been exposed to such an environment before."

"You will figure these things out soon enough. You are not used to this place, but I think in a week or so you will feel as though you have always lived here."

"Only time will tell." Elena sighed as she combed her fingers through her hair.

"Amir has given you a few days, yes?"

Elena frowned. She'd been so frightened that most of Amir's words had escaped her. "I believe he said a few days. I can't quite recall. He fairly took me by surprise."

"I do not know why you are afraid to spend time with him. Has he not shown you kindness in giving your son back, reuniting the two of you?"

"I suppose . . ." She shook her head, not knowing how to make Laila understand her plight. "You have to understand that I've never been exposed to any of this type of forwardness. We English are a little more—"

"Prudish," Laila supplied.

Elena couldn't help but smile back. Was she prudish? Most likely. Though it seemed insulting the way

Laila said it. Never had she thought it anything but an essential trait of any well-bred English lady.

"This is a different culture from the one you are used to. I do comprehend your plight, Elena. In time you will see that our way of life is a little more freeing than your old one. You can express yourself without fear of repercussion. No one will judge you for enjoying some of the things we indulge in."

"I should embrace my becoming a whore?"

That word no longer held the venom it used to. It didn't matter; the austerity of the words seemed lost on her new friend. Laila was contagious in her way of thinking.

"You see, you smile. I am right in this. Such a tact-less way of saying what we are. It is a prideful thing to be a harem girl who is well looked after. We enjoy what we do. Our life would not be so relaxed and sim-ple if fate had not intervened and brought us to Amir. We've all got a past we'd rather not remember."

She wholeheartedly agreed with that, and nodded. "My life might have ended in the slave market had I not been found by Mr. Chisholm. But that does not make this the better arrangement."

"How can you believe that? Are you and your son not safe?"

Elena frowned, then dunked her whole head under the water.

Laila was right. But one couldn't take a lifetime's worth of belief and reverse it overnight. Breaking the surface, Elena rubbed the water from her eyes and combed her hands through her hair once again. "It will take me a while to get used to this. Not everything will be easy for me to embrace."

"This is why Amir has me guiding you." Laila reached out for some of her hair and helped her untan-gle the snarls.

"Guiding? Is that what we call this?" Elena sat on one of the lower steps, wrapping her arms around her knees. She gave her back to Laila so she could brush her hair out easier. "You practically forced me to do your bidding yesterday. I would have cooperated had you given me some more time to adjust to the change I was thrown into."

"That was necessary according to house rules. I will guide you in how to please a man as well."

Elena coughed into her hand, choking on the spittle that went down wrong. When she caught her breath again, she said, "You can't be serious!"

Laila's smile was mischievous—a sly tilt lifted her lip. "I'm very serious. You must please a man in many ways . . . and in any way he asks once you've been sold at auction."

"I was . . . I was a married woman. I will not need instruction in these matters."

What was so hard about lying abed while her husband rutted above her? Not that she'd been a total deadwood in their marriage bed, either.

"You are familiar with the duties as a married woman, as your child goes to show. But do you think for one moment I believe your husband had you suck off his pego?"

Elena gasped as she turned to look at Laila, mouth hanging open in shock. "Laila, such words." Her husband would never have asked such a thing. Did women really do that?

Her only reaction was a wink. "I will have to teach you many words if this one makes you blush. Though I think Amir will like your blush; it gives a beautiful healthy glow to your cheeks and lends a certain innocence. This is something you lose over time. Even

Maram, young as she is, does not have this sense of innocence. Come to think of it, I'm not sure she ever did
have it."

"I hope to retain this innocence as long as possible,"
she mumbled. The declaration was lost on Laila since
the woman had started up the steps of the pool, calling
out orders to the slaves.

Laila turned to look at her when she made no move
to leave the water. "Come. There is nothing about your
person we haven't all seen. Modesty is lost among your
sisters."

"It's much easier for you to say, having grown up in
such a place. We don't go about London in this un-
clothed fashion, not even in our bath."

"Oh, but they do in the bawdy houses. I once asked
a patron."

Elena knew it to be the truth. Wasn't that one of the
many things that she thought separated genteel ladies
from harlots? It didn't matter; the two were one and the
same for her now. Never in all her days had she thought
to become the kind of woman to spread her legs for any
man's pleasure.

One did not wake up in the morning and wonder:
Will my husband lose me in a hand of cards today?

She shook her head in disgust. It did no good to
think about what her life should have been. As Laila
suggested, it was better to forget the past and embrace
this new life. Not that she could truly embrace it. But
she didn't want to be miserable—that would reflect
over time on her son. She needed to take Laila's advice
and forget about being a prude.

"Can we see Jonathan when we've finished here?" It
had bothered her all morning that she hadn't seen her
son before going to the bath. She wanted to snatch every

moment possible with him. The weeks they had spent apart had made her realize how precious spending time with her son was.

"Of course. He is too young to come to the baths. That is, until he has his legs under him. I thought it best to show you our days without your son between us. He would be too much of a distraction."

"You are likely right."

Before stepping out of the pool, Elena looked around the bathing area. There were about twenty women. They didn't seem to care about their lack of attire. Some brushed each other's hair, others lounged together at the edge of the room on wooden benches, laughing at whatever topic they found amusing, and smoking long strange pipes. No one looked at her. They all fairly ignored her as they went about whatever it was they did.

Elena took a deep breath; she could do this. She could rise from the water and bare herself, naked as the day she was born. What did it matter? They were all women, and she'd often stripped down to her chemise for her maids to help her bathe.

She rose from the water, and a passing slave gave her a small hand towel. How was she to dry with this? She looked at Laila, who paid her no mind as she spoke to another slave carrying a ewer of water. She couldn't understand the words exchanged. The language barrier was a handicap she'd have to fix soon.

"Reema will rinse your hair with rose water. It will help with the knots. Then we'll go back to the living quarters."

"Can you teach me how to speak this language with more confidence, Laila?"

"Of course. I can teach you many if it pleases you. I pick them up without difficulty. A talent that has made me well liked by some of the foreigners who frequent the Pleasure Gardens," she said with another wink. "I speak Arabic, Persian, Turkish, Armenian—my own language. You know I speak your tongue. I can teach you French if you like and some Russian, even German if you are so bold."

"Goodness. What a mix. One thing at a time if it pleases you."

They each sat on one of those wooden crates. Rather uncomfortable, but better than sitting on the damp tiled floor.

"It is easy to master a new one, when you've been surrounded by different languages most of your life. I've been with Amir for fifteen years now. It's all part and parcel."

"I speak conversational French. It has been difficult for me to grasp Persian and Turkish though I understand some rudimentary words. I think I have had such a difficult time because I was in seclusion shortly after we arrived in Constantinople. We English women don't go out while enceinte."

The slave's fingers were relaxing as Reema massaged her scalp, tipping her head back to pour the sweet-smelling water through it. The water was surprisingly cool as it sluiced through her hair. The rose scent was lovely and muted the sulphuric smell that clung in the humid air.

"Why do we spend so much time in here?"

"You do not like to be clean?"

Elena cracked one eye open, and raised her brow at Laila. "I believe you are teasing me. I don't understand why we have to spend hours in here."

"It is not about spending time bathing. We are here to bond. This is the only place we can express ourselves freely. Amir does not come in here. He has his own private bath. We can be women here without interference."

"Oh, I didn't realize." Elena looked around her again. Really looked. She spotted Maram on the opposite side of the room, a thread wrapped about her fingers and through her teeth. "What is Maram doing?"

Laila sat up to see what Elena was curious about. "Ah, this is the threading I told you of yesterday. We remove hair as soon as we see it growing back. That is another reason we spend so much time in here. It wouldn't be right to see a man with hairs on our body."

"But it's almost childlike to be so . . ." Elena looked down to her nether region. It was smooth and didn't feel as sore today. "Bare. Do you not want to be defined as a woman? I always thought it a rite of passage. From girl to woman."

"Not here. It is unsightly. Only men have hair. It is easier to clean ourselves, after men have taken their pleasure and we have had our own. Amir does not allow disease into the Pleasure Gardens. I have no idea how he learns the sexual proclivities of various lords, but none of the girls have ever become ill. The only strangeness is from Europe and your homeland. Men have a strange look to their penis."

Elena's brows furrowed in sudden curiosity. She sat up straighter on her crate. "Why are they strange?"

"They have a neck around them of loose skin. They call it a cap. Here, it is taken off when a boy comes into manhood."

"They take it off?" How grotesquely shocking.

"It is only loose skin. Useless, really. They cut it off."

What would a penis with its skin cut off look like? She couldn't begin to imagine. Would it be smaller? Did it not hurt to do that to a boy? She decided she didn't want to be enlightened.

They chatted about nonsensical things for another hour before they left the bathing area. Elena took a deep breath of the cool air when they exited the room. Would she ever get used to the heat in the public bath? It was something dreadful. How could one really be clean when one sweated while bathing?

This was how her days went for a week. Bathing every day, then sitting in their living quarters with her son and some of the other girls who weren't occupying lords in the other part of the palace. Eunuchs would come in at all times of the day and escort some of the girls to the Pleasure Gardens.

Elena went into the courtyard gardens daily. There were so many types of truly beautiful flowers. She couldn't imagine how many years it had taken to build the gardens to get it just right.

It reminded her of the Duchess of Glenmoore's gardens. She'd only ever set foot in them during the evenings, with her beau, Griffin, tugging her through the mazes, stealing her away to kiss her in secret. How those days seemed a millennia ago. So far away that she wondered if it was all a dream of what she had wanted with her life, to marry a man who professed great feelings for her. A man who made her heart speed the moment he entered a room.

She shook her head and took a deep breath. Silly nostalgic thoughts.

The sun beat down bright and hot today, so she sat under the shade of a cherry tree with the flowers blooming down on her. It was situated at the center of the court next to a great pond with orange and black fish swimming just beneath the surface. They were imported from China. White lilies floated atop the water and great tall grass reeds sprouted from the pond surface here and there. A stone ledge wrapped right around it so one could sit at the water's edge. She'd taken her son with her every day.

Whenever she threw in a pomegranate seed, fish swarmed to the surface trying to grab the tidbit into their big gaping, round mouths. Jonathan liked to grab at the wriggling fish and chortled whenever they came to the surface to feed.

A gentle breeze swept through the gardens, lifting her hair in its embrace before the warmth of midafternoon enveloped her again. She looked around her and took a deep breath of the sea air. It was refreshing and invigorating.

Tall flagstone walls covered with ivy climbed to the sky all around her, creating shade in the garden. Most of the shutters that covered the windows were open during the day. She could see into the bedchambers, mostly empty, and the main sitting area where many of the harem girls lounged, talked, smoked their hookah, and ate.

It was her very own paradise this afternoon.

Not all the flowers and plants could be identified in this little heaven. She'd always had a love for flowers and hadn't realized how lacking her knowledge was until her first day in this garden. It was peaceful sitting under this wide blooming tree, her son on her lap. She liked it when it was just her and Jonathan. It reminded her of days long in the past.

This wasn't so difficult a life to live. Not when such beauty surrounded you. But although she might find this peaceful for the moment, she knew it would only be a matter of time before she was expected to live up to her duties as Amir's personal slave.

Amir hadn't once called for her since that first night they met. She was thankful for that.

She turned at the shuffling of feet over the flagstone, surprised to see Amir strolling out into the garden, headed straight toward her as though her thoughts had called out to him.

He wore white linen trousers and a loose open shirt. Yellow and gold pointed slippers covered his feet. She kept her eyes plastered to the ground, not ready to meet his gaze.

"Laila told me I'd find you out here in the gardens," he said softly.

She couldn't find it in herself to look up, so she looked over to the slave, expecting the woman to take her son back inside. Elena was surprised when the woman nodded, not to her but Amir, and then turned on her heel. Leaving her quite alone with Amir and Jonathan.

She took a deep breath and raised her gaze as far as the top of her son's head.

Would Amir ask for her tonight?

She'd thought herself lucky to have so much solitude. This time of reprieve and bonding with her son had been healing for her soul.

Gathering what courage she had left, she raised her eyes to Amir's.

He hiked up his trousers at the knee and sat next to her on the bench. Balling up bits of bread between his fingers, he tossed them in the water. The fish raced to the surface, gluttons for crumbs to fill their bellies. It was like watching the slaves scramble for the bug-infested sludge at the slave market.

So focused on the past, she felt more than saw Amir lift Jonathan from her lap. She turned her head and watched him perch the child in his own lap. In awe of such a small act on his part, she watched Amir roll up more bits of bread, helping Jonathan toss them in the water. Amir laughed when half the crumbs went into Jonathan's mouth.

An endearing sight to be sure. Didn't every woman wish to see a doting father and son bond? Not that Amir played at being father. Her son was a means to an end for Amir, to win over her cooperation. But she still didn't know how she could surrender herself to this man.

"You have nothing to fear from me."

Is that what he saw? A frightened woman? There was a long pause of silence from both of them. Her son laughed at the rise and fall of fish from the top of the water.

"I only find my circumstances awkward."

Amir nodded his understanding, but his focus was on her son. "You will like my attentions in time."

"You seem rather confident. If I might say so," she added quickly so as not to seem ungrateful to what he'd already done for her. She must learn to temper her tongue.

"You will shed this cold exterior in time. It is a defense you use to guard your English pride."

"Who is to say it's pride that keeps me a gently bred woman? I'm not meant for what you have in mind." She bowed her head. "But I agreed to the arrangement for my son's future. I will stand by the promise I made."

Amir mulled this for a moment, his lips twisting as though he bit into something sour and not to his liking. "You did agree to this, otherwise Harry would not have gone to the trouble of purchasing you."

He turned away from the water and set her son on the ground, giving Jonathan the bracelet from his own wrist to play with.

"I won't let you leave here. We can come to many arrangements to make it more comfortable, but you will still be expected to warm my bed. If you find it reprehensible to have relations with a man beneath your station, there's nothing that can be done about it.

But you will learn to like it. I can be very convincing in acts of a more indulgent nature." His voice was soft and even, but there was no mistaking the edge of anger lancing his words.

"Please. Let me apologize for my behavior," she said. "I've said too much. I will do whatever you bid me. You are not a man beneath me. I never meant—"

He raised a hand to silence her protestations. "I'm glad for that, but your docile nature cannot cocoon you any longer. You need to come out of your shell. No one wants you to disgrace yourself. Everyone will help to support and strengthen your fledging wings as you learn your way around." He faced her and gave her a small smile, his anger no longer evident. "Only then will you find your missing spirit, little bird."

Such a strange way to word it.

She hated that everyone read her so well. But he was right. She hadn't been abused. In fact, she'd been treated graciously, thoughtfully; everyone wanted to help her learn this way of life. Amir reached his hand out to her son, who bashed the bracelet around in excitement.

He tickled under Jonathan's chin, and her son released the bauble and laughed at the man who played with him. How could a man who lived such an amoral way of life, owning slaves and whoring women, be this tender?

It wasn't a question she wanted the answer to.

Taking the delicate filigree between his long slender fingers, Amir bent the pretty band so the circle was smaller. Then he slipped it over her son's chubby hand, fitting it snugly around his baby-plump wrist.

Jonathan's eyes seemed to widen, and the bracelet went immediately to his mouth. Amir chucked Jonathan under the chin again until her boy laughed and chortled in his baby way. He seemed torn between sucking on the bracelet and grappling Amir's fingers.

Amir turned to her suddenly. "I want you in my bed-chamber tonight. Laila will prepare you."

There was no response to that. She lowered her head, not wanting to meet his gaze. The only sound was her son's laughter and the fountain that drained into the fishpond.

She would not argue. He could take away everything he'd given her and that might include her son. She must tread carefully so as not to ruin her last chance for survival. At least until she better understood this man.

His hand came down to rest on the top of her head, his fingers lifting a hank of hair, then releasing it just as quickly. He left her there, tears running down her cheeks.

Why was she crying? No use denying that she was grateful for all he'd done.

Maybe she cried because she was afraid to open up to him. Afraid of what she'd learn about herself when with him. She thought about that a moment longer. Her fear dissipated. She wasn't afraid of lying with a man who was not her husband.

It wasn't that the actual act of congress was terribly horrible; she had enjoyed it upon occasion. What bothered her was this strange intuition that she wouldn't find this a hardship in the least. Where had Elena disappeared to in the last week? She'd been so adamant and sure of herself before arriving at the palace. Now there was this new person taking over her body, her mind, telling her this was not a terrible fate at all, but a good second chance.

She slumped on the ground next to Jonathan and set him on her lap so that his wobbly legs stood on her thighs.

"Promise not to hate me when you learn that your mama has sold herself into this life."

One pudgy hand reached out to grasp her loose hair. She pressed her lips to his forehead, giving him a quick kiss.

"I will do everything in my power to give us both a life we can love. I pray to God you don't hate me when you understand what I truly am. But I tell you this now as a promise to us both; I will make this a life worth having. I will make this the best I can. For both of us. This looks to be our last stop before we're dancing in Elysium's fields."

Giving her son a raspberry kiss on his cheek and a hug that had him squirming as she tickled his sides, she picked him up and strolled toward Laila's room.

CHAPTER SIX

The Surrender of Reservation

A eunuch stood on either side of the double-door entry. Each pushed one massive wooden door inward and gave her a little push inside. She tripped a few steps forward and spun around to see the doors closing in her wake. She smoothed her hands over her arms as if warding off a chill.

So this was it. She'd known it was coming all day, so why couldn't she turn around?

Taking a deep breath, she lowered her hands to her sides and turned where she stood.

The room was empty. Amir was not waiting for her. She released the air she held tight in her lungs.

How long was she expected to wait? The longer she was here alone, the more nervous she grew. Her stomach was in knots and not all of it stemmed from fear. There was a note of anticipation that made her sick to her stomach. It was like her wedding night all over again.

Instead of worrying about his arrival, she focused on the opulence of the room. Lush carpets cushioned her feet, inviting her to curl her toes into them, but she wouldn't take her slippers off. She'd keep every last transparent thread on her person until she was forced to reveal more. There was no bed in the room, only a wide comfortable divan and cushions that could substitute as seating on the floors.

This room was no different than hers, except for the writing table that occupied one corner. There was a ledger open and resting on it, a quill sitting in the inkwell next to it. She turned to the windows. A warm breeze brushed over her in gentle reassurance before it was gone. She shook her head at her silliness and walked over to the ledge to look out at the grounds. She stood above the garden, the very one she frequented with her son.

How often had he watched her from this very spot? Goose bumps rose on her arms at the thought of him spying on her.

She smoothed her hand over the wall, caressing the rough stone to ground her to reality, the now. He had an unfair advantage by knowing more about her. It made her uneasy.

She looked away from the dark foliage. It was a clear night beyond the palace walls, stars twinkled bright and beautiful in the sky, and no walls impeded her view of the ocean perhaps a mile or two off.

Not wanting Amir to sneak up on her, she backed away from the call of freedom the night sang, and retreated to the divan. Sitting down, she hid her bottom. A small taffeta pillow in green edged with pretty glass beads went immediately into her lap.

It was more uncomfortable by the minute.

How she wished for the fortification of wine or even the swill of a fine brandy. She'd asked for some earlier to ease her nerves, but Laila told her that was impossible; alcohol was forbidden to the women. No sense in arguing the matter; her nerves would be on edge, mind on tenterhooks, hands trembling no matter how hard she clutched the pillow with or without wine.

Low voices came from the second, smaller door in the room moments before it swung silently open. Her heart thudded so hard in her chest; she was nearly deaf from the pounding of it in her ears.

Amir wore his usual white linen trousers, white shirt with loose sleeves, the collar cut down the center to reveal the fine lines and hairs of his chest. She tried to swallow back the lump in her throat, then pinched her eyes shut.

She didn't hear him approach, his steps were so silent. Courage hadn't surfaced in her when he stood within a handspan of her, knees bumping hers. He removed the pillow from her lap with a quick tug. The beads jangled as it was tossed behind him and hit the floor like the final blow of an axe.

Taking one of her fisted hands in his, he unfurled her shaking sweaty palm and placed it flat to his chest.

"Fear not." Leaning forward, he whispered into her ear, "I will treat you well this night."

She nodded, afraid to speak. She could do this. Whatever *this* was. Though she still fought to keep her eyes tightly shut. If they were shut, she could pretend this was an ordinary visit from her husband.

Amir smelled of musk and sandalwood, a masculine, rich scent that made her heart trip. He was so close, and her body tensed. She felt the low rumble of his chuckle where her hand rested over his sternum.

"If it makes you feel better, keep your eyes closed. But I cannot show you how this is best done if you play shy." His voice was soft, not accusing.

He pulled off the tie around her waist in one smooth swish of fabric. The warm silk slid open. The knot in her throat was bigger than ever, her body tight as a bow-string.

His touch was light, reverent. He didn't grope. His fingers were warm and surprisingly soft. She cracked her eyes open and was startled to see him staring back. She was locked in those dark eyes of his, unwilling to break away. The fear of moments ago now clouded her mind in a mantle of panic.

She couldn't do this. She really couldn't. Yanking her hand away from his chest, she scooted over on the divan, and turned her body to the side so her breasts were not in the direct line of his gaze.

It said a lot that he let her escape. Even if it was only for the moment.

"I know you are frightened." His finger trailed a circular path over her arm. "I will be gentle as this is your first night."

He held his hand out toward her, in invitation.

Seeing his face, his expression, she could read what he wanted. See the desire burning in the black depths. There was no mockery, definitely no pity. His relaxed stance told her he would wait, patiently if need be.

She crossed her ankles, squeezing her thighs together as she turned her head away from him. He sat beside her, their arms and legs touching. Taking her hand, he placed it on his thigh.

"Lie back," he said. The swish of his shirt being removed came next.

Her head shot around till her eyes were level with his. She shook her head, hands trembling with edginess where it gripped his thigh.

Tipping her chin up with his knuckle, he rubbed his thumb across her lower lip before releasing her. Gently, he picked up her shaky fist, his strong hand massaging the tips of her fingers as he pulled them loose. Warmth eased her frozen nerves.

"My touch is not so bad, is it?"

She hated that it wasn't horrible. Why didn't he force himself on her? If he did, she could hate him, hate herself for choosing this escape instead of suffering in the slave market like any well-bred English woman would've done. Instead, she'd embraced the opportunity to become a woman of loose morals. God, she'd agreed so easily to this. Too easily.

"Turn around. I want to see you."

She hesitated, not sure what to do. He grasped her calves, twisting her until her feet were in his lap. She was tipped back on the pillows piled on the divan.

"I assume you do not know all the ways to pleasure a man. Aside from a little shove and pull. I doubt you'll ask any necessary questions because it is beneath your breeding."

"This *is* improper. You aren't my husband."

"Improper." He smiled and grasped her foot to press it to the hardness of his groin. "This is improper by your standards?"

He raised his eyebrow, daring her to pull away. She didn't and for the life of her she didn't know why. He massaged her calf and around her knee. Her foot was still pressed tight to his *rod*—one of the words Laila had taught her. The only one that didn't make her cringe internally to say.

His hand molded and caressed the curve of her hip, the slight roundness of her stomach.

He pushed out one of her knees, forcing the folds of her sex open. Cool air met her flesh. She let out a small squeal, helpless to hold all her reservations inside. Biting down on her lip, she fought the urge to close her legs, to hide the shameful nakedness he exposed.

He rubbed the length of her thigh as one would a skittish mare. Smooth, firm strokes, up and down her flank.

"I won't take more than you are willing to give."

"I am forced to do this. How can you think I'd want to disgrace myself so completely? I'm a lady of noble birth and here you have me acting like any lewd doxy."

"Ah, but you belong to me now."

She pulled out of his grasp and hugged her arms around her knees, trying to cover as much of her nudity as possible. It was all she could do to preserve the last of her modesty.

Amir looked at her, head cocked to the side. "I did not think you hated my touch."

"You are mistaken to think I welcome your attentions."

"Yet you agreed to come here of your free will."

"I was not free. I was a slave, I'd been beaten and half starved and I was desperate to see my son," she said as calmly as she could.

"You try my patience. I do not want to force you. I want to teach you how to pleasure a man and how to take your own pleasure."

"I cannot be so free with my body."

"Yes, you can."

He grasped her ankles and yanked her legs down hard until she lay flat on the divan, Amir resting atop of her. "Perhaps I should show you the joys to be had in the full brunt of passion before teaching you the finer details."

She pushed at his chest. He didn't budge but gave a low sultry chuckle at her pathetic attempt to push him off.

He studied her face carefully, surely waiting for the veneer of her prim nature to crack. Laila's term for her swam through her mind: *prude*. She tried to remain passive even though her lip trembled between the clench of her teeth. She barely managed to hold her sobs back.

He forced her legs open farther. His rod sat firm against her inner thigh. His hand molded to the curve of her breast. Deft fingers plucked at the tip, bringing the nipple to a firm peak. "You like this. Otherwise you would not respond so beautifully."

"I do not." She couldn't even look at him. She did like what he did and hated herself so much for it.

Before she could protest, he placed her fingers at the juncture of her thighs. She gasped as he forced her hand to slide through the slickness of her folds.

"This is why your body cannot lie to me. Other men who take their pleasure in you will see this willingness. Listen and learn, Elena. No matter the humiliation you feel. By touching yourself, you inflame a man's desire.

"I do not think you will resist my attempts now." Before she could give a denial, his finger slipped, with ease, into her passage. "This pleases me, little bird."

CHAPTER SEVEN

Auction Block

"Stop moving and wriggling around. I'll be done before you know it."

"It tickles. You can't expect me to hold still when I have this constant desire to scratch."

Laila sat up and put her brush on the wooden tray laden with pots of pressed henna, some still in its powdered form. The designs of ivy and flowers covered her feet and palms, the back of her hands, and halfway up her forearms. Laila had taken the time to henna her areolas, and, to her great embarrassment, her nether region with a dulled rust-color paint. Elena stood and gave a shake of her arms to get the tickle to go away.

"Stop pacing. You make me agitated, too."

Elena stopped and turned. "When was the first time you had this done?"

Laila smiled. "The harem women did this to me a few days before my virginity was taken. Amir had me the first time when I was sixteen."

She looked at her sister with a raised brow. "The painting isn't the reason I'm fussing."

"You'll be fine. Amir will keep you close to his

side," Laila said with a nod of understanding. "You do not have to talk if you are not confident in your Persian. Only a few words here and there and the men will think you an enchanting creature. Your shyness will win them over, and I'm sure they will pay no heed to what you say. They will be busy looking over your other attributes." Laila pulled a sun-yellow scarf from the foot of the divan. "Yellow will complement your skin tone, don't you think?"

Elena rolled her eyes and carried on with her pacing. "I had a feeling that would be your response. I don't like the idea of being on auction and sold to another— it's rather sickening. And I was thinking the green silk. The one with the gold embroidered around the edges."

Walking over to her, Laila placed the scarf against her thigh. "Hmm. Maybe yellow doesn't go with the paint. Yes, I think the emerald is nicer."

"Do you think all men are so shallow and unintelligent that they won't figure out who I am sooner or later?"

"Elena, you forget this isn't a typical English soiree. You won't need to talk about the weather. You might not even talk." Laila grinned as she folded the yellow scarf and set it on the divan. "You know very well Amir will expect nothing more than your attendance for your first year here. Your only duty is to look sweet and ripe enough to bite into."

Elena flopped down on the divan and held her unfinished hand out to Laila. "Finish it then. I wish I only had to amuse Amir. That would be easier. Besides, I feel like I'm going to my first ball and I'm going to step on suitors' feet or dribble punch down the front of my gown."

"This will be nothing like a ball. Fear not, the men will not care what the veil hides, only what they can see beneath your scarves." Laila leaned back on the bench she used and looked at Elena's chest, a puzzled expression in her eyes. "Maybe we should paint them darker?"

"Is that supposed to be reassuring?" Elena shook her head and threw her free arm over her eyes to block out the light. "It's not. You are making me more nervous by the minute. I might make a fool of myself and embarrass Amir. I couldn't live with that. It doesn't matter what he thinks, it'll be me that's the fool. If you think painting my privates will keep the lords more concerned with my breast size and pertness, by all means paint them darker."

"Hmm . . ."

"Would you stop with that incessant 'hmm'?"

"I'm thinking how we should present you." She clucked her tongue in annoyance, another habit of hers. "You forget we've all been where you are. Someone had to rear us into this life as I am doing for you."

"I do not know what to expect here. I have nothing remotely similar to compare this to. I'm surprised how free I've become with my body where Amir is concerned. Though it's taken me some months to even allow that."

Laila bent her head to the task of finishing her hand without answering. Elena knew Laila contemplated her answer carefully. The soft tickling strokes of the brush resumed. Another twenty minutes and it would be done. The markings would stay for at least a month, maybe two.

"When you came here, you never thought you could endure pleasuring Amir, either. Now you are happy, no longer a frightened lady. This is a good life. You spend time with your son every day. You see your sisters and bond with us every day. What is it that really bothers you? That you will not adjust to the auctioning and the Pleasure Gardens?"

"I don't know. Maybe I'm being difficult. I don't mean to be. Things are comfortable right now. I don't want my life to keep changing. What if I stop adjusting? What will happen to my boy then?"

"You worry for nothing, then. You want this to work and not just for the sake of your son. Otherwise you wouldn't have accepted this life."

"What happens if Amir tires of me and finds me to be a disappointment?"

"Ah, so is this at the root of your fretting? Amir does not tire of us. I've never seen such a thing as that in all my years with him. You over-worry. Trust me, you will have other capable lovers." She frowned, her nose scrunching up in distaste. "And some not so capable. You will not mind pleasing others when your time comes. And Amir has never been disappointed in any of us."

"But none of you have ever given him reason to be disappointed—"

"You won't, either. Stop with this fussing. The more you worry the more likely you *will* upset Amir. He wants you and Jonathan to be happy. You must see how he treats your son. You'd think the boy was his."

"He does adore Jonathan. If he cares for us so much, why doesn't he marry us? I know I've said I won't marry again, but if he asked me—I would not refuse. Why is a wife so distasteful? It's not as though he is stuck with one, he gets his pick of four wives. How would a man get bored with four wives and a harem full of women ready to please him?"

Laila clucked her tongue again and set her brush down so she could blow over the design, to help it dry faster.

"You were told before you came here that this was the way of our life. Amir does not want children. He is sixteenth in linc for Sultan. He does not want his children to grow up as he did, locked behind the palace walls."

"Yet we are trapped here, as much prisoners as he himself was."

"This is different. You cannot understand how many princes go mad before they reach adulthood. Amir counts his blessings that his mother protected him as best she could."

"I still don't understand what that has to do with marrying any of us."

"He cannot marry us unless we are pregnant. It is the rule of the Ottoman culture. This is why we take every necessary precaution against a man's seed from taking root. He does not want us to fight for status within the harem. Amir's mother was not a happy woman. She loathed this life because she had had a privileged up-bringing in England. Like you, she did not choose this life. And because of his mother's hatred and distress at being confined to a harem, the things she was forced to do to keep her son alive, he will never shun you. Do you not see this?"

Elena bowed her head, a little shamed by her words. She hated to say she didn't see it that way, not in the least. She was a prisoner here just as she was in the slave market. Better looked after, but still a prisoner.

She was complaining too much for someone who was new here.

She also knew Laila was closest to Amir as a friend because she had been raised to be a part of his harem. If she wanted to voice excessive feelings in these mat-ters, she should take them to Maram. Laila was too close with Amir; she often chose the side of the prince over that of any of her sisters.

"I understand perfectly. I just wish things were dif-ferent."

"Do you? Do you wish your old life back? With its uncertainties and a husband so callous as to have sold you? This is a great insult in my eyes since you English abhor the slave trade. Your men take one wife; this is a very dishonorable act committed by your husband. Do you wish to go back to that life? Where your son might not stand out from the shadow your husband cast over your family? To a life where your son might have turned out to be exactly like his father?"

Elena shook her head. "No. I do not wish to go back, nor do I wish my husband to have found his end as he did." She let out a frustrated sigh. What use going over this topic again with Laila? She needed a change of subject.

She lifted her chin and gave a small smile in silent apology. "What is the word for paradise, Laila? I seem to have forgotten."

She needed to stop this prattling and bemoaning of her duty as a harem girl. Every one of her sisters had done this. Every one of her sisters had already been on the auction block and their favors sold to someone or other. She could do this, and hold her head high while she did it.

"Jinan. Is this the name you choose?"

Jinan. It rolled off her tongue in her inexperienced Arabic enunciation. Paradise.

This place. This life. It was all her paradise. Ironic, really. She could be Eve in the garden, offering the fruits and sins of her flesh. A fallen woman, to be sure.

Jinan. A very pretty name, indeed. A name best suited to her circumstance.

"I think so. Yes, definitely so."

The name defined the woman she'd grown into. And the name suited her more than Elena. She was Jinan. No longer the shy and proper Elena.

Laila patted her dry hand then lay back on the divan next to her. "You are finished. We will touch up the designs as they fade. I will teach you how to put the scarves on later." Elena turned to look at her sister. Laila scrunched her forehead in thought. "We will say you are a Turkish princess. This is believable because Amir's brother would only send the best of the women he buys. Being a princess will raise your value among the lords."

"Do you think they'll believe such balderdash?"

"Why wouldn't they? You have been sitting in the gardens during the day and your skin has only grown darker over the months. You now wear an Indian design, and Amir will dress you in plenty of gold and jewels beneath the gauze of your costume."

"What should I do if I recognize someone? I'm afraid I'll falter despite my disguise."

She motioned down at her painted body and the silk wrap tied about her waist. But Laila was right in her assessment that she no longer *looked* English. Her mannerisms had altered since coming to this place, too; she was less stiff in her carriage, more relaxed and at ease in this strange setting.

"You will not falter. Tell yourself that you are playing a grand trick on those men. You can laugh at them when you are back in the harem quarters. Laugh about how silly and superficial they are with their posturing and Western airs. They will only see what you present and what you are willing to reveal of your body. Never forget this."

"I know. Amir already assured me they would be looking over my goods, not wondering about my background," she lamented, barely keeping the unease from her voice.

"You see, you are taking this well now that we've

had a laugh. In all seriousness, you needn't worry. You will not be expected to leave Amir's side for many more months.

"Come." Laila sat up, pulling Elena's hand with her. "We'll go spend time with your son. Amir will know by now that we've hennaed you, and he may ask after you earlier than usual. He'll want to make a thorough inspection," she teased.

Elena smiled. What would Amir think of these designs? He'd probably trace every last swirl, and with more than his fingers. The thought made her shiver in . . . not anticipation, but something distressingly close.

She paused at the door. Why was she growing so attached to Amir? She'd never thought like this before. Her heart didn't flutter whenever she thought of him, and she knew she wasn't falling in love with the man. But why did she have this reaction?

She didn't question it further. What use was there in dwelling on such thoughts?

She knew it had everything to do with the fact that he was the sole man holding all the cards to her future. And her son's.

"She's lovely." The stout Russian gave her rump a good patting.

She squirmed out of his grasp and closer to Amir. Amir's hand squeezed reassuringly at her waist. It didn't help to calm her nerves in the least.

The portly man assessed her silently—more likely speechless—his mouth gaping like the koi in the pond as he strove for words more brilliant.

"She is lovely," Amir said. "Though shy, she's very talented in the arts of submission."

That caused the man to flush, but she didn't miss the

hunger that flared in his blue eyes. He pulled out a handkerchief to wipe away the sweat beaded on his forehead—apologizing all the while and complaining about the heat in this part of the hemisphere. He licked his lips, equally as plump as the rest of him, and gave her a glazed look that made her stomach roll in nauseous waves.

She stepped away from him, hoping to escape his keen look.

The overly thin, tall man keeping the Russian company nodded in agreement. Looking glass held in one squinted eye, he took closer observation of her nipples, showing clear through the gauze she wore. His eye was made obscenely larger by the round lens, so she avoided looking at him straight on.

Amir looked sidelong at her—brow cocked in amusement at the various men handling her—and translated to Persian what the men said even though she understood the gist of it. How could she not with the way they leered at and touched her? Amir turned to talk to another patron who'd tapped him on the shoulder.

Taking a deep breath, she told herself she could get through this. A few more hours and the auctions would be done, then she'd go back to the safety of the inner harem.

Someone came up behind her, grabbed her hips and thrust his hardened groin into her backside. She squealed and fell out of his grasp, knees banging on the hard stone floor, her palms smacking out to stop her face from hitting the stone.

There were too many people here for her to escape.

Smoke and opium filled the air, making her light-headed, slow.

She squeezed between the legs of a patron and one of her sisters embracing. On hands and knees, eyes and mind only focused on escape. She'd been so close to an alcove, a safe hiding spot, when she tumbled to the side and the heavy weight of a man pinned her down.

The man spoke some guttural, throaty language she didn't understand. She tried to squirm out of his grasp and cried out for Amir. The clamor in the room was too loud. Patrons occupied all the floor space available for their hedonistic indulgence; she was just another part of the game. She pushed at her captor's chest but that seemed to inflame him further. He grasped her neck tightly and found the opening between her thighs with eager fingers.

She tensed, knowing the intrusion was coming.

Maram's voice was songlike, breathless. "Adrien, she is Amir's toy. Let her be, come to me, love."

The man pulled himself up and Jinan scooted away, stood, and made her way blindly through the throng of patrons and harem girls.

These were the type of men she was expected to lie with?

She *couldn't* do it. More men groped at her as she passed them in a whirlwind of excess bitterness and feeling. She felt as though her nerves would crack at any moment.

Would she be in trouble for this hasty escape? Would Amir come and find her? Punish her? She ran headlong into another man, this one younger and handsomer than the patrons she'd seen thus far.

"*Ma petite*. Let me take you somewhere quiet," he murmured. But she didn't trust the kindness of his words. The only thing she could do was shake her head in disagreement and stand tall for his inspection.

He tugged on the end of her veil—just enough to make the coins jangle, and plucked at her breast, pulling the nipple taut between his fingers. "You are a magnificent creature, mademoiselle."

She must have stared at him doe-eyed, with a naïveté not usual for a woman in a whorehouse, for he was pulling her closer, his fingers slipping between the cheeks of her rear and sliding to the crux of her body. She shrieked as she fell away and into another patron's arms.

Looking over her shoulder, she saw it was Amir and hated the breath of relief that escaped her. She didn't want to be helpless or in need of his rescue at every turn. He had let her come to this pass!

Amir's hand fanned over her stomach, pulling her back to his chest. He nuzzled into her neck and inhaled deeply.

"When can we bid on her? She's rather ripe for the plucking." This came from the Frenchman who had tried to take her moments ago.

"She's mine for a while yet." Thank the Almighty for that, she thought. "You'll have to wait till I tire of this little bird." Amir thrust possessively against her backside, causing her breath to hitch. She bit her lip, afraid to give voice to her fears. He was a devil at her back.

"No doubt. She's handsome. But what are you hiding beneath the veil? A disfigurement, perhaps?" The Frenchman reached out, fingering the side of her neck under the edging of the silk.

Amir laughed, shaking his head. "Ask yourself if I would bother with such a creature if she were deformed? She's come by way of my eldest brother. Too timid and not cunning enough to survive his harem." Amir smacked the younger man's hand away from her chest "Besides, my brother prefers the pale odalisques, not the natural beauties of Turkey. Is she not a fine specimen of a woman?"

Amir's hand trailed over her breast to pluck at her nipple with the last comment. The action screamed of his possessive ownership. She let loose a surprised gasp, one that came out more a frightened squeal. Laila had warned her beforehand of the events that took place in the Pleasure Gardens—but she still wasn't prepared to act openly provocative.

"Will she remove the silk?" the Frenchman asked excitedly.

"No. I've allowed her to keep it since she came here thinking I was to be her husband. She did not know what her fate was to be. So I give her this much as recompense of sorts."

She lowered her head as though shamed by how she'd been put on display—when in fact, Amir had been very direct with how he would introduce her and how she was to react to his every touch, his every word.

The men laughed, thinking her a silly creature.

There were nooks all around the room to where the patrons could whisk off for privacy with their beauties. If they were so daring, they openly indulged wherever they pleased. She saw Sana, on all fours on the divan, her lord taking her from behind. Jinan looked away, disgusted with her open curiosity, when Sana acknowledged her being audience to her act.

When they finished laughing at her expense, Amir drew her close to his side and whispered, "You are doing very well, Jinan. It pleases me that most of the lords can't stop watching you."

"This is what you wanted," she said for his ears alone. What she didn't say was that she hated every moment of it.

"Yes, it is. And if this wasn't your first night in the

Pleasure Gardens"—his hand lowered to brush over the plumpness of her rear—"I'd take you right here."

Was he serious? She'd faint from embarrassment. "Please don't."

"Maybe when the patrons are focused on the auction, I will. Do you know how much I want you? How much I want these men to see only you in this room? You'll be well received, little bird."

Were his words supposed to make her more comfortable in this new setting? A strange way to go about it, if that was his goal.

She turned in his embrace, lowering her veiled mouth close to his lips. Surely he could see how frightened she was to be displayed in this fashion. Did he see that fear skittering across her wide eyes? She hoped so because there was another lord but a foot away, and she didn't want to risk saying anything to show her fear in a room full of lusty men.

Amir's lip lifted in a knowing smile, then he turned his head to the lord she'd nodded toward. "They are so nice when they are skittish, eh?"

Jinan didn't turn her head to see what the lord thought of that. Amir spun her around and walked over to a divan in the center of the room. He pulled her between his thighs when he stretched out behind her.

Placing her hands in her lap, she played the demure harem girl—though it wasn't all an act. She remained aware of all that happened around them. Laila was flitting around the room in her wispy silks, the rope tied around her center barely holding the thing together.

Laila had forewarned her that clothes were not permitted for the auctioning. The lords wanted to see what they spent their fortunes on.

Beside the podium, which the eunuchs had carried out not half an hour ago, Harry Chisholm made an appearance. He didn't glance her way. In fact, he seemed to purposely not acknowledge any of the harem girls.

Did any of these rich lords know what Mr. Chisholm did for Amir? That he was the sole man responsible for finding additional flesh for the Pleasure Gardens? He looked like any well-to-do Englishman. His clothes were impeccably pressed, his neck stiff with his heavily starched cravat. His shoes were shined so bright it was an obscenity in this boudoir of voluptuous proclivity. But he wore his usual pleasant, no-nonsense smile—though she didn't think it was really a smile.

Amir clapped his hands above his head, calling the buzzing room to semi-order.

"Gentlemen, if you please, I'd like the girls to dance, then we'll proceed with the auction. Come sit, play, fuck, do what you will."

Jinan slouched a little when Amir slid his hand around to her belly. All eyes were on her, but she didn't want to look at anyone so she trained her eyes on the beady dead gaze of the lion skin stretched before the divan.

A dozen girls came out wearing coin belts and chimes around their waist, ankles, and wrists. They were all veiled, wearing scarves as she did, strategically placed to bare the parts that aroused and titillated men most. Their bellies were bare and of every shape and color. Hair was worn loose for this dance, so it swayed alluringly around their hips.

Jinan had practiced this seductive dance from her first week onward and been surprised by her ability to move so easily and naturally through the dances without personal censure to impede her advancement. Though she doubted she could dance this way for a room full of men.

Amir displayed the most luscious and experienced dancers for the auctioning events, but each and every girl knew how to do this in private should their patrons ask. Hips thrust in time to the primitive beat of the drum, one of the girls sang out a high-pitched nasal chord—the sound astonishing in its melodiousness.

Maybe the mood of the room added to the seductive quality of the song?

They all twirled together, thrust together . . . bright shades of yellow, purple, red, blue, orange fanned out and pulsed as they stopped and clapped their hands above their head and put their heel to the stone floor, the sounds of bells chiming in harmony with the drum and tambourine.

Amir pressed forward, his chin resting on her shoulder, his hand still splayed on her lower belly, kneading her with increasing thrusts as the tempo of the music intensified. Looking around the room, Jinan expected to see eyes trained on her but none were. Everyone was focused on the dancers or the paramour keeping them company.

She gained more confidence with every breath she took. With a tilt of her head to the side she rested her cheekbone to Amir's and closed her eyes. In another time, another place, so long ago she could remember another man that held her close like this. A man too high in the instep for a woman of her nature. Proof of that lay in her current profession. It mattered not that he'd proposed to her on their final night together.

The heavy scent of jasmine wafted through the open room, wrapping her in its cocoon as Amir pressed his arousal into her lower back. The memory was lost then.

Amir's hands never ceased, even being so bold as to brush over her naked mound with his seeking fingers. She could almost forget they were in a room full of men assessing her every charm.

"You have done well thus far," Amir whispered, his breath raspy. "I knew you were ready for this."

She said nothing in response, only inhaled deeply as his hand grazed over her peaked nipples.

"Let us leave this lot to their own devices. I have plans for you tonight, Jinan. I will show you a little paradise."

She nodded her head in agreement, her breath held in her lungs. She was almost worried he'd take her here against her wishes. With a push on her bottom, he had her standing, the jut of his arousal firm against her backside as he slid off the divan. They went slowly, their steps timed to the music as he walked her back into the harem's private quarters.

This evening hadn't been so terrible a task after all. Amir had already told her she was expected at his side for the next auction in six months' time. After that she'd take her turn being bid upon. She wondered what he'd do to her next when in the company of these depraved whore-hunting men. It was only a matter of time before he was more daring, pushing her to the edge of her comfort levels.

She knew his plan was to force her to get used to this life. Otherwise she'd never come out of the ignorant shell of what her life really was, as Laila pointed out all too often.

Did it really matter what he did to her in public or private?

The answer shouldn't surprise her—it didn't matter.

As they walked past the eunuchs she realized *Elena*—the woman she used to be—had been left behind in the throng of overzealous pleasure seekers. She didn't know where exactly *Elena* had left off. But somewhere along her path tonight, she ceased to be.

Elena no longer existed.

In time she knew without doubt that she'd accept this way of life. Would she ever again give thought to the destructive nature this seemed to have on her moral personality?

What else would she lose of herself in the coming months? In the coming years? Would she even remember the person she was? Maybe Jinan was who she was always meant to be?

The ease and grace with which she was slowly accepting this life went against her proper English sensibilities. Did this mean she harbored some character flaw, some fissure in her morals? Maybe the flaw had been festering and had finally overcome her gentle nature once exposed to the vices offered here. It must have always been within her if she'd so easily turned into this woman.

If she had so easily embraced this way of life.

Every step toward the private harem quarters, toward the bedroom with Amir, reinforced that conviction. This was not duty but something she had accepted over the months.

With every step away from the men she felt a thrill pumping in her blood. Instead of the repulsion Elena should feel about catering to these men's desires in the near future, Jinan felt liberated.

This was her. Jinan. A woman hiding beneath a veil but willing to take on any challenge, not a simpering miss hiding behind her fears.

Was it perhaps because she felt safe here? Because she knew her son was safe in this wanton world of sex, scandal, and strange proclivities unfathomable to her as of yet?

Coming to terms with this life felt good in her soul. She'd been unleashed from her old restrictive life and felt a strange freedom of her senses, heart, and mind.

Now she was and would forever be Jinan.

Ironically, this *was* paradise.

Her paradise.

CHAPTER EIGHT

Recognition and Vulnerability

1846
Isle of Corfu

She should have no qualms about such an innocent act.
Her modesty had been stripped from her long ago, and
the marble dais was not unfamiliar to her. She stood
up here once a year. But she still hated looking down at
her bidders like the great whore of Babylon. The most
irksome thing about taking her place up here was she
couldn't wear anything aside from her jewelry and veil.

Who would purchase her favors today?

Jinan leaned toward her harem sister, who stood on
the floor beside the dais. "Asbury talked with me earlier. As interested as he is in spending time with me,
he seems to lose at every auction. Do you think he'll try
again?"

"I've got my eye on Asbury, Jinan. Don't you think
of stealing his attentions." Sana rolled her eyes and
snorted under her breath, whispering, "He can't afford
you. Maybe when you're saggy, wrinkled, and gray."

Jinan gave a deep laugh and shook her head; her

dark hair, which hung in loose waves, tickled her backside. The small coins that edged her veil clinked together with the movement. She searched out Asbury. "Where is he, Sana? He arrived with another gentleman. I didn't see his friend, did you?"

"I don't know who *he* is. But I'd love for him to play some games with me." Sana stood on tiptoe and pointed to the outskirts of the room. "Handsome as the devil. But you won't see him clearly, he's too far off."

Jinan followed her sister's finger. Sana was right; all she saw was Asbury's outline. He turned from the man shadowed by the arched pillars and strode toward the podium. Asbury was a young tradesman with a long, thin nose that didn't quite suit his face, but handsome enough that it wouldn't repulse her to spend time in his company.

As Asbury came closer, his gaze became more pensive. He would bid on her today; she could tell by the stance he took with his finger and thumb worrying his chin. It was in the way he studied her from head to toe, already imagining what he'd do to her once they were alone. He wasn't her first choice among the men here, but he wasn't the worst option, either.

He looked over Sana, then turned back to her. "Looking ripe as usual, my pretty doves."

Jinan cocked one brow. "Yes, but the question is whether or not you're interested *enough* to pay handsomely for our time?"

"I'd be more than happy to lord over you, princess."

"I don't think you'll be testing her wares for a while yet," Count Villieux called out, "you old goat."

Asbury whirled on his heel to glare at the younger man. Really, they couldn't be more than a few years apart. "Have some respect. And pull yourself together before talking to your betters, you French swine." There wasn't much venom to his words. The count laughed and continued his ministrations to Maram.

Maram was staked to Count Villieux's groin. His jaw was squared, eyes clouded with lust, as his concentration slid back to his mistress. His hands grasped her hips, moving his rigid length within her as she leaned forward on her elbows. Maram smiled up at the podium and winked.

Jinan shook her head and winked back. The more she flirted with everyone around her, the more the patrons would pay. The more they paid, the more Amir would tuck away for her son.

Other men watched the auction with lovers in their laps as well. Some embraced rather provocatively, uncaring of the greater audience, others were more modest—relatively modest for such a debauched setting. Asbury found a divan close by and crossed his ankle over his knee as he settled in, waiting for the proceedings to start.

The chairs and divans stretched out before her were filled with the evening's pleasure seekers. Bold colors were brazenly displayed in the bolsters and throws. Animal furs cushioned the floor near the furniture; rich Turkish carpets covered the rest of the floor in various shades of reds, oranges, and browns in the center. The lively colors incited the lustiness of the patrons currently in coitus. Her first time in this room she'd thought the welcome ironic—a showy, gilded prison for the harem girls.

Now the flashiness was just another facet of the place she considered her home.

The room boasted a great domed ceiling with holes pierced through the roof allowing daylight to shine through. Three eunuchs blocked the only door that led to the outer palace, and scimitars flashed at their waists in warning to any man who thought to take more liberties than tolerable. The only persons permitted through that door were Amir and the gentlemen who purchased the girls' favors. She had no desire to leave through that door, except to perhaps see the rest of the palace. She'd been content staying in the harem quarters. The eunuchs were no threat to her—not to any of the girls—only to the patrons who did not abide by Amir's rules.

Through the clamor of chatter, grunts and groans sounded from the pleasure alcoves, which were off to either side of the room. Silk hangings covered what took place behind, but did not stifle the sound. Not all the lords were interested in publicly displaying their libidinous acts.

She could hear the laughter of her sisters as they flirted with the lords.

She looked down on the melee of debauchery around her.

Even after all these years, she still had the urge to cover her body from the men's carnal perusal. Her hair only covered her backside. Her ankles and wrists were adorned with thick gold bracelets to complement her golden skin tone. Her hands were henna-covered in the ancient designs Laila painted on her every few months. Black kohl lined her eyes to lend them a mysterious seductive quality. Her high cheekbones, eyes, and forehead were the only parts of her face exposed. The veil covered the tip of her nose to her chin as part of her ethereal disguise.

At least there was no touching while she stood up here. A small relief, but a relief nonetheless. She needed no reminders of her days in the slave market—the days before Amir had rescued her and given her son a second chance at life.

There looked to be some thirty men here tonight.

Lord Somerset, a widowed earl in his late forties, leaned forward on the divan with Laila behind him. His face was flushed, his paunch revealing a taste for things other than women. Laila's hands were busy massaging his fat shoulders, but he was looking at the auction block with a keen eye. He was quick about rutting, then falling into slumber. She didn't want to amuse him again, he was worse than a sweating, grunting pig above her.

Amir spoke with the Russian in regalia next to him. Amir had his newest acquisition sitting in front of him between his opened knees with her legs tucked under her on a jaguar-skin rug. Amir's hands never ceased caressing his Italian beauty's breasts, bared to all.

Jinan remembered when she had been in that position—so long ago. She missed pleasing only one man, only having to warm one man's bed. She sighed and looked away since she couldn't catch his eye.

Sana leaned in closer to her, seeing where Jinan's gaze focused. "The man he talks to came in with Chekhov. I think he's negotiated to purchase Aysun for the next two moons."

Jinan twisted the gold filigree around her wrists, making the bracelets jingle together.

The harem girls were not oblivious to the dealings of the men around them. Amir spoke freely with them, so they understood how profits were made, for the money was to everyone's benefit. Some men preferred to settle their fees in advance.

A gentleman she didn't know walked around her pedestal and Sana, looking back and forth between them with equal fervor in his dark irises. She hated to look into the eyes of her bidders—too much of their intentions could be read there. But it was better to know their intent than to remain naïve.

This one wore a cruel expression, his face set in what looked like a permanent grimace, eyes troubled. She could see the promise of harsh enslavement with a leaning toward dark sexual acts in that gaze— something she was known to accommodate, because she felt nothing for these men, no matter how they treated her. He'd bid, too. She shivered in revulsion.

She preferred the most common expression worn by the lords—carnal hunger—such as the way Villieux eyed all his mistresses. Such as the way her old Russian lover, Chekhov, devoured her with his gaze. His finger ran along the floor of the podium, carefully abiding by the house rule of no touching those who were being auctioned. It was a paid privilege to touch those who stood where she stood now. She gave him a doe-eyed innocent look.

"You are interested this evening?"

"Yes," Chekhov said in thickly accented Persian, the common language in the harem. "But I've no time to play, my beauty. I've brought a friend to find company. I head out when the evening concludes."

"Next time, then."

"Yes." He turned toward Sana. "And do you go to auction? Or will you be the house plaything tonight?"

"No auction for me. Do you wish my company?" Sana wrapped her finger through the button on Chekhov's vest, leaning forward so her breasts grazed his raised arm.

He grasped her by the buttocks and pulled her into his groin. "Let's find a pleasure alcove, my dark beauty."

Jinan gave a snort. Chekhov's type was the most harmless here. The women might not live in fear for their lives day to day, but this wasn't an existence Jinan would wish on anyone.

She exhaled noisily, pushing out her veil with the

puff. She tried to ignore the swarm of eager men at her feet.

The man who'd been talking with Asbury earlier walked toward her. He looked familiar from this distance, his blond hair a bit too long to be fashionable. Not that she knew what fashionable was anymore locked inside the palace walls.

Her breath hitched in surprise, and she froze, her fingers clenching the bracelet she'd been twisting. Her heart gave a great leap in her chest. She narrowed her gaze, bringing him into focus. It couldn't be *him*, could it?

Oh, it was definitely *him*.

A man she'd never expected to see again. A man from her youth. A man, really, from another life altogether. Her breath caught, and all she thought—all she hoped—was that he did *not* recognize her. She mentally chastised the absurdity of her thoughts. Why should he recognize her? They had spent only a few weeks in each other's company. Their laughter and budding love all those years ago under a darkened sky were too distant to hold on to. Besides, what kind of man proposed to a woman he professed to have feelings for, only to leave the next day? She doubted he would remember her. Especially in a place like this.

Without the cover of clothes, her dark skin tone labeled her anything but English. Her areolas were painted a medium brown, her skin a deep bronze aided by the sun in the gardens. She'd taken her mother's Spanish coloring, and right now, more than ever, she was thankful for the exotic look that had always made her unfashionable in English drawing rooms. With her altered accent and natural Persian tongue, he would never place her as English.

The Marquess of Rothburn stared thoughtfully up at her. He didn't study her nude body or stare at her breasts with their hennaed areolas and her painted naked mound as others had. He stared directly into her eyes. Those brandy-colored depths assessed her as his dark blond brows drew together in deliberation.

Lord Rothburn had aged well; he must be thirty, now. His shoulders were wider and sturdier than she remembered, his waist trim, legs firm beneath tight trousers. After her perusal, something she rarely indulged in, she raised her eyes and stared back.

His lips thinned slightly. Did he try to place her as he studied her?

Cocking her hip to the side, she curved her palm around it to draw his eye. His gaze dropped and she breathed a sigh of relief when he turned and walked away, leaning against one of the pillars at the edge of the room. This time she could see him at a distance.

Jinan couldn't look at any of the other prospective buyers after seeing *him*. Lord Rothburn wasn't the first man she'd recognized over the years, but he *was* the first man she'd fawned over—dare she say felt the first tingling of love?—as a young girl. What a foolish girl she'd been, to think he'd follow through on his offer of marriage. Yet to see him now . . .

It was humiliating to stand before him as if she were some sacrificial lamb.

She was being silly, of course. He would never recognize her, let alone remember her. She caught Villieux's eye and held it in silent plea. She prayed he won her favors tonight. If Rothburn did . . . it didn't bear thinking.

Harry Chisholm finally came into the room, the click of his shoes echoing. He tapped his little stick to the marble dais to call attention to the auction.

"The auction commences now. Gentlemen"—he pointed toward her—"some of you are familiar with the

exotic and most luscious Jinan. You'll find this Turkish princess most compliant for anything you wish to
play. She's trained in the darker games of submission
should you so fancy. Bidding to start at a thousand
pounds."

That amount was low, but it would buy any one of
these men a week of her undivided attention. The price
would climb, of course. It was always interesting to see
how much profit she'd bring in for Amir. A profit that
would help pay for her son's education. Amir had
promised that her son would live outside the harem with
enough riches to support him when he was ready to
leave.

Asbury nodded, taking the opening bid.

The man with the harsh gaze stepped forward. "Two
thousand."

"Three." This from another gentleman she didn't
know.

"Five," from Villieux. She exhaled in relief. He had
a voracious appetite she was more than willing to appease if it meant escaping Rothburn.

"Seven."

"Eight and a half." Asbury was at his limit, his face
red with anger at losing her to another yet again. She
wondered if he would ever win her favors.

Villieux looked insulted by the drop in bid incre-
ments and bumped out Asbury. "Ten." They often bid
against each other, since they shared the same taste in
women.

All was quiet. A good price. Spending the next month
and some with Villieux was no hardship. He was a con-
siderate lover.

Maybe Rothburn hadn't recognized her.

All eyes were now on Mr. Chisholm. "Excellent. Well,
then, gentle—"

"Twenty thousand."

Heads turned away from the auctioneer and toward the deep voice. Jinan could have sworn she heard a hiss from Asbury's direction. But she wasn't looking at him. She was looking at the pillars straight ahead. Jinan didn't need to see the man who had bid the outrageous sum. She remembered his voice, the deep baritone that had had many a woman swooning in her ballroom days.

Intention impossible to decipher from his blank, unemotional look, Lord Rothburn stepped forward. Jinan's gaze slammed into *his*. If she were the fainting type, now would be the ideal time. A shame that she wasn't. How could she lie with this man? There was no bidding price great enough to make up for a broken heart. Because she well knew, the cost of lying with him was her heart.

The smoldering stare he gave her could not be defined. It could have been a look of sexual appetite, annoyance, or anger. Perhaps it meant nothing at all. She bit her lip, knowing her display of nervousness was hidden beneath the veil. The knowledge of being purchased by him roiled uncomfortably through her body, right down to the pit of her churning stomach.

Jinan turned to look at Mr. Chisholm with a silent question in the curious scrunch of her brow. *What is this about?*

Mr. Chisholm gave his usual sneer—lifting the right side of his mouth—jolting her understanding. This deal was done long before she stood upon the dais.

Strange, she hadn't seen Lord Rothburn before now. When had he ever laid eyes upon her? And after he'd had such a short perusal of her person tonight, had recognition had time to settle in? Impossible. She was thinking too hard and took a deep breath to clear her head.

It didn't help. It made her more nervous.

What more could he want than to taste the olive-skinned princess? One he would never dare enjoy among his own kind.

The distance between them shortened faster than she was prepared for. She searched her inner thoughts for a memory of any man who was as remotely closed off in emotion as his lordship seemed. There must be some chink in his exterior, into the shield blinding her to his true intent. Did he know who she was? It was disconcerting, to say the least, and more than a little alarming that she did not know how to deal with this man, for fear of revealing her true identity.

Her hand clutched feebly at the air before she stilled her obvious unease and fisted her hands at her sides. He stood but a handspan away. His attention was not on Mr. Chisholm but her.

For how long would she amuse this man? Jinan, the "Whore of Paradise," was a favorite of these lords. How long did Amir expect her to keep Lord Rothburn company?

How *terrible* to be put in such a predicament. To be fair, it wasn't as though Amir knew the whole of her past . . . her prior association with this particular lord.

No use dwelling on it now. She made too much out of nothing. Any one of her sisters could have caught this man's attention. His being here was happenstance, not *qismet,* as the Turks said. All Amir did was sell her well, probably highlighting her carnal abilities with an explicitness that made even the most salacious lord blush while bargaining.

She would treat this lord as she did all others. And keep him at arm's length from her heart.

This was like any transaction of human flesh that went on within the Pleasure Gardens. Jinan—not Elena,

since she no longer associated herself with her past—
would give Lord Rothburn his sterlings' worth and play
the dark, exotic princess he craved.

Mr. Chisholm gave a succinct nod, and Jinan unclenched her hand and held it out to him. It wasn't Mr.
Chisholm's slight, cool hand that grasped hers. Lord
Rothburn's firm, warm fingers slipped over her hand.
Her heart nearly tripped right out of her chest in trepidation. His hold was strong, as if he were afraid she'd
vanish if he didn't hold tight enough.

He helped her down the steps of the dais. When she
was eye level to him he released her hand and clasped
the back of her knees to swing her up in his strong
arms.

Her arms went automatically around his wide shoulders. Tilting her head back, she gave him a hooded
gaze, one that showed the depth of her desire and willingness to fulfill his deepest yearnings.

It was wasted.

He stared straight ahead without so much as a word
to Mr. Chisholm. She looked over Rothburn's shoulder,
seeing the envious crowd of outbid gentlemen, then
raised an eyebrow at Amir in question, but he paid no
heed to her misgivings. Then everyone's attention returned to the auction. She was forgotten as the men
sought to purchase their pleasures with another of the
forbidden women.

Rothburn's gait was smooth, his strides determined
as he carted her off to one of the private, sari-covered
alcoves.

Sweeping the gauzy silks aside, he stepped into the
small nook.

His arm slid away, releasing her knees, forcing her
to stand in front of him in the darkness. The soft scent
of jasmine filled her nostrils, as did the smell of man,

sending her heart aflutter. The beating of it was so loud
in her ears she wondered if he could hear it. She could
smell a faint aroma of olive oil, probably from his soap,
and a little bit of sweat, not at all unpleasant. It was
nice and so very masculine. He stood a full head above
her, a towering, imposing figure. Taller than she remembered. Even though they'd once danced a cotillion and a
waltz together. Even though they'd spent every night of
their two-week courtship in any secret place they could
sequester themselves.

Conjuring the details of her past was dangerous.
Besides that, it wasn't like her to take to these flights of
fancy. He was her lord for however long Amir said.
She'd do her duty. No more.

Pushing the old memories from her thoughts, she
began to play her part in the seduction.

The lamp was unlit in this room. It was too dark to
make out his expression so she raised one hand to
sculpt his face. He said naught as she felt the prominent
planes of his cheekbones, smooth and defined with hard-
edged lines. Her fingers were slow, feeling every con-
tour as she stroked his smooth-shaven jaw and the cleft
in his chin.

Curious, she raised the other hand and caressed the
soft plumpness of his parted lips. An even stream of his
hot breath met her exploring thumb. He seemed in no
rush to stop her, standing still while the tips of her fingers molded lightly over his closed eyes. A small sound
of ecstasy escaped him as she put the tip of her thumb in
his mouth, touching his tongue. He bit down lightly to
hold her in place as his tongue swept around it.

Her resolve to banish the past from her thoughts was
as futile as denying Rothburn her body. How she wished
her life had taken a vastly different path.

Concentrating on the physical and not the memories

that stole her ability to seduce, she pulled her thumb from his mouth and trailed her fingers lower. The column of his neck was strong, manly, the pulse that beat there erratic, telling her an entirely different story than that of the sound of his controlled breathing. Did he know she was just as aroused as he? He'd know it if he touched her. As the thought slid into her mind, he raised his arms, hands reaching for the veil placement at the back of her head. She pulled away, shaking her head no, the copper coins at the edge ringing like distant wind chimes.

His hands dropped away from her hair, falling loose to his sides. The outline of his head, barely visible in the dark, cocked to the side in question. She put her finger to his lips and said in Persian, "Amir would have been explicit in this. My veil stays for the duration of the contract."

He didn't argue, and seemed to understand the meaning of her foreign words.

She opened her mouth to ask how they should continue when his finger crossed over her lips. "Shh . . . no words between us this night. I want you silent, no matter what I say to you. Your owner will discuss the contract we've agreed upon when I leave. Just give me all of your true self this night," he responded in English.

What did he mean by such words?

The only indication he had moved was the sound of sliding material. She thought he had removed his vest or unbuttoned his trousers to take them off. She was mistaken. His hands reached for her arms and after a gentle squeeze he turned her around, pulling her back flush to his cloth-clad chest. He burned hotter than the summer night, yet goose bumps rose at her nape where his breath fanned through wisps of her hair.

It took her but a moment to understand what piece of clothing he had removed.

Complete darkness blanketed her eyes as he tied his stiff neckcloth around her head, locking over the clasp that held her veil in place.

His message was clear. She'd played the submissive often enough that she understood the significance of the blindfold. He forbade her to see him when denied the privilege of viewing her. Now more than ever it was imperative she not remove the veil for fear of revealing her identity. So be it. It was better this way.

If the moon awakened from its sleepy hollow in the clouds and illuminated the room, he would be able to read her flitting thoughts in her eyes. Read the hunger that went beyond her being a mere mistress of the night.

When the material was snug he pulled her in tighter. Her back bowed, bringing her shoulders to his chest and her derrière into his hardened groin. He didn't nestle his cock between the cheeks of her buttocks as she expected.

His hand made a downward arc between her naked breasts, caressing over her ribs right to the top of her navel. Then lower, his fingers spanned the sloping curve of her stomach. His other hand wrapped around her neck, his fingers turned her face till her ear was pressed to his mouth. His breath was rushed, uncontrolled as it rasped out in a needy thread.

He did nothing more than hold her in that position. She wasn't aware how long they stood there, both breathing hard in anticipation of the inevitable outcome.

It was as though nothing existed but him in the dark world he had created with the blindfold . . . and that wasn't good. She needed to guard herself carefully. She would not lose her head or her heart to him again.

What did he plan to do with her?

He scooped her up in his arms again and strode over to the plush divan where he lightly deposited her on her back. She couldn't see so she listened to his movements, the shush of his quiet steps, the raggedness of his breath as he came closer. The press of his body between her thighs dipped her forward. He pushed her knees out with his hands. She was quick to spread her legs wider and place her heels close to her rear to give him at least a slight view he could appreciate even in the darkness.

His groan was barely audible, but she heard it and grinned. Some men liked the vulnerability of a woman's body. Men were aroused by the raw, unadulterated liberty a woman gave them in the intimacy of sexual congress. That was the most important thing Amir had taught her. And that was what she offered Lord Rothburn by exposing the core of her femininity without fear or reserve.

She was not an untried English miss. Not once would she give him reason to believe they had a previous acquaintance. A previous engagement, no matter how brief it had been.

She waited for him to release the buttons on his trousers, but he only pressed his clothed body to her naked flesh. His weight came down fully upon her; his hands pulled her hips up off the divan and snug to his arousal. How she wanted to rub up and down that length until she found her own release.

Afraid to show too much desire, too much of her own need, she held still in his grasp.

With his hands still clasped to her hips, he bent over

her and rubbed his cheek over the delicate skin between her breasts. His pace was indulgent, languorous, and meant to excite her senses and increase her arousal. Why didn't he take her? Why didn't he thrust inside her and lose himself in what she offered so willingly? Perhaps she needed to take him in hand, rub him off—some men could only find their bliss this way.

Jinan lowered her hand toward that prominent thickness but was stalled when he grasped her hand. Manacling her wrist and throwing it painfully to the bed, he said, "Do not touch me this eve unless I give leave to do so."

She nodded her understanding. He released his hold and let her arms fall on either side of her. Some men liked to know how a woman reacted to certain touches, to better take complete control of a woman's desires.

His lips touched the plumpness of her breast before he bit down—not too hard—just enough to test her limits. She moaned and arched higher off the divan, wanting him to take more, do more. How badly she wanted only to pretend she wasn't just an agreeable whore. With a desperation unlike her, she needed to mean something more than a frig and passing pleasure to Lord Rothburn. She needed tenderness drawn from caring and . . .

Love.

The only thing she needed was to banish these indulgent thoughts.

Even so, she stretched her arms above her head to find purchase against the wall and pushed closer to that warm, inviting mouth of his. The kisses were featherlike, followed intermittently with the sharp nip of his teeth. He bit her shoulder, his breath hoarse, hot and heavy against her fevered skin. A deep appreciative moan passed her lips when his teeth plucked at the flesh on the underside of her breast, then did it again and again until he'd covered the whole underside of that tender flesh with his mark.

He pulled her in harder against his cock, grinding at an even, unhurried pace. He was intent on their finding their climax just this way.

She should stop this madness. It was she who should be pleasuring him, touching him.

As if he had read her thoughts, Rothburn said, "Thread your hands together above your head."

So, he was the type to bind his ladybird. Was that what she should expect this evening?

Her nether region was soaked. Her slit slid easily against the material covering his cock. His grasp never lessened as he held her hips, riding her along his rigidity.

Her hands flung out to grab the throws and brocaded silk beneath her. Sweat beaded under her veil, around the back of her neck. The scent of sex and her cream was heavy in the heated air around them. She needed to hold on to something. Her orgasm, her release, built rapidly as he rocked her along his hard groin, his tongue and teeth nipping, tasting the flesh of her breasts.

Her knees fell wider apart and she planted her feet on his hips, surely opening the folds of her sex and completely exposing the rosy flesh unseen in the dark, to his beautiful strokes. The pearl hidden in her folds swelled and throbbed with every stroke.

"By all that is holy . . ." The words slipped out, as her back arched impossibly higher off the divan and her release washed through her body as her heart filled with impossible longing for more than sex games. More than a mere contract with Rothburn.

She felt a release of fluid from her center drench his trousers more thoroughly than they already had, the slickness further aiding the slide of her naked body over his clothed form. His lordship stilled then jerked twice against her. He let her rock her hips—barely—in his unrelenting hold. His fingers gripped the flesh of her hips with bruising intensity. The pain of his grasp was dulled by the intense pleasure that clenched her womb. She was unable to stop herself from riding out the completion of her bliss.

After her peak she'd worry about the possibly destructive aftermath of the storm that had swept through her life this past hour.

When the tremors subsided and the thrilled clench of her womb eased, his hands came under her knees in silent demand that she stretch her legs out. She did, leaving enough room for him to fall into the vee of her body. Instead, he turned her on her side, pulled her back to his chest, and wrapped his larger frame around her slight one. She couldn't feel his hardness anymore. The dampness of his trousers slid against her every now and again as well as the push of his linen shirt against her back. Had he too let loose his seed while she'd been helpless to stop the desperate thrusting of her pelvis?

She hadn't noticed.

That was worrisome. She was trained to take notice of her master's needs, and she had failed on her first night with Lord Rothburn. Though he'd demanded control over the crisis of her body. She'd forgotten what *that* bliss felt like with a man, for she hadn't done that in more than five years. She banished any further thought of her long-dead husband.

The veil felt hot against her mouth. Clasping the edge with the tips of her fingers, she pulled forward so it parted at the back of her head and let the night breeze fill her lungs. The heavy musk of their union was strong in the little room. It would take a long while for that sweet muskiness to dissipate in this dry, unmoving heat. What did it say about her that she liked the smell of their sex?

Closing her eyes, she waited for Lord Rothburn to fall asleep—it was a man's prerogative after these things took place. She wanted to go back to the harem quarters and collect her thoughts before she had to face him. What had just happened? What had she let happen?

What a fool she was.

Lord Rothburn's breathing deepened and calmed. But he did not sleep; his hand plucked at her peaked nipple. She would not be sneaking away any time soon.

Over the years she had done strange things for her patrons but never this. Was this all he wanted? This seemed more intimate than the sexual act alone. More intimate than any depraved unnatural games she played with others.

By some perversity, or maybe even some self-flagellation, she did not want *this* to end. Just for a short moment, she wanted to pretend that she was not this man's whore. All too soon the truth of the situation would hang its weight around her heart.

But that didn't mean she couldn't live with the lie for as long as the night allowed.

When both their breathing steadied, Lord Rothburn whispered into her ear, "I will take the same liberty you took. Do not flinch away."

A quick tug at the back of her head released the tie bound about her eyes. She didn't move as he pulled the cloth from under her head; a soft whoosh sounded as he tossed it away. The tips of his fingers traced her brow, smoothed along the curves around her eye, then down her cheek. He didn't attempt to slide his fingers beneath the veil as he felt every part of her face. She barely breathed as he touched her; afraid to stall—or even stop—the moment of bizarre intimacy they shared.

So like the kiss they'd shared in the Glenmoores' maze all those years ago.

She was trying to live in a past better left buried.

A past that had been so far removed from her mind in this setting that tears came to her eyes—but they did not fall. She wouldn't allow them to. Was this what it could have been like? Was this what marrying Lord Rothburn might have brought to their marriage bed? This—dare she say it?—affectionate, almost loving touch?

Why did she hold on to what could never be?

What use was there in *that*? Except to shed tears, revealing the depth of her despair.

It wasn't as though she could ever admit the truth of her identity. She was only Jinan here. Elena had died long ago when the last shred of decency she once esteemed in herself had been stolen. By the man she'd been forced to marry in the end.

Men never brought her love. They brought her misery upon misery. Loneliness.

His hand caressed her naked hip, higher to her ribs. "After you take your bath in the morning, we will spend the day here. I leave in two days but will be back by week's end."

"For how long have you purchased my contract—" A small gasp escaped her when his hand grasped the fleshy mound of her breast tightly in his hand.

"Hush. You will only speak when I've given you leave to do so." His reproof came lightly, but she shut her mouth nonetheless.

He released her breast and rolled her onto her stomach. His knees came between her thighs and pushed them out.

"Put your hands above your head, Jinan."

The way he said her name sounded different and foreign, rolling off his tongue with his crisp English lilt. He made it sound more exotic than any other man who had whispered it.

She wanted him to say her name again. Instead his leg came up firm to her mound, causing her to groan. She raised her hands above her head and grasped the edge of the divan, nails clawing into the material for purchase as his knee rode up farther, splitting her sex, exposing it to the abrasion of his trousers. Her desire flared anew.

There was indeed more than a mutual rubbing to be had between them.

Now, he would start his real games.

"I'm going to have you so many ways, you won't remember where you are, my sweet *Jinan*. My name will be the only one you can speak for weeks, wishing for *my* company." He bit her shoulder, not too hard, but enough to leave the flesh stinging when he released her.

"You'll want no other." He growled so low in her ear, she thought maybe it was her imagination. Those words held deeper meaning for her. Did they for him, as well?

She unclenched her fingers from the couch and reached back to hold his head against the flesh bite. He rewarded her with a deep groan of appreciation. Pressing her bottom up to his groin, she gave herself over to him in complete animalistic supplication. He ground their bodies together and pushed her down so her stomach was flat to the soft, cushiony velvet, his breath hot in her ear.

"You'll never want another after me, Jinan."

She made no response. She knew the truth of those words without having to say them.

Pulling his lower body off hers, he centered his fingers at her core. "Say it, damn it. You'll want only me." He drove his fingers into her, slamming the flat of his palm against the damp lips of her slit. The slapping, moist sound made her writhe against him for more.

This was so different, so primal and raw, compared to the innocence of their courtship ten years past.

There was something more decidedly pure, real about this.

"Say it." He pulled out and thrust his fingers back in, causing her to arch her back as she tried to get closer to his warm body.

"Only you, my lord."

Those words held a finality.

Without a doubt, *this* man she was to play mistress to still held her heart in his hands. The light, fragile beat could be easily crushed in his grasp. She buried her eyes into the divan so he couldn't see her tears. She suffered under the heat of her veil in the dark room but didn't care.

She didn't deserve comfort. She didn't deserve *him*. Even if he was nothing more than her master for however long her owner said. She had done the one thing all the girls here feared. She'd fallen in love. Not tonight. It wasn't so simple as that. But years ago.

Her humiliation was complete.

She was to play the whore for a man she loved and yearned for.

And he would never know the truth of it.

"Much better," he said.

Damn her foolish heart. She was still in love with him and that was the most dangerous thing to ever happen to her. Tomorrow she'd try to break the contract. Tonight . . .

Tonight she'd live the dream.

CHAPTER NINE

The Heart of the Matter

"Why do you hide yourself from me?" His fingers brushed along the edge of tiny, bronze coins hanging beneath her jaw.

Jinan turned to face Rothburn. "I do not."

"Then why won't you remove your veil? You are the only harem girl who holds to this tradition. It stands between us as a very ineffective shield." He dropped his hand away. "You only wear it because I allow you to. There will come a time when it will be removed." He just hoped she would remove it before it came to that point.

She made to stand from the bench, but he clasped his hand around her wrist. "Sit down, Jinan."

He didn't release her till she sat, reluctantly. "The contract you've agreed to stipulates my being veiled at all times. It is the only condition you must adhere to, or I will have Amir cancel the agreement."

"That's not what stops me from removing it," he mumbled, and leaned against the vine-covered wall. They were in the gardens, in one of the many secluded nooks off the flowered paths. It hadn't escaped his notice that they were very, very alone. Plucking a pink clematis from the vine hanging over his shoulder, he ran the flower over her bared arm.

"Is there no way for me to convince you that you'd be better without it? What secrets do you possibly mean to hide beneath a thin piece of silk?"

She looked at him for a long moment. "None."

A lie, of course. He saw the tenseness in her shoulders, the affronted stiffness to her posture. You could incorporate the ways of a harem girl into an English woman; but some habits of an insulted English woman never completely disappeared. He almost smiled, but was still too angered by her refusal to unveil to do so. How was it that he had made no headway in this argument? They'd been playing this pretense for two weeks.

He'd tried to get any number of secrets out of her since their contract started. But she was closemouthed about her past. She'd only repeated the tale Amir had given him.

Sometimes Griffin wondered if she was truly Elena. It wasn't as if he weren't capable of imagining her to be someone she was not. In all seriousness, how could she deny their acquaintance so completely if she really were Elena? Why would she wish to deny it when he could find a way to take her from this place, if she but asked? He'd do anything for her, yet she seemed to want nothing from him. Nothing! All his years of needing her and she didn't want him with the same ferocity.

"I have to leave again. I won't see you for at least a month, Jinan. I have business to attend to in the East."

Her finger stopped drawing an invisible pattern on the stone bench. Her breathing stilled. Would she miss him? It was going to be a torturous month for him, without her touch, her soothing voice, the simple comfort of her presence. She would become a dream again, and he hoped like hell he didn't fill the void with something else.

She looked him in the eye, stopped the trail of the flower by covering it with her own hand. Her head tilted to the side in question. "Why did you purchase me if you cannot be here for the majority of that time?"

"Are you saying you'll miss me?" He placed his hand to his chest. "Be still, my heart, I think there is feeling in you after all."

Her brows drew together in disapproval. "What should I say? I find it perplexing. You spent a great deal at auction to have these three months."

He sat up suddenly, worried about what she'd do with her time, and whose company she'd keep. "Will you warm another's bed when I'm gone?"

She shook her head. "Not for the duration of your contract. And not for at least a year following that. We are not treated so poorly here as you like to think."

Griffin gave a sigh of relief, for she was indeed his alone for the next while. Then he asked, "Will you be happy to have a reprieve from me?"

"I like the time we spend together. You are kind to me, my lord."

He pulled her into his lap and pressed his forehead to hers. "I could be more than kind to you. You need but ask me and I'll take you anywhere you wish to go." She raised her head from his and pressed her silk-covered lips to the top of his head. He nuzzled closer to her breasts, pressing kisses to the exposed skin above her vest. At least she didn't say no when he mentioned whisking her off this time.

"Where in the East do you travel to?"

A clever change of subject. He let her have it. "I'm traveling my trade routes. There have been some problems along China's border between the locals and the Redcoats stationed there. It'll probably have settled by the time I arrive. I still need to make sure business is running as usual."

"Can I ask what you trade in?"

"Silk, these days."

"And on other days?"

"You are inquisitive today, Jinan. To what do I owe this marvelous change of character?"

"My apologies, my lord. I just wondered what you'd be doing once you left."

"Ha! So you will miss me. You are a darling girl."

"Is it so wrong to be curious about you?"

"Not at all, but I don't want to enlighten you if you won't enlighten me. I think it only fair that we both share a piece of ourselves. Are you still up for a game in this?"

She nodded her head once, her long lashes caressing her cheek. "I am."

"I made most of my fortune in trading opium. It was not an easy life, and very dangerous at times."

"Is that why you stopped?"

"No. I stopped because I started sampling the shipments."

"An opium swallower, then. I've heard of such things happening. It is not so uncommon in some harems. Amir refuses to stock it in the inner harem for obvious reasons."

"Then count him among the more intelligent. I did not swallow it, though. I smoked it. Constantly. It was not a good time in my life. At the time, I couldn't change my reliance upon it, even knowing that it was slowly eating away at me."

"Then how did you stop?"

"A friend found me. On one of my bad days. I don't

recall much of it as I was in quite a state when he took me from the opium den." He shook his head, not wanting to go into all the details of that day. It was not fit for her ears at any rate. "I've not touched the stuff since and one of the only guarantees that I would never touch it again was to stop trading it."

"This is a part of yourself you do not share with others, isn't it?"

"Outside of the friend that found me, you are the only person who knows I was reliant upon the drug."

"This is a great gift you've given me, then." She bowed her head, twirling the flower she'd taken from him. "What is it you wish to know of me?"

"Do you have no deep dark secrets? Something no one else knows?"

"It is not so easy for me to share my past. I will give you one secret. While life here in the palace has not been my greatest hardship, it was not the life I planned for myself. I cannot hate that fate's hand turned me down this path when it has brought you to me. There is great danger for someone in my position to say such a thing."

With a press of his lips to her fast-beating heart, he said, "It is enough to hear you whisper those words." He stood from the bench, pulling her to her feet, as well. "Come inside before I ravish you out here under the sun and bright blue sky. I'm leaving early tomorrow and will need my fill of all your loveliness."

"We have all night, do we not?"

"Yes."

"Walk with me in the garden." The look in her eyes said she wanted to remember today with more than coupling. He was willing to oblige her every desire. "You may have the first fill of pleasure there."

"Whatever you wish."

"Come, then," she said, taking his hand and leading him deeper into the walled garden. "It's like a maze, don't you think?"

He stopped walking, remembering the night he'd proposed to her. He'd dragged her down the dark hedged path at the Duchess of Glenmoore's maze to steal kisses and an embrace with her. How those days had been filled with innocence.

He took his steps slowly as they walked under the shade of flowering trees. Seizing the moment, he pulled her to him, released her hand and lifted the bottom of her veil to take a real kiss from her lips. When her hands came between them it was to give a slight shove but she was soon pulling him closer, her fingers curling into his shirt and guaranteeing he wouldn't escape. Not that he planned such a thing when she gave him this much.

They both broke away from the kiss, the veil slipping between them as if he'd never done something forbidden. Jinan put her forefinger over his mouth, closed her eyes, and tipped up on her toes to place a veiled kiss against her finger and his lips. Before he could snake his arm around her waist and hold her close, she took off at a run down the cobbled path, her red scarves fanning out like little lures pulling him along in her wake.

He caught her and turned into a private alcove. Snagging her hand, he pulled her into his hard body and lowered his mouth to hers. She didn't fight him, didn't turn away, but met him with equal fervor. Fingers fumbling at his trousers, she slid her hand beneath his clothes and stroked his hardened length. Taking some steps backward, he hoped the back of his legs met a bench of some sort. When they did, he sat. Jinan set her legs on either side of his, then impaled herself on his length. He groaned with his upward thrust.

"I'm going to miss you, Jinan."

"I think I'm glad for it, for I will miss you, as well."

He laughed and grasped her hips to control the slide of her body. It had taken him two weeks to get her to reveal even this much to him. Hopefully their time apart would not put the walls back up between them.

He'd been gone some six weeks. Hadn't planned on being gone that long, but it couldn't be helped. Less than a month left on his contract. He was soaking in the Roman baths that were built for the visiting gentlemen; he seemed to be the only one in here so damned early in the morning. As he leaned his head back on the tiled ledge, a slave woman pulled the blade of the razor over his whiskers. On concluding his tour through Foochow up the river to Nanking, he had but one goal in the end: to get back to Jinan.

He was slipping. His mind never went far from her. What a sad existence he lived; his contentment was based upon her whims, and she didn't even know the power she held in her hands. He needed to be careful to never reveal this weakness. It would cause her to think less than she already did of him. It would shut her off more.

The slave patted his freshly shaved face dry with a soft linen cloth. He rubbed his hands through his hair and stood from the bath. Slaves came forward to wrap him in bath linens. Two Nubian women ushered him out of the bathing room and to his private sleeping quarters, fussing on him the whole of the way. He turned them around when he came to his room and shut the door before they could follow him in. Pulling on smalls, he sat on the edge of the bed.

Griffin looked over to the sideboard. The decanter was gone, in its place a pitcher of water. He'd had the brandy and the hookah removed while he'd gone down to freshen up. If it wasn't one addiction, it was another. One obsession traded for another.

It made him a weak man. Or was he stronger for refusing it?

He pulled his shirt on and stepped into his trousers.

Might have been better had Asbury left him to rot in his own spoiled mind all those years ago. But he was no longer flawed in that sense. He'd stayed true to Jinan while surveying his routes, despite his need for something more. Hellfire, he'd been on a straight path for a good four years and some now. Though that old recklessness was peeping through his careful control. It was *her;* she could so easily destroy him. Still might if she refused to acknowledge the truth of their past. If only she'd admit the truth of who she was. Give him something to go forward with—to do what with, he didn't know. He could be patient, he'd woo her, court her; he'd do whatever it took to win her over these next three weeks.

He left the room. A eunuch waited for him outside the door to lead him to the Pleasure Gardens. Griffin would forget himself in Jinan's arms. Elena's arms. He really didn't know who she was anymore. Perhaps he'd dreamed her up; turned her into something she was not, twisted some incarnation of his youthful love into this woman.

Her back was to him when he entered the large, domed sitting room. She was talking animatedly with two other harem girls. His approach was slow. He wanted to take in her form; imprint it on his mind. Lord, had he ever missed her.

The gauze she wore was a creamy champagne color; gold braiding tied around her middle accentuated the curve of her hips and the dip in her waist. There were a few thin plaits in her hair, woven with strips of yellow silk. The veil was in place, of course. He saw where it clasped into a pair of jade hairpins.

He pushed her hair aside and placed his hand on the back of her neck. Whispering next to her ear, "How've you been, darling?" And because he hated to hold back certain things with her, certain actions when he'd been craving her for too long, he kissed her temple, let his hand drop away to grasp hers, and whisked her off to a secluded alcove without so much as a greeting to the other women.

He pulled her close, framed her face and kissed her brow. His body was strung tight. With desire, need, emotion. Threading his fingers through her hair, he inhaled her familiar scent of rose water.

"You were gone for so long, I began to wonder if I'd ever see you again."

Was she breathless, or did his ears play tricks on him?

"I will always come back for you, Jinan." His voice was muffled, his lips pressed to her forehead.

She pressed her hand against his erection—there was no hiding the evidence of his desire.

"So you have missed me, then?"

"A great deal." She ducked her head as though embarrassed to admit even that much.

"I thought of you every day I was away from you, so do not be uncomfortable to admit the truth to me."

She nodded. Perhaps his extended time away had made her want more between them. Maybe he wouldn't wait to ask if she wanted to leave this place. He'd steal her away this very night if she so much as hinted her longing to escape.

"Let me ease this, my lord," she suggested with a firm caress over his cock. His ears weren't mistaken, her voice was thready, aroused.

"No. Not yet. I just need to soak you up. God, Jinan, how easily you get under my skin."

He thrust her head back tight between his hands, and placed a hard kiss against her veiled mouth. He felt her lips part under his, her hands clasp the material of his shirt on either side to pull it free of his trousers. There was no sense in delaying the inevitable. He let her remove his shirt, and loosen his trousers. She managed to push them and his smalls so far as his hips, before he hiked up her silk scarves and pressed her back to the carpeted floor.

He sank into her wet, tight warmth and held himself still, burying his face between her breasts as he pushed them together. Gently biting the side of one, then the next, before he thrust up deep inside her, eliciting sweet sounds of pleasure from her lips.

He moved one hand up to clasp her throat, not too tight, but enough to feel her swallow against his palm. She arched up into his body, taking him deeper. Then his control snapped, and he was pounding into her, the sound of wet flesh slapping together almost as loud as his groans and her mewls. He came to his crisis after a few quick strokes, his body jerking the last of his seed into her womb as he collapsed atop her. He stayed that way, long enough to catch his breath, long enough to be comforted by her soft, pliant body. She said nothing, only breathed in rapid unison with him, running her hands over the length of his back.

Pulling himself to his feet, he shucked his clothes off, helped her to stand and yanked on the material that held her scarves in place. With the sharp tug, the golden rope fell to her feet, then she helped him slide the material down her shoulders, over her hips until it, too, pooled on the rug.

She looked at him a long moment. "How long do you stay this time, my lord?"

"For the remainder of the contract." He ran his finger along the veil's edge. "I won't leave for more than a day or two with our time coming to an end."

He held his hand out to her, inviting her to join him on the divan. She placed her hand in his, and let him lead her to the bed. He lay down on his side and pulled her body in snug to his, till her back pressed flush to his chest. "What did you do while I was away?"

She turned her head enough that she could see him. What was she looking for in his gaze? She seemed reluctant to say something. Or perhaps she needed to edit her words. "I spent my days in the garden. It's beautiful this time of year, with the fruit trees flowering."

"Is that all there is to do in the harem quarters?" He trailed a path down her arm with one finger, watching the gooseflesh rise as he did so.

"We spend our mornings in the harem bath. Our afternoons are either spent teaching new girls to dance, or in language lessons."

"Did you have to learn to speak the language when you came here? What's your first language, Jinan?"

She stalled too long to make it a believable lie. "Turkish. Why do you ask?"

So they were back to this game. Griffin rolled over to his back and tucked his hands under his head. "You'll have to do better than that to convince me you speak the truth."

Jinan turned to face him, her head resting on her fist. "Why do you care to know so much about me? I should think you'll find another beauty once you've finished with me."

He gave her a long assessing look. "Do you really think that? I'm not a callow youth, my fine beauty. I should hope we can renew our contract until the time comes when you are bored with me."

She gave a low, husky laugh. "I don't think one would easily be bored with you. You are a generous lover."

"Is that all I am, Jinan? I try to uncover even the smallest of your secrets and you shut yourself off from me. You're like a damned impenetrable treasure chest."

She placed her warm palm against his chest, her fingers drawing circles through the blond hair there. Placing his fingers under her chin, he tipped her face to the side. "Remove your veil for me, Jinan. I want to see the real woman."

"This is the one thing I cannot do, my lord. This is who I am and who I will always be, with the veil in place."

"Is it? After everything that has passed between us, you won't remove a simple piece of cloth? How can it mean so much, when it does so little?"

She pulled away, sat up, and gave him her back as she swung her feet to the floor. There was no chance of him letting her escape so easily; she must have known it because she didn't try to leave the divan.

Didn't she know he would persist on this issue? Running his knuckles down her spine, he asked, "Tell me why this secrecy is so important. Who would I tell about you, Jinan?"

"It's not that."

"Are you afraid I'll see something familiar in you? Recognize you from somewhere?"

Her back stiffened, her hands clenched the edge of the divan. "How could you know me?" she said so low he barely caught the words. "You from England, me from Turkey. We are worlds apart."

I don't think so. You give away too much with your actions. But he did not say it aloud. Not yet. Why he held back was anyone's guess. Maybe because he was still trying to come to terms with the power she had over his will, his control. Maybe while he was away from her his obsession had turned into something else. Something more freeing. More feeling.

Was there really a difference between obsession and love? Maybe for some people. Not for him. They were two extremes. In a person where one addiction led to another, it only seemed natural that he would form a deeper, more affectionate attachment to her. She'd long been in his thoughts and fantasies. She'd long been the root of his self-destructive path. Maybe not *the* root, but definitely the catalyst. And here he was, given the chance to clip her wings and keep her for himself after all their years apart. If only she'd let him.

He sat behind her, his naked thighs on either side of hers, his chin resting lightly on her shoulder.

Griffin resolved then that he would convince her they needed to stay together. To go on somehow. Grow together. Because he didn't think he'd survive leaving her behind. Or having her leave him behind.

He sighed and pulled her in tighter against him. "I'm tired. Lie with me a while."

No, he wouldn't survive leaving her behind. She belonged with him. At his side. He'd do everything in his power to keep her there.

"I've upset you. I did not mean to."

"All the traveling has worn me down. I barely slept through the last stretch of the journey. My thoughts were filled with you."

"Then I've a confession, as well. There was not a day I didn't think of you."

"Three weeks isn't nearly enough time with you. What will you do when the contract has finished?"

"I try not to think about it. If things were different—

if our lives were different—I wonder if we would have ever come together."

"Tell me something. What damage would be done in revealing your true self to me?"

"Is the contract, the time we spend with each other, the passion we share, not enough for you?"

"No. You are holding a larger part of yourself back from me. Your true self. I'm a greedy enough man to want all of you. Whatever the truth is, you can't frighten me off."

"We both know the truth. Yet we both choose not to speak of it. At least not outright." She turned in his arms, wrapping her legs around him and locking her ankles at his back. One hand stretched up and she brushed her fingers through his hair, massaging his scalp in the process. "Nothing more can come of this, Rothburn."

"Because you refuse to share the full truth." He closed his eyes, enjoying her soothing touch.

"No. Not at all. The truth will only hurt us more in the end." Her fingers trailed down his arms till she found one of his hands at her back. Taking it, she placed it behind her head. "Remove my hairpins."

His eyes drowsily looked into hers as though he could lock her in place. He didn't give her a moment to change her mind and gripped both ends of the pins and pulled them free. The weight of the brass rings at the edge of the veil pulled it the rest of the way down.

His first thought was that she really hadn't changed much over the last ten years. What was revealed was definitely his Elena. Her mouth was still full, her chin dainty and pointed. His second thought was that he now understood why she'd insisted on the veil. Anyone with a good eye for placing a face from the past would immediately recognize her. When she looked at him, he read sadness in her eyes.

"Is it so awful to reveal the truth to me, Ele—"

"Shh"—her hand covered his mouth before he could finish speaking—"that name is no longer mine. I told you the truth would do neither of us any good. I have given you more than I have given any man. Let that be enough between us."

"Let me take you away from here."

She shook her head, her eyes filling with tears. "I'm afraid that is not possible. I've gone to great pains to make this my home. The women do not leave this place once we've set foot inside the palace walls. It is perhaps our fate to be star-crossed lovers. But I don't regret your coming back into my life, even for this brief, fleeting amount of time."

"Jinan. There is no amount of money I won't pay to release you from this place."

"And there is no amount of money Amir will take to let me soar free. We have three weeks left. I suggest we make the most of what we have left," she countered.

"I'll ask you every day until you change your mind. I can be a persuasive man when necessary."

"Ah, but you must promise not to share the truth of my identity with anyone. You cannot let Amir know of our past. He would certainly have you removed from the palace. I told you my most frightening secret before you left. That I had feelings for a patron. It is forbidden. In truth, it is the only thing aside from leaving the island that is forbidden to us. Let us have this time together."

"I will not give up hope on us." When she gave a nod in understanding, he lowered his lips to hers. "You've given me more reason to pursue this."

PART TWO

CHAPTER TEN

Confinement

"Does this please you, my lord?" Jinan asked in a docile, exotic voice, fingers seductively skimming her bared thigh.

His gaze followed the view she presented—one pointed toe in front, revealing the long line of her leg. The jewels and copper coins that adorned her ankles twinkled in the amber sunset that settled around the room. Rothburn's face was shadowed so she couldn't read his emotions. He inclined his head, his jaw squared as he concentrated on her forward progression.

The *dumbek* beat its alluring thrum. The sound vibrated through the whole of her body, triggering a lustful throb in her veins as her senses were intoxicated with anticipation. She danced and swayed to the music. Everything in the background fell away as the drums, tambourine, and vocalist enveloped her and Rothburn.

Every thrust of her hip landed on the timed beat of the drum's *doum*. Two thrusts to her right and the drummer caressed the skin, one thrust to the left—another stroke ended the sound, then the process repeated.

She knew this tune well. It allowed her to display

her body to all its advantages—her generous hips begged for a man's strong hold, her breasts jiggled, demanding a man to latch on and suck them deep into his warm mouth. The naked glimpses of flesh beneath her scarves titillated his lordship into finding the treasure beneath the silk . . . taunting him to search out the glistening pearl.

This was her art form, her body painting a picture only to entrance and excite the observer. Though she loved to tease and play with him, she performed this seductive dance as a parting gift to him.

The *kuchi* bells chimed with every step as if to praise her coordination in this dance of seduction.

"You're very pleasing tonight, Jinan." His reply was hoarse, his pupils dilated in arousal.

He seemed relaxed, but she was no fool. Both were aware of the drummers in the main room and the other patrons in the Pleasure Gardens. Eunuchs stood guarding the exterior entrance, and her personal attendant stood outside the alcove, waiting to take her to her private quarters once the session concluded.

Other patrons would see her silhouette moving through the wind-caressed silks hanging around them.

There was no privacy here.

And on this night—*her last night*—with Rothburn, she wasn't sure if that was a blessing or a curse. She opened her eyes and focused only on him and none of the distractions around them.

He was aroused. His hand cupped the bulge pressed firmly against his trousers. He worked one big hand over his straining rod in long, slow strokes—how she wanted to place her hand there, though she was equally aroused watching him thus. His head rested against the high-backed chair—the only piece of furniture besides the divan in the room—and his eyes were lowered to watch the thrust and grind of her hips.

Jinan bit her lip to muffle a sound of pleasure. She loved pleasing this man. Time spent with him was a chance to live the life she'd wanted and imagined all those years ago when she'd first laid eyes upon the Marquess of Rothburn. But that life was no more.

For their last time in each other's arms, she would give him everything. She'd indulge in every pleasure of the senses he offered, simply for a memory. One that would have to last the rest of her life.

Fingers trailing up her inner thigh, she pulled aside the sheer fabric of the blue scarves. Rothburn, obviously pleased, grunted. Shrugging off his jacket, he made short work of his waistcoat. When it fell to the floor, the sound was reminiscent of the bells worn on her ankles. Perhaps a new bauble jangled in the pocket—a parting gift to bestow upon her.

"Take your veil down."

She shook her head no.

"I want to see you tonight, Jinan." His tone was oddly pleading. This man rarely pleaded. He ordered and took . . . all part of his disposition that she loved most.

Ignoring his request, Jinan reached for his lordship's neckcloth and pulled the simple knot loose. "Do you wish to tie me, my lord?" she whispered against his lips, a scant inch from touching them.

Oh, how she wanted to take possession of his tempting mouth. The need to press her lips to his burned in the pit of her belly, branding her insides as hot as the desert air that swept through the palace during high summer.

Did he understand the power he held over her love-hungry heart?

Her warm breath mingled hot with his as she waited for his answer. The silk separating them shifted back and forth with each of their exhalations, tickling her jaw and chin. So tempting.

One of his hands brushed over her hip, her breast, down her arm, causing a delightful shiver in its wake. He relieved her of the neckcloth and remained silent for some moments. "Turn around." The firmness returned to his voice.

Her eyes met his in what felt like an eternity of longing, of lost time between them. A flicker of regret reflected in his gaze. Oh, how she craved something fresh. To keep her remembering what it was to be touched by this particular man.

She needed something more to remember him till her dying day.

Though in reality, he was impossible to forget.

This man made her *feel*. Feel as though her heart hadn't shriveled and died long ago. Feel as though she could afford tender emotions for someone aside from her son and harem sisters. What a fool she was to have fallen in love with him.

Thank God above, this was the last time she would see him. She'd become too attached these past months. Too excited from a mere glance of Rothburn. The sight of him gave her hope for a different life, one which included him, and *that* was impossible after all her years in the harem.

She turned her back to him, her hips again moving erotically to the music as his hands grasped her tapered waist and squeezed. His fingers pinched just under her ribs. That one sweet touch made her breath catch and her dancing stilled in expectation. She wasn't sure what she wanted and swallowed back the emotion that threatened to crack her carefully erected façade.

He dropped his hands with a sigh, and she immediately missed the strong, supporting feel of them. But he wasn't done touching her. Hands skimmed the bare flesh of her calves, her thighs, her buttocks as he gave each cheek a light squeeze. Then he pushed the blue silk of her scarves forward and over her hips to expose her rear. He didn't rise from the chair as he sat motionless behind her. She moved in time to the music again. At least her body knew what to do. Her mind seemed lost in the high seas of hopefulness.

Dancers' bells could be heard from the other pleasure alcoves. The beat of the drum was savage, primal, and echoed around their niche, rousing the animalistic urge to sit astride this man until they both writhed in mutual ecstasy. Rothburn restrained her hips between his hands, his breath searing her already overheated skin.

Her slit was slippery and aching to be caressed by his clever hand

She wanted him to kiss her. Bite her. Mark her as his as a parting gift.

She waited, breath held tight in her lungs as the stubble of his jaw scratched over the smooth flesh of her bare buttocks. She pressed back in invitation.

He took his time, his tongue laving where his beard abraded her skin. The sharp sting of his bite made her tighten one cheek.

"A shame this is to end so soon." His hand dropped from her hip to knead into her backside. Was it to gauge her reaction to his firm touch or for her to react to his regret-filled words?

"Yes, my lord." She arched forward. She was helpless to stifle the mewling sound that escaped her throat.

She needed him so badly.

His fingers slid higher between her thighs until he

cupped the smooth, hairless flesh of her mound. The air whooshed from her lungs as longing was replaced with desperate desire. Teeth marked her hip in a feral, primal gesture; he slipped one finger into her wet core as far as it would go and left it there unmoving, teasing her. Inner muscles clenched around him.

He must know she wanted so much more than this. She rocked forward a minute amount, breaking his phantom hold on her mind as her body moved in need of deeper penetration. He pulled his hand free.

"You will receive pleasure at my command only, Jinan." Then more quietly, "Unless you remove the veil for our last night together."

"You know I cannot."

Lord Rothburn stood and spun her around, putting his body flush to hers and aligning their pelvises. The jut of his cock was a firm demand against her belly. His bigger body engulfed hers, sending a driving, aching buzz to her clitoris, urging her to savor his potency, his virility, for the last time.

Instead, she placed her cheek to his pectoral muscle for a moment and inhaled his comforting, familiar scent. He never wore the cloying perfumes of the upper class. The scent of his musky, manly sweat acted stronger than any aphrodisiac she'd been exposed to. She pulled away and stood tall, held herself motionless and awaited his bidding.

His fingers brushed through the long tresses of brown hair that hung in a loose wave over her back. His breathing was deep and even, an indication he was in complete control of his desires, while she was not. Cupping her shoulders, he pulled down the vest that cinched under her breasts. The ties were already slack in the front, so it came off with a sharp tug. He stepped away, allowing the delicate silk cloth to fall between their bodies, and then crushed her breasts against his chest. All the air left her lungs with the motion. Fresh craving blazed through her veins hotter than cinders.

Gripping her hair tightly, he tilted her head back far enough that her neck arched and exposed the vulnerable skin beneath her chin. The stubble of his jaw continued its sweet assault against her, his tongue lashing out to taste her overheated flesh. Arms loose at her sides, she submitted to his touch. He would bring her pleasure despite any of his firm reproofs or actions stating otherwise.

His kindness was another of those blessings and curses all tumbled and knotted together, further confusing her feelings. She wished he had been cruel or demeaning at least once in their time together. It would have made parting from him that much easier.

"Kneel on the divan," he commanded as he stepped away to strip his shirt off and toss it to the floor. She loved the play of muscle under the blond tangle of hair on his chest. That hair trailed downward, inviting a woman to explore. Her fingers stretched in perfect memory of what it was like to take him in hand.

"Jinan," he reprimanded when she continued to stare.

She sauntered to the divan, complying with an exaggerated sway of her hips. Pulling the silk scarves behind her, she faced him and kneeled, spreading her knees wide, buttocks resting on her heels. Wrists held out, she waited for him to bind her. He tied his neckcloth tight around both her wrists, lifting her arms above her head where a pole with hooks was installed into the wall.

He pulled down on the material to make sure she was secure and caressed the length of her arm reverently, her body bowed toward his. To her disappointment, he stood at the edge of the divan, his gaze following the stroke of his hand. Despite the warm breeze that came through the low window, her nipples puckered with his gentle touch.

Hunger for her body flashed briefly in his eyes before he raised them to hers. The smoldering in his amber-colored gaze matched the heavy pulse of awareness ravaging her body.

"I like that you remove all your hair, Jinan. Have I ever told you that?" he said hoarsely. "A woman with skin as smooth as yours makes a man mad with passion."

She let the hunger show in her eyes, telling him she was more than happy to please him.

His touch lingered under her arms and then moved lower to lift the weight of each breast. He leaned in and pulled the taut peak with his teeth, his tongue flicking out to wet the tip. Moisture gathered at her center, the engorgement and pulsing of her hidden pearl building by the moment.

Only his touch inflamed her senses this way.

Only Rothburn made her yearn for the love a man gave a woman.

How did he have so much power over her? Why had she surrendered her every sense to this man? How easily he had passed all her carefully erected defenses.

This was her last night with Rothburn—she needed to keep reminding herself of that.

But parting was so much easier said than done.

She could play this game one last time. There were no attachments to the patrons, no *tendre* allowed to mature. It made her want to weep that she would lose *this* man who long ago stole her heart. How she, a trained whore, had let this unnatural attachment go on so long, she wasn't sure.

But Rothburn was an addiction more dangerous than cantharides.

It did not help that she became more intoxicated, more obsessed by him, with every moment spent in his arms.

She was foolish to refuse his attentions at a later date. But with her son growing up so fast, any connections with the English could have her discovered. It was too risky. He'd already torn down many of her defenses. If anyone found out the truth of her whereabouts . . . the shame it would bring to her name—Jonathan's name— was unacceptable.

She was Jinan. Could only ever be Jinan.

Elena had died years ago. There was no possibility of resurrecting her from the ashes that bore her shame. She'd never be able to live with herself and what she'd become if forced to face her past. The path she'd readily accepted for her child's future.

There were no more yesterdays. There was only the present. The now.

She wrapped her fingers around the cloth that tied her to the pole and hauled down hard with all her weight, tightening it. A small pain shot through her wrists, down her arm, and brought her back to the game. She couldn't afford to think of anything but the man in front of her. He was always quick to note her inattentiveness and to question her until he knew the train of her thoughts. He already knew too much.

He gave her a long assessing look and an awakening pinch to her nipple. "Spread your knees farther apart."

She did as told because she wanted to concentrate on the moment and to stop thinking about what she gave up in ending their contract.

"Close your eyes and arch those pretty breasts toward me."

As she leaned her head back against the wall, his mouth trailed hot kisses over her flesh. He shifted, and with his weight no longer pressing into her, she raised her head to see what he was about.

He retrieved a few lengths of silk, giving her that warm smile when he noted her curiosity. It was his boyish, naughty smile. Where the dimple in his left cheek winked at her.

"Do you remember our first night together?"

As if she could forget. All that had gone through her mind that night was a hope that he didn't recognize her. Blindfolding her was a game they'd played often—until she'd finally removed her veil for him.

He wanted her helpless. Did he feel helpless when she refused to show her face? If he couldn't see her, she wouldn't be permitted to see him. It was that simple. Her price for shielding her true identity.

"That is how we will start the evening. You were so abandoned to your sense of duty that night. Will you free yourself to me again?"

She'd been some wild creature living in a fantasy that night, but managed to say, "Yes, anything for you. You know that."

A few more hours and she'd leave her heart in his hands. She wondered if he had other games planned. Regardless, he would have to live out the last of his fantasies—she'd lived out all but one of hers.

Loving him. What was love anyway? There was no love here. Not for her. Love played naught in this game.

This was Lord Rothburn's last session. His last night in paradise.

What Griffin would give to know Jinan's mind right now.

He could see her thoughts scattering to the wind; her eyes were expressive enough to show him the truth of her state. Her gaze was distant, unfocused, and looking beyond him to the window.

It was in the way she no longer watched and anticipated his next move. The haze of the drug he'd given her was gripping her mind. Dragging her under. He hated that this was the only way to keep her. Hated himself for reducing her to his mercy, making her so helpless. But it was necessary.

No matter how often he tried to convince her it was better for her to leave this place, she refused his assistance. He could help her. Though she might not think he did just that after tonight. He was drugging her to remove her from the island. What did that reveal about his character? Aside from his being an ass?

He watched her bear down on the material around her wrists. Those dark eyes of hers focused on him again. They were cloudy, sleepy, the pupils dilated for reasons other than arousal.

Sure that her mind no longer wandered, he said, "Spread your knees farther apart."

She complied, of course. She always did. Very rarely did she disobey a direct command. He wished she would, just to give him a better idea of her willfulness. In the coming weeks she was bound to fight him, but to what extent?

Her eyes slid shut for a brief moment, and he thought she might be holding back a moan as his fingers slid between the lips of her sex. Did she realize her whole body trembled when she fought to control her desire?

She looked him full in the eye. Her gaze seemed sad, melancholy. Did she regret this being their last night? He should feel guilty for what he planned. Though he wouldn't forget any time soon that she'd been the one to refuse the renewal of their contract in a year's time when she stood on auction again.

Drastic measures for drastic times.

Hadn't he made it clear that he could not let her go? Hadn't he warned her there was more than a contract between them?

"Close your eyes and arch those pretty breasts toward me."

How did she bury her past so easily? Everyone had hardships to overcome in life. He'd been in his own personal hell and back; he knew all about it. He'd tried explaining that on more than a few occasions. Tried to open up to her. Not once had she admitted to the truth of how she'd ended up on this island.

Sometimes, he was sure she longed for something deeper between them. It was in her gaze, her touch.

She didn't realize there was no giving her up. Not for anything in this world would he do such a thing. He'd always been a one-woman man. Even in the arms of other cyprians over the years, his mind was never far from this one woman.

Could she comprehend what a reprehensible act he was willing to commit to have her? How he hoped her hate would abate after a few days in his company. Time would tell, he supposed.

He hated doing this to her. He was selfish enough to steal her away from this life whether she genuinely liked it or not. He'd prove to her, somehow, that a life with him was better than this place could ever be!

He stood up from the divan. He'd bind her eyes; pretend this was like any game they had played in the past. Really, enjoyment was impossible, so overpowering was the disgust and anger he felt toward himself. Anger against the act he was forced to commit in the name of the woman he loved.

He pinched the bridge of his nose as if that would relieve the stress clouding his mind. He retrieved the silk strips hanging over the chair he sat on earlier. It would be easier on him if he didn't have to watch her eyes cloud under the hazy hold of the drug. He turned to see her studying him with an avid eye. As avid as her drugged mind could be.

Silently cursing his stupidity, he managed to ask, "Do you remember our first night together?"

It was there in her expression. Such an easy woman to read.

It was easier to pretend a repeat of their first night than to reveal the depth of his deception. It was for the best, he had to keep telling himself that. She'd forgive him in the end. He had so much more to offer her than did this gilded whorehouse. This sad, low life. If she'd asked, he'd have given her the world. She never had. And he had to know if it was because of fear from living on this island with her owner. The only way to do that was to take her away from this place. He'd make it up to her in the end. He promised himself that.

Strange, though, there was still that niggling feeling he shouldn't deceive her this way. That he should take her away from the island without the cloak of lies he was relying upon. It was too late now; there was nothing that could convince him this wasn't better for her . . . for him.

In the long run, better for their future.

Because he wasn't willing to part from her again.

In a few days she would be free from this place. Free to live the life she was meant for, and in time, any fear from being a slave should dissipate. Never had she given him reason to believe she'd been abused here. Not once had she shied away from his attentions, nor had she ever cowered in the presence of her owner.

What was unfathomable was her wanting to live out the rest of her days here.

His plan was simple: give her a few weeks to adjust to life outside the harem, then take her back to England. How he was to reintroduce her into society, he couldn't guess. But he was resourceful enough to find a way.

Tying the silk around her eyes, he watched the last of the daylight rays filter through the window. Dusk wasn't coming soon enough. His hand smoothed over her stomach in a soothing, coaxing motion; anything to make the drug-induced state come on quicker.

She started to nod off. Her head sagged to one side and then jerked back up as she tried to fight off the tiredness weighing her down. She must never have been under the influence of opiates; she didn't put up much of a fight as the drug pulled her beneath the surface of consciousness.

Pressing her legs closed, he braced his thighs on either side of hers in support. Her body finally giving out with the tincture, she slumped, her wrists tightening in the truss he'd slung her in. Pulling her against his chest, he loosened the knot easily and stretched her out on the divan.

The eunuch stood waiting on the outside of the room. The bribe had been negotiated a week ago. Griffin didn't care what reasoning the eunuch had for his deception against Amir. This was his last chance to take Jinan out of here.

Tucking her body into his, he watched the entryway. He didn't move until the eunuch's hand appeared under the silks in the arch of the alcove. Griffin was given the count of five. He was off the divan, had shrugged into his coat, and had Jinan in his arms before the eunuch's hand reached one and then lifted the silks aside.

Sliding under the material, Griffin nodded when the

eunuch came into view. He kept to the wall until he hit the exit. There was only one exit out of the Pleasure Gardens, and Griffin had chosen the alcove closest to that door so he could make a quick and easy escape. Amir kept a tight watch on his harem girls. How the eunuch had rid the entry of the other guards he wasn't sure, nor was he inclined to care.

Very few people wandered around this room after indulging in their sexual escapades. It was just after the dinner hour now, only a few hours of light left. This was the quietest part of the day here—so far as he had noticed. Amir had warned him this was his last night and that he wasn't welcome until the next auction.

It was that simple for Amir.

Not so simple for Griffin to give her up.

He had paid handsomely for Jinan.

It was better this way. No use dragging out an inevitable conclusion. Anger faded in time.

Once in the main hall of the palace he found his way. His sense of direction was faultless. The eunuch took him to a servants' entrance, seldom used when the palace wasn't full of patrons, and led Griffin through a private garden.

The only room that looked out this way was Amir's, and he was currently occupied in the inner harem. Or at least Griffin hoped the man was busy elsewhere, as he had been for the last three weeks.

Situated at the far end of the gardens, the door was well hidden by the shade of tall flowering trees. It opened to reveal the rocky embankment of the beach. There was no hope of safely making it through the main exit undetected; that area would be crawling with servants and guards alike.

Outside the palace walls, Griffin almost breathed a sigh of relief.

Not yet. They were not out of harm's way yet.

He turned and looked at the eunuch. Jerking his head to the right, he motioned for the man to follow. Griffin had left Jinan a week ago and arrived back at the island yesterday, bringing his fastest ship with him. He had a feeling he was in for a race to escape Amir's attempts at recapturing Jinan, the favorite harem girl. Or so Griffin was led to believe. She was his favorite girl, and he had so much more to offer than Amir.

Two days and he'd be at his private villa. Two days, and he could release Jinan from the servitude of this life. No one would look for him there, since he rarely set foot in his Brindisi villa; he'd seen it for the first time when he'd inherited it from his uncle. He preferred his own villa outside Florence, where the weather was more hospitable.

He carefully made his way down the stony terrain of the coastline. It was a difficult path to descend but this rock facing proved to be the only place to hide a skiff. Finally making it to the water, he saw the first mate lying in the bottom of the boat.

"Lord Rothburn." The boy sat up quickly and took the oars in hand. He couldn't be more than fourteen years.

Griffin nodded, deposited Jinan in the bottom, and turned to the eunuch. The man's hand rested on his scimitar. Griffin pulled the emerald from his pocket, a five-carat family heirloom he'd had removed from a necklace. He held it toward the eunuch. It was pinched from his hands, pocketed so fast he didn't see where, and the eunuch turned and trudged back up the rocky ledge.

Griffin stumbled down into the skiff and took the other set of oars. There was no sense in dallying. They needed to move.

"We move as fast as your arms can carry us, Jimmy."

"Aye, my lord. We'll be on the *Belladonna* in a jiffy. Timed it meself how long it was. Not more than a hundred pulls to get us there."

Griffin looked down at Jinan. There was too much skin exposed, her belly and thighs visible. Why hadn't he thought to wrap her in a blanket before making his way down here? Though the boy tried not to look at her, he was blushing a furious red seeing so much female flesh. Griffin clenched his jaw and cleared his throat. The boy tugged at his neckerchief when he caught Griffin's angry expression.

"You're sitting on the *ferace* and yashmak. Hand it to me, boy, and look toward the *Bella*."

Griffin clenched his jaw, angry for the furious outburst toward the youth. But he didn't want anyone looking at her. She was so much more than what she appeared. What did it matter? Once she was dressed in English fashion, no one would know she'd ever been brought so low.

He released the oars and snatched the muslin out of Jimmy's hand. Pulling the silk robe, made for this occasion, over her head, he settled her more comfortably between his legs and put the yashmak in place over her existing veil. The less everyone saw of her, the easier it would be for her to adjust to her new life. He longed to be in the privacy of his villa. Clothes awaited her, both in Turkish style and English. He wasn't sure what she'd choose.

He picked up the oars and put all his weight into pushing the skiff faster through the unsteady water. The sooner they were on the ship, the closer they came to reaching safety. When they hit the side of the *Bella-donna,* ropes came down to haul them up.

In passing the captain, he informed him, "We sail to

Brindisi as fast as you can." He hadn't taken any chances by telling anyone his plans, except his man of affairs, prior to abducting Jinan.

"Aye, me lord." The captain seemed at a loss for words as he looked at the wrapped package carried in his master's arms. The captain's jowls wobbled, then he seemed to think better of saying anything and turned on his heel, barking out orders to raise the sails.

Griffin wasted no time in taking Jinan belowdecks to his own quarters. Sequestered there, she'd be safe from having to reveal her identity to anyone but him. His crew probably had figured out at some point today that he planned on bringing a mistress home since he'd had Jimmy placed ashore out of eye's view.

Once in his quarters, he laid Jinan on his bed and went for the skin of water he'd set on his desk earlier. He trickled a few drops of water down her throat, then hung the skin on a hook beside the bed. The drug would dehydrate her so he'd have to keep giving her fluids.

He went about stripping her down to her scarves and placed a light blanket over her. It wasn't that it was cool—it was rather warm in his cabin—but he didn't like the possibility of anyone seeing her in a state of undress.

Tomorrow night she'd be awake. He expected her to be confused, angry, and maybe even frightened. He'd deal with it when the time came, whatever her mood. Right now, he need only worry about keeping her hydrated.

The aftereffects of the laudanum would not be pleasant when her mind finally swam out of the fogginess that had taken her under. Never had he been a fan of the stuff, but it was the safest sleep inducement he knew of.

So lost in his thoughts, he didn't realize he'd been

staring at her unmoving form until moonlight filtered through the porthole.

He stood and flattened the creases in his trousers. Leaning over the bed, he pressed the back of his hand to her forehead to make sure a fever hadn't set in. She was cool, but not sweating. He retrieved a warmer blanket and tucked it around her prone form.

He needed to get himself abovedeck to see if anyone followed his ship. Amir would have noticed the absence of Jinan by now. It wasn't as though Griffin could trust the eunuch to remain quiet when his association with a missing harem girl could be construed as grave defiance.

Griffin was confident enough to know there wasn't a ship on this side of the hemisphere that could catch his clipper. He'd brought the *Belladonna* down from Liverpool where he shored her. Those Americans made a nice, fast sail.

One Amir could not catch with his best *xebec*.

Taking the skin down from the hook, he trickled more water into Jinan's mouth, then hung it back up before leaving the cabin.

Griffin wasn't sure if this sickness was the effect of the laudanum or something else.

She was running a high fever, sweating profusely no matter how many times he mopped her off with a cool cloth. He'd spent the greater part of the night trying to cool her skin down, using half the ship's store of fresh water. She'd been frighteningly ill, vomiting throughout the early morning. He couldn't imagine what was left in her stomach to expel but still she heaved.

He'd not been on deck for more than an hour last night. He'd come down to check on Jinan only to find her in a fever state, sweat soaked through both blankets he'd wrapped about her. Frantically he'd checked and examined the vial of laudanum to make sure he hadn't given her too much.

He rubbed at his dry eyes and stood to pace the small quarters. What if he had given her too much? What if her body just couldn't handle the substance? Catching movement from the corner of his eye, he turned to see her hunch into a ball. *God, please don't be sick again, Jinan.* He was at her side in two strides and took her in the cradle of his body in case she started to heave again.

He didn't want Jimmy to watch this unfold; it was time to send him off. Jinan was his responsibility. Jimmy had helped him slop up the mess of her sickness, but the smell of it lingered repulsively sweet in the air. It probably didn't help to keep Jinan's stomach at ease.

"Still no tail?" he asked the boy. He needed another distraction. He was worried sick about Jinan. What if she died because of his stupidity? He'd never survive if something happened to her, especially if it were by his hands.

"No one follows her. They'd be hard-pressed to catch us."

"Good. I assume we are still on track." He had only been on deck long enough to ask for Jimmy's help. The captain would send someone down if they were being followed. But he hoped they were ahead of being only "on track." He might need a doctor to attend Jinan as soon as they reached his villa.

"We'll be there in record time, 'morrow morning be my guess. Cap'ain says 'tis the fastest he's ever taken *Belladonna*. Says she needed a good runnin' since yer brought 'er down from Liverpool."

Good. That put them at least twelve hours ahead of schedule.

"Excellent to hear. Now get out of here and find

some fresh air. She seems to have settled down for now."
And he wanted to be alone with her. Take the rest of her
silks off so her body cooled properly. What had he done?
What had he done!

"Yer sure? I don't mind stayin' to help yer."

"Go get something to eat. If you can stomach it at this
point." He grimaced; he couldn't stomach food, though
he'd force some down soon if only to give himself
enough energy to sit up with Jinan for the remainder of
their trip. "I doubt she has anything left to expel."

The boy nodded and was out the door in an instant.
Probably more than thankful to get away from the
scent of vomit lingering in the air.

Her fever seemed to have subsided; the worst effects
of the drug had been purged from her body. The re-
maining tincture was tucked in his vest pocket. He'd
toss it when he was off the boat. Had he known she
couldn't tolerate the stuff he would have done something
else. Anything else, even met the damn end of Amir's
scimitar. Anything but cause Jinan such harm.

Walking over to the door, he turned the key in the
lock. Alone at last, even if the room had an unpleasant
sour smell. He'd strip her down to wash away any remnants of the fever. Well, he'd take off what was left of her
harem outfit—most of what he'd put on her had had to
be removed when she'd thrown up.

Releasing the ties on her vest, he pulled it off and
tossed it on the floor. He brushed the scarves around
her hips aside. Her skin was a deep bronze even in this
lighting. Touching her cool and still sweaty stomach,
he pushed the scarves up. Should he take them off? It
wasn't as though he'd never seen the whole of her in the
nude.

Everything she wore probably smelled of the sickness. Feeling around to her lower back, he tried to find

a tie but there was nothing in the delicate layers. How had he never noticed the intricacies of this costume before? Perhaps it came off over her head. As gently as he could, he started to push the scarves up. Revealing her naked mound, he groaned and closed his eyes. He couldn't strip her down right now. He was tired, frustrated, and anxious to have this over with. Anxious to have her well and healed.

His head falling forward, he rested his forehead between her breasts.

"Even now I can't keep my hands off you." He placed his lips to her breastbone. "You're going to hate me. I know it. But I'll be damned if I take you back to Amir now. Just live through this, Jinan. Hate me when you are alive and well, just pull yourself through this."

He turned his head to the side, pressed his ear to her chest and listened to the steady beat of her heart. Surely if she wasn't strong enough to survive this, her heart wouldn't pound so strong. It was a sign. It had to be. She'd pull through.

He pressed a kiss where her heart beat strong. Another against her breast, his arms tucked under her back to pull her up close so he could hug her tightly to his body. How he wished her arms would fold around his shoulders. Instead, his folly had her lying there limp as a rag doll.

He needed space. He needed her clothed. Forcing himself to rise from the bed, he walked over to his chest by the door and rifled through it for something sexless.

He had brought a caftan with him in case they needed to hide from pursuers before they hit the shores of Brindisi. Without ceremony he pulled the linen gently over her head and settled it around her legs before walking away from her. She hadn't been ill for at least an hour

now. It was safe enough for him to go see what was prepared in the way of food, and then go abovedeck for
some fresh air.

Pulling out the vial of the drug one more time, he
measured the liquid. No more than the tip of his nail
had come from the tube.

He locked the door behind him and headed toward
the galley. After that, he'd get his hands involved in
some manual labor on deck. Hopefully by the time he
returned to his cabin he'd be too tired to think of touching Jinan.

His mind had obviously gone wrong after all those
years of overindulgence. Was he really any better than
Jinan's owner? He'd taken a woman against her will—
or at least he assumed it was against her will; he'd have
affirmation of that as soon as she woke.

Asbury should have left him to rot in that opium den.

CHAPTER ELEVEN

Awakening

The fog that had wrapped around her mind seemed to have eased. She'd been fighting it forever. At least it felt like forever.

Her eyes seemed too heavy to open. Her world spun in darkness. Never-ending circles, dancing round and round behind her lids. Her stomach clenched. She was rocking. It was as if she were swaying with the motion of a boat. Her stomach cramped some more, and a groan escaped her dry lips.

"Shh." Someone whispered close to her ear.

She opened her mouth to speak, but her tongue was thick, dry and swollen. There was no saliva in her mouth to help aid her voice. She let out a croak, and the swirling circles came back with a force all their own, dancing viciously, nauseatingly in her head.

She groaned again and flung her arm out. The other arm felt like dead weight; maybe she was lying on it. Someone was with her. She hadn't enough strength to open her eyes. She wrapped her hand around a big, hard male body. An arm?

"Amir?" she choked out.

The spinning got worse. Her stomach heaved, trying to expel its contents; but nothing came up. A hand wrapped around her stomach as she pitched forward, holding her in place.

"Give it some time. Be still." Such a gentle, soothing voice.

She couldn't *be still*. Did Amir joke? She only ever felt this ill when she was on a boat. "Amir," she groaned again.

Buzzing in her ears made it hard to hear; her head was not only spinning, it was pounding unrelentingly.

Wetness touched her lips.

Water.

Her tongue touched the tip of a water skin. Fresh, so fresh and cool against her parched mouth.

"Drink," the voice said.

It was so far away, as though someone were yelling to her through a wind tunnel. She sputtered, water flowed over her lips and down her chin.

"Slower . . ."

Coughing out the refreshing sustenance, she lurched forward and tried to vomit again.

She was on the floor, rocking back and forth. Someone held her tight from behind. Was that to keep her from moving? From falling?

"Water," she tried to say.

He must have understood since the skin brushed across her mouth.

She took smaller sips. Her tongue felt less weighty, her lips less sore with the liquid swilling through her body. She felt so empty. As if she hadn't eaten in a week.

"Sleep," the soft voice said.

But she couldn't sleep. Her head hurt, her eyes

wouldn't open, her stomach roiled with every wave of nausea that clutched her body. She must have come down with some illness.

"Amir?" Was she dying?

"Shh . . ."

"What's happened? Dying?" She sobbed and heaved up nothing again. She sucked in great gulps of air only to heave once more.

"You are fine. We'll make port in a few hours."

"Port . . . ?"

She tried to open her eyes again. They seemed so heavy, so swollen. There was only darkness when she managed to crack one lid halfway, then she closed it when the pounding behind them worsened.

She was on a boat. That explained the sickness, and it also meant the man holding her was not Amir. Pushing her arm behind her, she tried to dislodge him but he held fast. She was so weak right now, how did she expect to fight him off?

"A few hours at most. Hold on till then. Please, Jinan."

Rothburn.

She should know that voice anywhere, pounding head or not. How was it possible that she was with Rothburn on a boat? A new fear washed through her body. She felt herself shaking and shivering but couldn't seem to say anything. Where would he take her? What would he do to her?

How had he stolen her from the palace?

Her son.

Her Jonathan.

She was without her child and knew it as sure and stinging as the vomit-scented air she breathed.

"No . . . no . . ." The denial finally made it past her lips.

"Shh . . . Everything will be fine soon. Shh. I'll arrange for a doctor as soon as we're on land."

"No. Amir. Must go to Amir . . ." Though she tried to speak firmly, it came out in a croaking, wheezy noise.

Her son. How could her son survive without her?

How could she survive without her son?

How had this happened? Reaching up to her face, she was only more dismayed to realize the veil was gone. But what did that matter when she'd been taken from her son? He knew. Rothburn knew who she was because she'd been foolish enough to share that part of herself.

Futile as her struggle was, she relaxed in his hold, breathing in deeply through her mouth and out through her nose so the smell didn't make her more ill. Yet her stomach knotted impossibly tighter. Everything inside her was hurt, raw. Sad. Oh God. Her darling boy was alone.

The rocking over turbulent waters became a gentler sway; the motion still sickened her but it lessened in slow degrees. The pounding in her eyes didn't ease, and her mouth was so very dry. So dry there was no spittle to swallow and ease her sore throat.

She was lifted. It made her squeeze her eyes tighter, to shut out the pain racking against her brain in never-ending, throbbing waves.

Tiredness swept through her, her body grew limp, heavy, and started to drift with his every step. Her captor said nothing as she fought the fog dragging her back into sleep.

"Jonathan," she thought . . . she whispered . . . she didn't know.

"Sleep, love. Sleep."

The voice was so far away.

Too far to lure her back into consciousness.

* * *

She shouldn't have slept this long, even under the influence of the drug. Why was she so ill? Was she prone to boat sickness so severe? Her body had been tense until he'd stepped from the gangplank to solid ground. They'd gone to see a local sawbones before heading to his villa. The man said she should sleep it off, eat light and rest easy. Why didn't Griffin feel reassured by the words?

His man stood solemnly by the whole time they waited for Jinan to be looked over. Peters had come down from England at Griffin's insistence that they sojourn in Italy for an unknown length of time. Peters was one of the few men he trusted with private matters. Griffin had been vague about his real reasons for having his man of affairs here until he'd left to retrieve Jinan. His man of affairs knew who Jinan was, had known about her since arranging the money transfer to Amir three months ago.

Peters opened the door to Griffin's apartment. He didn't fail to notice Peters's look of disapproval. The man thought the bundle of cloth Griffin held to his chest was nothing more than a ladybird. And that the extreme measures employed to retrieve such a creature were highly unusual and completely unnecessary.

Peters nodded and gave a slight bow. Was there reluctance in his steps as he took his leave?

Before Peters attempted a heart-to-heart, Griffin said, "Have water brought up and a light repast prepared."

"My lord," Peters intoned with an air of annoyance.

Griffin paused. How to get Jinan to eat? There was no possible way for her to stomach real food. "Bring some vegetable broth as well."

Kicking the door shut behind him, he grimaced. His mood was black enough that he might lash out at Peters if another snide remark was so much as hinted at. After a meal, he'd have a clearer mind. Then he'd bathe and sleep, in that exact order. Jinan would need those things, too.

With a quick yank, the coverlet landed at the foot of the bed. He placed Jinan on the clean sheets and set himself to stripping her of the caftan that smelled of her sickness. The blue scarves of her dress were a tangled mess about her hips. He yanked them down to cover her mound. He was no hedonist to make her eat completely naked. Though they'd done it frequently enough in the Pleasure Gardens.

New beginnings. He needed to stop dwelling on what they had had and focus on what their future held.

If there was one thing he was determined to do, it was to reacquaint this beauty with her true heritage as an English lady—of course, only outwardly. He liked the free sensuality she unleashed when playing the Turkish princess. But he wanted her free of the life she must have been forced to live.

Putting her foot in his lap, he looked to see how the coin anklet came off. There was no clasp. Did she never take them off? He didn't want to break the golden chains in fear they held sentimental value so he left them. He pressed his thumbs into the ball of her foot, massaging them until she curled her toes forward.

With a slight clank of the silver tray, a hiss passed Peters's lips at the sight of the exotic woman in Griffin's bed. Her veil hid her features; he made sure he'd secured it around her face before leaving the ship. Her dark brown hair wrapped around her shoulders and arms in a tangled mess. She looked like a Gypsy harlot in her scarves and bands of gold, with painted designs around her hands and feet marking her as a heathen. But she was no heathen to Griffin.

"Good Lord, Rothburn. You can't seriously expect to introduce her into society."

"If you know what's good for you, you'll hold your tongue." He hadn't told anyone her identity. He wasn't sure why, but her true origins were his secret for the time being. It would be up to the lady in his bed to decide to whom she revealed her secrets.

"My apologies, *my lord*. But have you really looked at her?"

Griffin wasn't in the mood for prejudices. Peters had no way of knowing his past associations with Jinan. And for that reason alone, he didn't lash out at the man.

He lifted some of her hair, trying to pull his fingers through it. There were more pressing issues at hand then dealing with an overset Peters. "I'll need a brush and comb to pick out these knots."

Dismissed, Peters clicked his heels with the announcement. "Bathwater will be prepared in your bathing room." The door shut softly, and Griffin was happy to be alone with her at last.

"How is this going to work, Jinan?"

Her only answer was to snuggle deeper into the pillows. He sat her up, propping her between the stacks of pillows, and retrieved the glass of water.

"Jinan," he said, next to her ear, one fist planted at the side of her leg. She moved a little, her thigh pushing against his wrist as she tried to stretch out, as she fought her way into consciousness.

Her hands fisted at his chest, burrowing into his shirt.

"Jinan," he said louder and with more firmness. He needed to get fluids into her. When she was filled with water and broth, he'd let her sleep as the doctor ordered.

"Amir?"

Her voice came out as a croak, not that he expected it to be any better since they'd left his ship. He almost hadn't caught whom she asked after until she said it again. It made jealousy flare in his stomach. Why was it always Amir she called after? And who the hell was Jonathan? That was the last name she'd whispered before sleep had overwhelmed her earlier. He couldn't remember her husband's name, but he did know it hadn't been Jonathan.

Still, it was another man she called after. Had Griffin not shown her how gentle and kind he was over the past few months? Did she think Amir so kind when he owned and auctioned his women off as no better than slaves? There was no kindness in reducing women to harlots.

Nor was kidnapping her to make her see *his* reason a kindness, he admonished.

He clenched his jaw and swallowed his pride. In time, she'd see how much more he had to offer. He vowed he'd prove it to her. "No. Amir's not here."

He placed a cool glass to her lips. She took it in small mouthfuls.

She pushed the glass from her when she'd had her fill. Her eyes remained shut. He knew she suffered a headache of massive proportions—a nasty side effect of the opiate. What she needed was to get some broth in her. Two days without food and fevers ravaging her body was too long.

With less of a catch in her voice, she asked, "Where is Amir?"

So she still played the princess speaking her Persian tongue. No more games, he was bloody well sick of games.

"Jinan"—he wrapped his hand around hers and held tight—"you well know Amir isn't here. You are at my villa."

She looked at him through squinted eyes for a long

moment. He'd closed all the curtains in here so she wouldn't be pained by the midmorning light. Whatever comfort she asked for, he'd give her. To an extent, of course.

"Where is your villa, exactly?"

Her fingers rose to her own face. Griffin hated to admit it, but he was used to the scrap of silk covering her features. It didn't seem important to remove it when he knew damn well who she was. She sighed in what he could only imagine was relief when her fingers found the cloth still tightly secured through her knotted hair. "Has anyone else seen me?"

"No. I've kept your veil in place. Here. Drink this, it's broth. It will give you some of your strength back."

He brought the warm bowl up in his free hand. She shook her head, refusing.

"If I leave it on the table here, and give you a moment to collect yourself, will you drink it?"

She only stared at him through narrowed, sleepy eyes. "You need something nourishing, you were sick on the trip here."

"The boat—"

"Yes, we came in my clipper. We only traveled for a couple days."

"I cannot travel by boat."

"I'm well aware of that." He gave her a small, reassuring smile. "So we will start with light fare. It's a celery-based broth, not meat. I don't know if you even eat meat." With a gentle squeeze to her hands he stood from the bed. "Please drink the broth. You've had me worried, and I just want to know you are on the mend. I'll be back in a few minutes."

He didn't go much farther than the sitting room of his apartment. He couldn't leave her for long, he was sure she'd try to escape. And in her state, that could be dangerous. He paced back and forth, his hand tangling in his hair as he silently cursed himself for being all kinds of a fool.

What was he going to do with her? Damn it, why did the first words out of her mouth have to be her owner's name, and *his* whereabouts?

He went into the bathing room. A maid sat at the side filling the tub. He wanted to sink into the inviting water with Jinan, but he didn't think she'd appreciate that sort of attention right now. He so badly wanted to hold her, reassure himself that she was well.

The maid ducked her head. "It'll be ready in a minute, my lord."

He backed out of the room and paced the sitting room again. The dull thud of the bowl told him Jinan was done, and he went into the bedchamber to check on her.

She sat up without the support of the pillows. She hadn't bothered to cover her bared skin. The silk of her scarves had shifted to cover the naked flesh between her thighs. It pleased him that she wasn't a skittish miss. That she could sit baring her body so freely. And it made him hot and aroused at a most inconvenient time. Did she tempt him purposely? Or was he that much of a cad? Oh, how he knew the answer to the second question.

She pointed at the curtain-covered window. "Where have you brought me?"

Still in Persian—not that he expected otherwise.

"We are in Italy." He leaned against the chaise off to the side of his bed, giving her space but not too much.

She cocked her head to the side in question. "Italy? What did you do to me?"

"Laudanum."

"Laudanum," she repeated. The English word rolled

off her tongue with the ease and intonation only an English woman would use. "You must take me back to Amir."

He frowned. He had to remember to be patient. It was most certainly a shock for her to find out she'd been stolen away from the only home she'd known for God knew how long.

"I'm afraid I cannot do that."

"You must. He will find me here, then he will kill you."

He wasn't buying that excuse. Did she think to frighten him into releasing her? Patience, he reminded himself. "He doesn't know where *here* is, Jinan."

"He will find me," she said with a hint of defiance. "We can never leave the palace."

"You are free now. You never have to go back to him." He moved to the bed, perching himself on the edge.

All the air seemed to escape her lungs on a rushed exhale. Quicker than he thought she could move in her weakened state, she threw herself at his feet on the floor. "Please. You must take me back. Before it is too late."

She stayed on her knees with her hands gripping one of his shoes as she pleaded.

"Jinan," he said, trying to gently remove his foot from her hold. She only grasped it tighter.

"You must take me back. Amir will be very angry. You don't know what you've done. You can't possibly understand."

"You are free, Jinan. He won't find you. I won't let him find you, do you hear me?"

"You don't understand. I cannot stay here." He heard the tears in her voice now. What had Amir ever done to make her fear leaving the island so much? At least it was Amir that made her cry, not him. At least not yet.

"Jinan"—he hooked his hands under her arms and hauled her up to stand in front of him—"stop this line of questioning. I'll not take you back. I can't."

Tears trailed down her face, wetting the veil so it stuck to her trembling lips. "Take me back before Amir does not forgive me. Take me back before it is too late."

Maybe it was the defeated look in her eyes. Maybe it was the tears flowing so freely down her face. Maybe it was his damned idiotic adoration for her. Whatever it was, he couldn't stand to see her so torn and scared of her owner, who kept whores aplenty. She was safe here. And if there was one thing he could prove to her, it was that no harm would ever befall her under his protection.

"I'm sorry you are upset."

"You are not. You can't possibly understand the wrong you've committed."

"Then explain it to me."

She looked at him for some minutes, wiping the back of her hand against her cheek to remove the wash of tears. "You've taken me from the only thing that has ever mattered to me. You've left my son behind."

Had he not been holding her still, she would have crumpled to the ground with the admission. Had he not been sitting, he probably would have gone down with her weight. A son. He'd bloody well screwed this up. How was it she had never mentioned the child before now?

"Your son?"

"You must bring me back to him."

"It's too late." He watched tears wash down her face. "I'm so sorry. Why did you not tell me sooner?"

"How could I? We had a three-month contract. There was no reason to tell you."

"What of the things I shared with you? Did it not occur to you that I could help both you and your son get out of the harem?"

He set her on the bed beside him and took to pacing the floor. Shitfire. What had he done? This was a disaster. This was unexpected. Brushing his hands roughly through his hair, he tried to think. What was he going to do? Jinan still cried, although her sobs were silent as she watched him pace to and fro with an expectant look in her sorrowful eyes.

"I would assume this is a younger child we are talking about?"

She nodded.

"I'm sorry. God, Jinan. I don't know what else to say. I will find a way to fix this." Which meant facing the man he'd stolen property; although Griffin did not think of Jinan as property.

He raked his hand through his hair again. "Come, we'll get you washed. We can't do anything right now. You are tired and worn from the trip here. You need sleep and food so your body can heal from the ordeal. I need to rest, too. I haven't since you've fallen ill, and I'm afraid I'll fall over from exhaustion soon. We'll take care of your son as soon as we are both fit to."

"These things are unimportant. You must take me home."

"I can do nothing about it right now, Jinan. Had you been more forthcoming with your circumstances, I would have moved heaven and earth to take your son out of there with you. Do not test my temper right now."

Because he was in a right fit. He wanted to hit something. Wanted to release some rage from such a simple yet stupid act. Had he listened to his gut instead of his prick, this wouldn't be a problem. No, he'd not been thinking with his cock, he'd been thinking with his heart when all along she didn't give a damn about him. Certainly not enough to tell him she had a child.

She came to her feet and pushed her finger into his chest. "This is *your* fault. How dare you do something so despicable, so awful to me! You are a beast of a man and you need to right this immediately!"

Temper finally getting the better of him, he scooped her up into his arms and carried her to the bath. He'd had enough of her desires for Amir, and her equal dislike for himself. She should be thanking him! The man who had saved her from a life of prostitution. Had she given him more to go on, he would have removed her son, too. What part of that promise did she not understand?

"You won't be going anywhere right now, Jinan." His next words took him more by surprise than her. "If you won't listen to reason, then hear me now. You belong to me. Not Amir. Me! I'll find a way to get your son out of the harem. Trust me, please."

She hissed in a breath as he set her on her feet on the tiled floor of the bathing room. She looked at the water in the tub with wide eyes

"The water is warm," he offered in apology. Though it was going to take more than a warm bath to apologize for what he'd done. Goddamn it. How was he going to get the child out of there? It must be Amir's because she'd been careful about preparing her body to avoid pregnancy the whole time he'd been with her.

Her head whipped up and she stared at him with terror. What was the problem now? She had never had a problem bathing in front of him before. She'd done it often enough in the public bathhouse on the island.

She tried to make a dash past him, but his arms came around her, lifted her, and before he could temper his fury, he dumped her into the water. She needed to wash off the smell of sickness and sweat. It was that simple. She landed with a splash. The water spilled over the rim and even more spilled as she tried to scramble out of the tub.

It infuriated him that she insisted on this disobedience, when he did nothing more than try to help her.

"Jinan, I'm a patient man. But you are testing my tolerance to the utmost."

"It is standing. I cannot be in standing water." Her voice was high-pitched, scared.

He held her down and dumped water over her head with the pitcher. "I have no idea what you are talking about. Hold still or I will join you in there."

"You do not understand anything." She flung her arms out, giving him a good thumping on his chest, knocking some of the air out of his lungs. "Stop this!"

He paused, gazing down at her. She wasted no time in pulling herself out of the tub to stand beside him on the marble floor, dripping everywhere. She was breathing heavily, one hand holding on to the lip of the tub as she panted out, "This is bad luck. I do not bathe in standing water. You have ruined everything in my life today. Leave me be."

He knew it for the truth so said nothing, just ground his teeth together and gave her a long look. Could she be so immersed in Turkish culture and the life of the harem in general that she'd forgotten what it was like to be English? He stood, his pants and shirt sopping wet, both sticking uncomfortably to his legs and arms.

She must have read anger instead of frustration in his stance because she backed up until her back was firm against the wall. "Send me a slave, and I will do as you wish."

"There are no slaves here, Jinan." He closed his eyes for a brief second and took a calming breath. "I know you know this. You are no longer a slave. Do you understand me? I won't have you playing these games now that you aren't in the palace."

"There is nothing to understand. You will take me back to Amir once I can travel by boat again. I will bathe, and you will go pen a note. If you will please send me someone to help with the bathing."

Griffin pursed his lips. There was a time to argue, and a time to cede what wasn't important. He would do as she asked. Straightening his clothes, he gave her a slight bow, then left the bathroom, making sure to close the door firmly behind him. The hinge on the door creaked, so the second she opened it, he would know.

He went and changed his trousers. That gave them both some time to calm their tempers.

Then he went about finding help for Jinan. A maid was bound to walk by his room sooner or later, so he stuck his head out to see who happened in this direction. There wasn't a chance of him leaving Jinan alone, not yet anyway.

"Donata, come here, I have a task for you." He motioned the maid into his suite. She came quickly forward and had fresh linens in hand. Perfect.

"My lord." She curtsied before walking through the door he opened wide for her entry.

He wondered if she already knew that a lady of questionable values occupied his chamber. The butler had been present when Griffin had carried in Jinan.

"I require your attention in the bath. Jinan speaks no Italian that I know of. She needs someone to help her with her hair and bath, and well"—he shook his head, not sure if he could explain what Jinan's needs were—"you will see."

When he opened the door to the bathroom, Jinan sat on a bench opposite the bathtub, staring at the water as though it would jump out and pull her under at any moment. The maid's inward hiss told him she hadn't yet heard about his *guest*. Or, at least, the strange overall appearance of said guest.

"Jinan," he said, switching back to English, "this is Donata. She will help you with whatever you need."

Griffin turned back to the maid and spoke in Italian. "Jinan cannot bathe in standing water. She'll not accept help from a man. Some strange custom of hers, I'm sure. So, she requires your help." He looked over to Jinan again, her fists clenched in her lap, her eyes narrowed in resentment. "Drain the tub for her, so she doesn't fear it any more than I've given her reason to."

Jinan looked up before he could retreat. "This woman is to help me? She does not look like a personal attendant. She will not understand my words or the ways of my people."

"Tell me what you need, and I will relay your message before I leave. She'll be most obliging. Besides, I think it is better she does not speak a common language with you. I'm sorry, Jinan, I didn't mean to frighten you by tossing you in. I have grown weary after such a long trip and after hearing the news you waited so long to enlighten me with. Though I don't deserve it, I beg your forgiveness."

Jinan stood there staring at him a moment, gave one succinct nod, and then pointed to the bathtub. "It must be drained."

"I have told her as much. Do you need help removing your scarves?" He looked pointedly down to her bared belly and what he could see of her curvaceous hips.

"No," she said, defiance making her voice harsh as she pulled a thread that held the delicate silk together.

No wonder he couldn't find the knot that bound it around her hips. It pooled in a silken mass of blue waves at her feet. She stood there naked as a babe, her henna markings clearly visible around her lower legs, the rust-colored paint that stained her mound and nipples further attesting to her status as a lady of pleasure. Had he been in a better mood, he would have smiled at Jinan's brazenness. She only demonstrated the willfulness she had kept under rein all these months.

He had a feeling she'd rebel against him at every given opportunity. God, he needed to sleep. Then he'd be able to better deal with her and process everything that had happened in the last few days.

She made no move to take down her veil. He turned to Donata. "She will require help with her hair." Skimming his gaze down the front of Jinan, he let the delectable image she presented sink into his mind. He'd sleep with that image in mind tonight. "I'm sure you two can figure things out," he said with a careless shrug.

He left them, clicking the door softly shut in his wake.

So, she was a fighter.

He had the best of intentions where she was concerned. He'd convince her of those good intentions when they both had rested and were of clearer mind.

While he figured out a way to get her son out of the harem, how was he to convince her she was, indeed, free? Convince her she was no longer just a mistress? Perhaps he should make it clear he wished them to spend the rest of their days together. Maybe then, she'd change her tune. Hard to say, since she never gave him reason to believe this was, in fact, something she might want.

Now more than ever she seemed to hate him. Would an offer of marriage endear him to her? Doubtful, he thought, especially with her unwillingness to listen to reason thus far. Unwillingness to believe he would do everything in his power to get her son back for her. Despite all the mess he had created, one thing was certain—there was no way Griffin intended to release her. She'd come to understand that in short order.

CHAPTER TWELVE

Secrets and Lies

She had requested a maid in hopes of befriending someone who might sympathize with her plight. But she hadn't
expected someone who only spoke Italian. At least she
knew they were, in fact, in Italy. One couldn't be sure of
these things when she didn't even know where the palace
she called home was located.

How was it that in all her language learning she'd
never learned a word of Italian? Well, aside from a few
words screamed at the altar of Venus.

She loosened her veil and smiled at the nervous maid.
It was only a matter of time before Rothburn forced her
to remove her cloth shield. She wanted to keep it on in
defiance, and she would. Until he demanded otherwise,
it would stay firmly in place.

The maid removed a stopper in the bottom of the
cast-iron bath. Jinan had seen such a thing in the penny
press once. Her husband couldn't afford a place with
the plumbing needs for such a device, so she was, in a
sense, a stranger to such a luxury.

As nice as it would have been to indulge in a bath,
she couldn't. Years of silly superstitions and the cultural

beliefs she was submerged in had been firmly instilled in her mind. In her everyday actions. She couldn't change those things so easily in her daily life; they were all part of the person she'd become. It affected everything she did. She could not just turn that all off and revert back to English ways.

She *was* Jinan.

But even as Jinan, she knew she'd given the maid a fright. It didn't matter. She'd find other ways to make his lordship's staff eager to help her. Pitcher in hand, she motioned to the young lady to help her rinse her hair. The maid took up the water, and Jinan leaned her head over the edge of the bathtub as the warm trickle washed through. Reaching out to the water that spouted from the swan-neck tap, she rinsed out her veil.

When she was finished in the bath, she wasn't surprised to see Rothburn waiting for her in his sitting room. He was pacing back and forth until he realized she stood in the room, a long bath linen knotted at her bosom and dropping straight down to cover her to the knees.

Damn the smile that slanted her lips at his immediate regard. She hated herself for it and walked toward the window to pull back a panel. The sun was settling on the horizon; it was probably well past the dinner hour. She wondered what day it was. Two days, he'd said, on the boat. So had she been away from the harem and her son for three days now?

"That'll be all, Donata."

His voice was calm, as he no doubt waited for the click of the door behind the maid. When she was composed and ready to face her nemesis, she turned and walked toward him with a seductive, confident sway in her step.

"Did you write that letter to Amir?"

He looked her over, his gaze lingering on the veil she refused to remove. "I have clothes for you. Come to the bedchamber."

So he would continue to be difficult. "You cannot keep me here. Amir will find me sooner or later. He has eyes in every part of the world. Once you go to him for my child he'll come down on your home, and none too gently."

He turned to face her; a smile that was not kind lingered on his lips. "Does he? I'm not overly worried about him finding us here. You will not be permitted to leave the villa grounds. There is a walled garden you can spend time in, if you so wish it, but you will be accompanied at all times by either myself or my man of affairs. I will pen a note to Amir tomorrow regarding your son. There is nothing that can be done about it now."

She would not be dismissed so easily.

"This is what you bring me to? You tell me you are saving me from some fate you think is not to my liking only to lock me in another prison? Have you not done enough damage to my life that you must dictate my every move?"

His jaw clenched. "I have done you no disservice. In time you will became accustomed to living here . . . with me."

"I will not," she said coldly, her chin jutting out in determination.

Rothburn seemed short on patience, for he took a threatening step forward. Could it be that he knew she had to return to the harem? Did he fear Amir? Maybe Amir was looking for her even now. Surely Amir wouldn't think this her fault; she had never shown any desire to leave. One thing she did know for a fact—Amir would not release her son to Rothburn.

What if his lordship spoke the truth? What if Amir

couldn't find her—wherever here in Italy was? Somehow, she needed to find a way back. For her son.

Only one immense and unsolvable problem impeded her. She didn't know where the Pleasure Gardens were. Perhaps Rothburn had had an accomplice. Someone else must know where she had come from.

"Please, I do not know what else to tell you. But I cannot stay. I will not stay here. Amir is short of temper, and you do me more harm than good by keeping me." The first was a lie, the second was not.

"It's not possible for you to leave. I've gone to a great deal of trouble taking you from that whorehouse." His cruel words were all but spat out. She refused to shy away from his brand of unkindness. His steps were determined, domineering, as he pushed her back to the wall of the sitting room. Refusing to cower, she stared him defiantly in the eye.

"I will do whatever is necessary to find my way home." What she needed was something extreme that would force him to release her. There was nothing else she could reveal. She'd already betrayed the existence of Jonathan. His reputation had remained safe these five years, until now. "If I do not go back, Amir will send someone to kill me. Probably you, too."

She shrugged as though the prospect of his demise did not trouble her. He seemed not to care. Infuriating man.

"They will not make it past the vineyard." His voice was low, dangerous. "I have eyes everywhere, Jinan—maybe as many as your old master. You might want to remember that. You are not leaving here and you'll be stopped the moment you attempt to do so."

"You will make me a prisoner for yourself?"

It was a cruel look he wore. Not the kind one he'd shown so often when in the Pleasure Gardens. "Yes."

She put her hands between them and pushed against

his chest, trying to make him retreat a step. He didn't budge. His hand slid over her arm and clasped around her neck, under the veil.

Turning her head to the side, his mouth next to her ear, he threatened, "You attempt to leave, and I'll have you chained like the curs in the slave market. Are you familiar with such a setting, Jinan?"

She ignored the jibe as best she could. Yet the old familiar revulsion twisted her gut, and her body went still as a board beneath his hold. She hated the show of weakness and disguised it quickly by letting her limbs slacken. They were only words to him; he did not understand their significance. There were a million tactics at her disposal to persuade him against tethering her. How many of them would she have to toss at his feet before he took mercy on her situation? Before he felt a modicum of regret for his actions?

"There is no one here to help me as my sisters would. Find the kindness I know you carry in your heart, my lord. Do not do this to one such as me. I cannot live in your world nor can I convert to your way of life. I belong in the harem with my son. It has been my home too long to abandon, even if it means I will live out the rest of my days as a whore."

Her words seemed only to anger him further; his pupils dilated in anger, his nostrils flared. "I will not release you. You belong to me—only me. If all you require is a woman's company, I will find you a companion. You can forget your harem, your sisters, your damned master! And I've told you enough times now that I will find a way to retrieve your son."

Jinan shook her head. "Your words are not sufficient." She tried to duck out of his hard grasp, but he tightened his hands around her arms and pressed his body against hers. "You do not understand what I need."

Her heart constricted painfully, she felt forlorn. This life in the Western world was never meant for her, she'd learned that lesson long ago. She was safer, more protected, even loved by her sisters, in the harem. Her boy wanted for nothing, their bellies were never empty. Surely, anything else, any other life, was certain doom for them.

"Harem ways, eh?" he said with a thrust to her core. She almost let out a groan with the move, but sealed her lips against the betrayal of her body. "These are the only ways we'll worry about right now. Do you understand me?"

His words, his intention to treat her so callously, should repulse her, but to her disappointment it did the opposite. She looked over his shoulder, refusing to acknowledge the effect he had on her body physically. Really, she wanted to cry out her anger, scream at his callousness. His stupidity. Her conflicting emotions derived from her desperate situation, she had to believe that. How could she want a man who was taking away her very life? This was something she should never forgive him for.

When her words came they were cold and as detached from reality as she felt in this moment. "I *do* understand, my lord. Perfectly."

He'd kidnapped her for no better reason than to be his personal sex slave—there was no refuting that. This was about him not wanting to share her favors since his contract was concluded. Her regard for him plummeted, but her heart still beat furiously for an entirely different reason as he leaned in closer, his mouth grazing her lips. She would not allow him to bend her so easily. She'd lost her son again, and that was something she had refused to believe was possible as long as she lived in the safety of the harem.

"Good," he said.

With a quick pull to the knot that held the towel between her breasts, he yanked off the material. His trousers were quickly undone. Her legs spread and hitched up and over his hips as he slammed into her, one hand gripping her buttocks, the other on her hip. He stilled inside her, his arms caging her in. "You were ready for me. You're wet. Don't deny it now that I've got you wrapped around me."

She looked him in the eye. "Then I make you the perfect whore, don't I?"

Malice as sharp as a dagger shone in his eyes. Then she looked away. Giving him nothing in return—no emotion, no action to bespeak the desire and hatred that tumbled around inside her. Unable to look at him, she stared at the vermilion satin-covered windows with their gold ropes and fringes and fought the tears blurring her vision. With her hands slack at her sides, she waited for him to finish. He proved nothing to her, not his dominance, his strength, or his authority, in using her this way.

The moment he turned a blind eye, she'd find a way to escape.

"Jinan, look at me."

What was the use in that? It did not matter that his voice was gentle, his grip loosening. Even the bite of cruelty in his voice seeped away as he worked his body inside her.

If she looked at him and he held remorse in his gaze, she might forgive him this. Was it possible for him to get as little satisfaction out of this as she? The crack in her heart splintered more with every hard thrust of his hips. As his tempo increased, she knew he was close to finishing. How could he enjoy this when she remained so unresponsive?

Then a realization hit her.

She had nothing to stop his seed from implanting in her womb. Pushing at his shoulders, she tried to relieve herself of his weight. But it only seemed to infuriate him on some primal level of being denied his victory. He thrust harder.

She cried out then, "Stop this. Stop!"

Determined to dislodge his member from her body, she pushed harder at his shoulders, trying to squirm upward. His hold on her hips was unrelenting. Were those tears coming down her face?

"Stop," she tried to yell, but the words came out on a choked sob.

With a growl of frustration, Rothburn pulled out of her. "Goddamn it, Jinan."

Giving her his back, he stalked away from her. His shoulders were tense, his hands probably shoving his machine back into his trousers. He walked to the opposite wall and smacked the palms of his hands hard on the surface. He hit the wall a few more times, uttering some good expletives while he did so. "You've turned me into a ravaging fucking animal. No. I think I've always been that."

On her knees, hands tense against the carpeted floor in case she needed to push off it for leverage if he renewed his attack, she waited to see what he'd do.

Red-faced when he turned, he gave her one last look full of remorse—a silent apology—before turning on his heel and stalking out the door. It slammed behind him, shaking the wood in its frame.

The relief that washed over her was instantaneous. Swiping her hand through the folds of her sex, she felt only the slickness of her fluids, not the heavier substance of a man's milk. Hysterical, sobbing laughter bubbled in her chest, but there was no time to feel sorry for herself so she squelched her fear and worry and stood. Pulling the linen around her, she knotted it between her breasts again and went to the windows.

Spreading hues of purple, red, and fading gold, the sun's final rays of the day settled over the darkening room. She tugged the material back to reveal an upholstered window seat. Kneeling, she tried to push the windows up. It didn't take long to see that the side and the bottom of the window frame had been nailed shut.

He had planned this.

It was tempting to break one of the glass panes. Someone was sure to hear her. She doubted the staff would come to her rescue; they were probably loyal to their master. What did it matter? Walking over to the writing table, she picked up the candelabra and threw it with all her might at the window. Two panes of glass shattered. She walked over to the window. A lot of good that did her. But she did feel better.

Looking out through the empty glass slots, she saw a walled garden below with a gnarled, heavy-trunked olive tree in the center. It seemed so desolate and empty of life even with its abundant leaves, but without flora and fauna to give it full life. The landscape looked dry, the sunburned grass unwelcoming. So unlike her palace home, yet the same. The only brightness in her life had been her son. Without him, everything was dismal, gray.

Checking the door Rothburn just exited, she tried to open it. There was no lock on the inside; he probably had the key tucked in his pocket. Away from her. She smacked her palms against the door and swore in Turkish.

She sat on a chair placed near the windows and stared outside. No stirrings, no movement, not a soul to be seen even after she'd thrown the candelabra at the glass. How much staff did Rothburn keep on hand? She wouldn't put it past him to have sent most of them away while he tried to acquaint her with this place.

But *that* wouldn't happen.

How could it? While she was here, Amir was either enraged or worried about her—maybe both—and probably frantic to find her. What would her sisters tell her little boy? Her son . . . God, her son, she didn't want to think about him. It hurt too much.

How had Rothburn stolen her out of the harem? No woman had ever left the palace. That was just how it was, and how she always expected it to be. Surely there were patrons in the past who adored their mistresses and wanted them all to themselves. Maybe they tried to negotiate their freedom. Maybe they'd stolen them from the palace but been caught. What of the guards who stood and watched over the patrons?

If the harem girls couldn't persuade the eunuchs to let them pass—it seemed none of her sisters had wanted to leave in all the years she'd been there—then how had Rothburn accomplished this Herculean feat?

She shook her head at the thought. Did it really matter how he'd secreted her out of her home? The only thing that should worry her now was finding her way back.

Even if she did escape Rothburn, where would she go? She had no money, no jewels aside from the gold bracelets around her wrists and ankles. And a few small diamonds and emeralds in the clip holding her veil in place. The best she could do was beg one of his servants for help. Maybe then they would be rewarded greatly if they helped her find passage out of this villa.

But where would she go?

Constantinople?

Harry Chisholm was well known in the slave markets, but it was too dangerous for a woman to go there without a protector. Women were nothing without their husbands or owners guarding them. No, she couldn't risk going back to Constantinople alone.

Was it possible she could persuade someone to go on her behalf? There must be someone—a youth who wanted to be a damsel's knight in shining armor— someone to take pity on her in her predicament.

There was just one major flaw in her plan.

How was she to communicate with any of the servants when she couldn't speak Italian? Had Rothburn deliberately brought that maid to her because there was no way for Jinan to confide her secrets?

So, Jinan, what are you going to do now?

Had the charade played its turn? She didn't think so. But she wouldn't wager on seeing her son any time soon if she didn't find the empathetic heart of some sweet maid or stable hand.

"Bugger it all to hell."

He'd been an utter ass to her. How could he have done that? What had gone through his thick head as he tore away her towel and thrust up into her warm, pliant, soft . . . fuck it all to hell!

His cock was still hard, straining painfully against his trousers. He'd had to untuck his shirt to hide the monstrous reaction he was having to the delectable Jinan. What kind of bounder was he to do such a thing to the woman he professed to love? Thank God he'd registered her refusal and stopped what he'd started.

If a man loved a woman, would he steal her like some barbarian thief in the night? He was a sick, twisted man. The smashing of glass rang through the hall as Peters opened the door. Griffin wondered if he should go to her, then discarded the thought. He needed to gather his thoughts. Cool his temper.

"What has the heathen done?" Peters asked as he entered the study.

His voice was light and teasing, but Griffin was irritated by the whole turn of events and not in the mood for such frivolous commentary. He turned to stare at Peters while continuing to pace to and fro in front of the great mahogany desk that took up one wall of the study.

"Refrain from insults. Unless you feel like being unmanned and picking yourself up off the street when I toss you out on your ass."

Peters only smiled at the threat before he sat down on a leather chair across from the desk. He watched Peters steeple his fingers and settled in for a lecture. "Has she gotten the better of you?"

"Damn it. Shut that mouth of yours, Peters." He made a frustrated noise in the back of his throat. "That woman's going to drive me mad."

Peters raised a brow in amusement. "Never did I think to see this day."

"Well, believe it." Griffin roughly brushed his fingers through his hair.

How could he have guessed she'd want to go back to that place? She was English, not Muslim, not a whore, and most certainly not the princess she pretended to be. When had Elena surrendered her life to play at being a sex slave? How was it possible for someone, more specifically a lady, brought up in English society, to throw away her beliefs and embrace the depravities of the darker parts of the world? He had practically handed it all back to her on a platter and she had had the audacity to refuse it, to throw it in his face.

Shouldn't she be grateful to him for her freedom?

Shouldn't she throw herself down at his feet in gratitude and eternal thankfulness? Not beg to be sent back to her master!

Had he misjudged her?

It wasn't possible. Or was it? This line of thought angered him to no end. Then there was the child. Had she had the child with Amir? With another patron?

None of it really mattered.

He knew what was best. In the end, she wouldn't choose the life of a harlot over a life with someone of his status. He had so much more to offer her. Life without servitude, for one. Though what he offered probably seemed no better to her. In time, it would. That was what mattered.

How in hell had he acted so harshly with her? He'd violated something sacred between them; it didn't matter that sexual relations had been a paid service beforehand.

He'd never done such a thing to a woman. Never.

Worse, he still *wanted* to do *that* to Jinan.

He was sinking in frustration, annoyance, and just plain anger because of her continuing charade. He'd outsmart her soon enough. Or it would be certain madness for them both.

"Arrange for only Italian-speaking maids to attend us in my room. In fact, it might be better to remove anyone from the property who speaks English. I have a feeling Jinan cannot understand Italian. I know she's fluent in English, Persian, and Turkish. I don't want her pleading her woes to the staff. They don't need to know any more than necessary."

"It's already been done. There were few here who have a handle on the English language. Those who could speak it are on paid leave."

"That's good. I have to go back upstairs."

Was that really a smart idea, though? Had he killed the passion in her? He rubbed at his eyes, wishing the image of her perfectly shaped form didn't keep him in a raging stiffness. What in hell had he just done?

He'd have to apologize. Maybe he could take her down to the gardens, let her have some fresh air and beg forgiveness for his actions. Would she forgive him? He could tell her his ultimate plan to marry her. Or was it the wrong time now?

Damn it. It did him no good either way. He was annoyed about what he'd done and how he'd taken her. Peters just watched him with amusement, further annoying him. What would happen if he went back upstairs? Would he force himself on her again?

He paused in his pacing and sat on the edge of the desk. Perhaps she acted spiteful in hopes he'd bring her back to her old master? Could it all be a ruse on her part? Inflaming his desires so he felt like a fool? Acted like a fool? Had she known he would do that?

In fairness, she'd probably acted the way she did out of worry for her son. Assurance that he would retrieve her son was the only way this could move forward. The only way she'd forgive him.

"Tell the staff dinner will be late tonight. Around ten. No one is to disturb me in the meantime."

Hopefully Jinan would settle in a little by that time. He was going to apologize. No, that would only prove he was in the wrong by kidnapping her. If he apologized, she'd still insist on him taking her *home*.

This was her home now. She'd have to get used to that idea. Once she realized how much freedom was within her grasp, how much more she was entitled to here—once he could trust her with said freedom—she'd be melting with gratitude.

"We must come to an understanding, Jinan."

His plan was not going as he wished. She paced before him, refusing to meet his gaze—refusing to listen to reason.

"There is nothing for us to understand. I will not change my mind. You must let me go home. Or you must bring me back to the harem immediately."

"Maybe we are starting this conversation—or negotiation, if you will—in the wrong place for us to come to an understanding."

"You will never see it my way, my lord."

"Please, Jinan. We've been over this a hundred times, if not more—stop addressing me as *my lord*. Use Rothburn, Griffin, I care not. Just stop *lord*ing me."

Pinching the skin between her brows, she closed her eyes. She was probably coming up with some reprimand to suitably knock him down another notch. He couldn't seem to sway her from this silly insistence that she needed to go back to the harem now. What had Amir threatened the harem women with, to hold to this notion that their lives were at risk? Interesting how she never once mentioned her son might be in danger. That told him—or at least he hoped that meant—Amir would not hurt his women.

She continued her pacing back and forth on the carpet, her hands always rubbing at her face, and driving him to distraction.

"Cease this pacing of yours, please." Griffin stood and took a few steps toward her. He'd force her to stop and look at him if she didn't do as asked.

She stopped, her eyes narrowed as she turned to him. That damned veil snug as ever over her lower face.

He was incensed by the mere sight of it. "Remove your disguise, Jinan. It's unnecessary at this point, don't you think?"

"No. I will not remove my veil. You see, it is very

necessary. You are not my husband, so you cannot demand anything of me." She continued pacing. "Do you know it is a disgrace for one such as I to come to such a transgression? I should never be seen by anyone but my husband, so your demands mean nothing. Even Amir will not marry me. He has made me this creature, yes. I despise what he thought necessary for my fate. But this is the only life I have known for a long time."

"How long were you in the harem?" One question he was curious about and had never asked her.

"Five years. Time is irrelevant, though."

"I've had enough of this arguing"—he held a hand out in invitation—"come to bed. We will figure these things out in the morning. You are tired from the journey, and your bout of sickness. And I'm just plain weary of everything."

He didn't miss her quick glance at the closed door.

"This is also another bad idea. You do not seem to understand the importance of contacting Amir."

"No, I do not. Nor do I plan to send the missive you requested. You could tell me the truth of why you are so eager to leave my company. Or we go to bed. Now."

He held his hand out to her again. Instead of taking it, she walked past him and into the bedroom. The *ferace* she'd produced from his wardrobe was loosened from where it was secured under her arm and dropped to the floor. She turned when he didn't make another move forward.

"Is this not what you want of me? I am a slave to you as much as I was to Amir."

"You are mistaken in that." He swallowed with great difficulty against the lump that had formed in his throat.

She raised one brow in disbelief and shrugged her shoulder. "If you wish to pretend so."

"I do not wish to pretend anything with you, Jinan. You are the one fabricating one lie upon another. I have given you a gift and you refuse my generosity. I've made a million promises to find a way to free your son but you think the venture foolish."

"This is not generous, taking me from my home. You think I will grow to like this, I see that, but it is not how it will be. My home is with my sisters. My son. With . . ." She didn't finish what she was going to say. He was glad for it, because another mention of Amir might set him off again.

"Do not deny there is a connection between us. It's been there since the moment we met. The very first time we met." At the Glenmoores' ball. Surely she knew that was what he referred to.

He wearied of this game. He was not the villain in all that had transpired between them since her arrival. At least he hadn't intentionally meant to be. Time was the only factor that would show her the very truth of his words, his kindness, his love. Why could she not see he wanted the best for her? It was nothing he could give a lot of thought to now; he was too damned tired from the trip here. This night could prove to be a long one if Jinan didn't cooperate.

"Do I need to tie you to the bedposts or will you stay put?"

She didn't answer as she crawled seductively across the bed and tossed the blankets aside.

"There are night linens in the wardrobe for you."

"I do not want these clothes of yours."

"I'm not in the mood to fight with you, Jinan. You did not want my attentions earlier, I cannot imagine you want them now. Put on some clothes."

"Stop telling me what I should do. You are not my owner."

Damn impertinent woman. Fine, let her have her way in this. Griffin pulled his neckcloth off and tossed his shirt toward the chair. There was no way for her to get out of his rooms should she leave the bed without him noticing. His key was well hidden. Sitting on the edge of the bed, he pulled his boots off and slid out of his trousers. He thought about removing his small-clothes and stopped himself from taking them off.

Letting out a great yawn, he pushed the blankets farther down on the bed and scooped Jinan into his arms so her back was to his chest. "Sleep well," was all he said as his fingers wrapped around her bared breast. Good thing he was too tired to do anything about the raging cockstand jutting out and pressing into her backside.

He'd fix that come morning. But for now, sleep washed over his mind, shrouding him in the cloudy mist of dreams.

She couldn't sleep like this. How could anyone sleep with a man thrusting into your backside while presumably asleep? He'd been *this way* for a while now, at least an hour as far as she could tell with the ticking on the mantel clock. His fingers pinching at her nipples, his cock strained against the material of his smallclothes, seeking entrance to her body.

If she took him in hand and let him frig himself off, would he just spurt out whatever dream he was having? Or would he wake up and want more from her? Because it was impossible to fall asleep when a man was blindly pawing and groping at you. She might not want his sexually deviant attentions now but come morning she'd be too tired and foggy-minded to push him away. Worse, she might even welcome him.

This was partly her fault. She didn't have to climb into bed naked as a newborn. He would have been less tempted—well, she couldn't really be sure of that, either. He *did* have a voracious appetite.

First, she needed to try to slide out from his grasp. Rolling over to her stomach, while his hand was pinned between the mattress and her breast, she inched toward the edge of the bed. She didn't even know where to go if she made it from the bed. Clothes would be the first thing to procure.

She'd heard the click of the lock when he came back up to the room, clear as a bird chirping at first light. The windows were nailed shut; maybe she could find something to pull them out.

Her options were few. Perhaps there was a panel door that slid open somewhere along these walls? She couldn't tell by looking at the ones in the bedroom; it was too dark, and the curtains had been drawn against the starlit night.

Hooking her knee over the side of the bed, she pulled herself slowly out of Rothburn's hold.

"Naughty, naughty," he mumbled hotly next to her ear, his hand squeezing her breast so he had a firmer embrace as he tucked her back under his body.

She stilled, wondering if he was asleep or fully aware that she was trying to make an escape. Better she just stay like this for a while, maybe even an hour or more, in case he was awake. She tilted her ear away from the pillows and listened to his breathing. It was deep and even, but he could be concentrating on keeping it that way.

She waited. When she thought it safe to move again, she waited some more.

It wasn't to be, she realized, when Rothburn's hand

slid from her breast and found its way between her thighs. The press of his hard cock against her backside made her release a brief, surprised screech. She couldn't feign sleep now that he'd heard that. Even if she hadn't made the sound, Rothburn knew her body too well, and she'd been wet since he pulled her in tight to his body. His fingers would find that moisture at any moment.

Damn her body.

He groaned his appreciation when his fingers slid between the slick folds of her sex, searching out her bud. He marked her shoulder with his teeth and rolled her fully onto her stomach. His weight came down on her, his knees spreading her legs farther apart.

He drove two fingers into her convulsing sheath before she could even think of objecting. Instead of giving him the satisfaction of a groan, she bit through her veil and into the pillow.

It wasn't fair that she still had some feelings of tenderness for him, when he'd taken her life away from her with the snap of his lordly fingers. She held her breath as his fingers drove harder into her. His free hand pushed her hair aside and his tongue laved into her ear.

What she wanted to do and what she knew she had to do were two completely opposing things. It was best to push him off. She still had no protection if he spurted his seed into her womb. And if he impregnated her, Amir might not take her back. Where would that leave her son? She didn't want to find out, she just wanted to go home, and with that thought she pushed all her weight up and tried to get Rothburn off her back.

He stopped his attentions to give her ear a sharp nip to the lobe. "Your body wants me, Jinan."

It was the truth, but she shook her head and tried to push her elbow back into his ribs. He caught and held her arm there.

"You want this," he all but growled. "Admit it."

His hand slipped between the bed and her stomach as he tilted her pelvis back and slipped his cock into her sheath in one thrust.

She grunted her surprise once, then made no other betraying sounds. Yes, she did want this. But she'd be damned if she would admit to such a thing.

"Damn it, just say it, you stubborn woman." His voice was calmer, but his strokes were still forceful, strong. His balls slapped against her nether region on each downward stroke.

She lay there, afraid her body would respond if she found and matched his rhythm. She let him take his pleasure as she lay beneath him trying to think of her escape. When his fist tightened in her hair, she knew he was going to come to his crisis. And hated him and herself for everything that had happened. Not just everything in the last few minutes, but since her supposed *last* session in the Pleasure Gardens.

Let his seed dry up and prove infertile. Please . . . Amir cannot banish my son and me now, not after all I've worked for.

She voiced a sob then. It didn't matter what she did, he came, great jets of his seed squirting into her channel. After a few small thrusts of his hips and twitches of his semihard cock inside her, he released her and rolled over to his back, his breathing hoarse.

In her haste to leave the bed she fell to the carpeted floor, banging her knee with the impact. She scrambled away from the bed, desperate to get his seed out of her. Retrieving the washing bowl she'd spied earlier, she put it on the floor and upended the pitcher in it, uncaring that it splashed on the floor around her.

The shadow of Rothburn came closer, but she paid him no mind. She had to get his seed out.

She was aware—barely—that she sobbed aloud as she squatted over the basin and submerged a small hand towel, soaking up as much water as it would take. She slipped as much of her hand inside her vaginal walls as she painfully could with the cloth. She felt his seed there, its consistency so different from hers as she wiped it out and frantically washed the cloth in the water below her so she could repeat the process.

Rothburn's face flickered in front of hers, a lit candle illuminating the space between them. His mouth moved, but she didn't hear his words. The roaring of her anger buzzed so loudly in her ears it drowned out her surroundings.

She looked to the basin and scooped up water to wash around the entrance of her sheath. She could still feel his seed there. Would it plant in her womb? Would she bring another child into this godforsaken world? She didn't want that to happen—it couldn't happen.

She'd get his seed out.

What were the herbs she was to use if she found herself with child? She knew only their Arabic and Turkish names. She couldn't even begin to translate their names to English.

Her sheath was sore and raw from her ministrations, as if it had had one too many fuckings without the aid of feminine lubrication.

She heard the hiss of his breath and his voice pounding through her ears.

"Jinan, let me help you. What's this about?" His hands cupped her face. So gentle, but shaking.

She stared at him a moment, not moving because

she had no cloths to dry her. "Why would you do this to me?" Her ears rang so loudly she wasn't sure what language she spoke. Her fist shot out and hit him in the chest. Then, because it felt good to assuage her anger that way, she pounded her fist against his chest again. He let her fight him, his hold staying light against her face as she took out her frustration and anger. Why did he let her treat him so? She did it a few times before he stilled her actions.

"Stop this." His hands pressed over hers, surprisingly gentle. "What are you doing?"

"Your seed is in me. I need to get it out."

Instead of commenting, he pursed his lips and went into the other room. She looked around for something to dry off with. It appeared that she had soaked both hand towels that were on the washstand, and she wore nothing useful to help her in this situation. Her bath towel was on the other side of the room, the scarves of her dress had been left in the bathing room.

Rothburn stepped back into the room, carrying another pitcher and a small cloth that looked like a handkerchief in the near darkness. Wordlessly, he handed it to her and gave her his back as she cleaned herself.

He mumbled something.

"What is it you are saying?" she hissed out.

"I can guess what all this worrying is about. When are your menses due?"

Oh, he knew his way around a woman of pleasure, all right. That angered her more than the seed he'd put inside her.

But she understood why he'd mumbled it the first time and seemed to have difficulty in asking her such a blunt, private question. It wasn't normal to discuss bleeding with a man in English society. Even in the harem, she was taught her menses were a dirty time in her month.

She had no reason to be shy about this, even though it was something her husband would never have asked outright, nor would have Amir—it was not their way.

"Three days past the full moon." And since she didn't really know what today was, after all the groggy traveling, she waited for him to tell her. She'd also not been paying attention to much besides this man while she was still in the harem. She'd been completely absorbed in the ending of their too-brief union.

"Full moon's tomorrow. You should be fine."

She was glad he still stood some distance away from her, or he'd have seen the blush that rose in her face. How embarrassing for him to know she'd be bleeding in four days . . . if she bled.

But he was right, it was a safe time, and she might not need to worry; she should not be ripe for impregnation. She released a long breath of air.

"Is there a wisewoman in the kitchen?"

She hoped he knew what she was getting at. She did not want to explain the necessary precautions she would take regardless of the timing of her menses.

He faced her then. "Yes. I know what it is you want."

She looked to her feet. It was chilly in this room—her nipples puckered into rose-tipped beads and gooseflesh rose along her stomach. Ignoring the awkwardness, dread, and irritation in her mind, she focused on the cold. On nothingness.

No sense in displaying her emotions by acting skittish. She stood tall and looked him in the eye. "Will you send her to me?"

He nodded, raised his hand to her cheek to touch her reverently, then said, "I'm sorry, Jinan. You did not fight me off. I thought it was all right."

"It did not occur to me until afterward."

Nodding, he walked away from her, saying something

about bringing her whatever tea they might have on hand. The jangle of a key told her he'd left the apartment. She listened to the sound of the lock clicking back over—sure enough, the *snick* was the last sound she heard for some minutes.

She needed to dress. She made her way to the armoire, threw the doors open and paused. Her eyes took in the bright silks before her. How had he done this?

Had his abduction of her been planned right from the beginning?

There were rich materials of every color, so bold you'd not see them worn in polite society. A heathen's sanctuary of familiarity within her grasp. Her fingers touched the brocade floral design on the white trousers. All in Turkish style. There were silk scarves of every color, perhaps as many as she'd had when back in the palace.

How had he done this?

It didn't matter, she reminded herself. He'd done a great injustice toward her. One that by all rights was unforgivable.

Her only worry right now was how to protect herself from becoming enceinte, then she needed to find a way back to Jonathan. She pulled out red scarves and an orange brocaded vest and trousers.

She slammed the doors on the armoire closed. What she really wanted to do was kick them. How could she not have understood his desperation before now? She was trained to read the desires in every man she played sex with. How had she not seen his obsession? It should have been apparent long before she had been abducted.

Jinan tugged the vest over her head and buttoned it up, and then the trousers. Then she tied the scarf around her hips, knotting it below her navel. She now wore sufficient clothing that his lordship would have to go to a great deal of trouble to remove them. That way she might have time to take precautions against pregnancy.

Though she doubted it would stop his lordship from taking what he wanted, she felt some peace of mind. Peace that had been absent since she'd arrived.

CHAPTER THIRTEEN

Enslavement

How in all the isles of hell had he done something so reprehensible? Worse, he knew he'd do it a hundred times more, if only to prove that they were the pieces of a long unsolved puzzle joining in a unity long denied.

She'd denied him in so primal a fashion that it made his blood boil in a rage such as he thought had died with his autocratic uncle. His fingers tangled in his hair, pulled it tight until he felt something . . . *anything.*

It was a damnable act on her part. To deny his seed. It was a damnable act on his part for wanting to force it on her. Was he not good enough to have her? Even if she were his mistress, shouldn't she want such a gift? Not once had he shown her any unkindness. Not once. He was irritated. He knew she was fuming. But his anger now affected his thoughts. He'd been useless for two days straight because of Jinan.

Because she'd turned their congress into an act of filthy debauchery.

Why did he care? Why did this bother him? He'd freed her. There was no kindness greater than the one he'd given her. Now he offered her a life by his side and she refused him?

She dared to refuse him?

He squeezed the plump breast in his hand.

Jinan was sound asleep. She had been for some hours while he'd mulled over the prelude to their evening. His hand didn't meet soft flesh, of course. She'd dressed when he'd gone to retrieve some herbs from the cook. The cook he'd dragged out of bed and down to the kitchen.

Jinan had gulped down the nasty-smelling concoction in a trice, wiped her lips, given him a disapproving once-over, then slipped between the turned-down, ruffled bedding. She hadn't said a word. He deserved an explanation.

What was so wrong with his seed? Would she not want his children, should one come of their union? Did she hate him so much?

This wasn't working. Nothing was working. They fought at every turn. He reacted distastefully at every turn. There was nothing he could say to persuade her that he'd made a good choice for her. The right choice.

What did the harem have to offer that was better than this?

She couldn't seriously want to go back to that lair of vice. His contract had ended, meaning she was game for any other patron. It was unacceptable, and he'd be damned if he'd allow another man to occupy her time, her bed, her body.

She was his.

Jinan was his alone. Weren't his feelings for her apparent?

He pulled her in tighter, needing to ground himself to the here and now. Everything to this point seemed to have gone wrong in her eyes and he needed to correct that.

He had debated saying something to her last night about their brief engagement so long ago. It seemed as though she'd forgotten about their courtship. There were moments when she would say something to trigger those memories again, like that afternoon they'd spent in the gardens at the palace.

Releasing her, he rolled to his back and stared at the inside of the canopied bed.

He had to believe she would come around. She was just inexplicably angry—anger passed with time, or at least he hoped it would pass.

Griffin gave his eyes a frustrated rub. As if that could relieve his mind of the image of her shoving the towel inside her quim to rid herself of his seed. Acting as though it burned and she was desperate to douse the flames that had licked up inside her. Her eyes staring bloody daggers at him for his treatment. It wasn't as if he'd done anything he wouldn't have done at the Pleasure Gardens.

He rolled out of bed, shoved his feet in his slippers, and pulled on his dressing robe. Cinching the tie around his waist, he made a quick decision to give Jinan something to alleviate the tension between them. Opening the armoire, he pulled out the velvet box tucked down on the bottom shelf.

Would this make her rest easier? Would this help rein in the look of loathing she shot his way, every chance she got?

Walking back to the bed, he placed the box on the pillow next to her and left the room. It would either infuriate her further, or make her see reason.

Some coffee was in order at this early hour; then maybe he'd send up Donata to see to Jinan's needs.

* * *

The curtains were open; the sun was high in the sky. Jinan rolled over to her back and was surprised to see the place next to her empty. Rumpled but empty. Uncurling her hand and arm, she stretched her fingers out. It was stone-cold next to her, so Rothburn must have gotten up a while ago. Stretching her tired arms above her head, she touched something hard above her head. She sat up and looked down at the red box, smaller than her hand, set on her pillow. Filigreed gilt swirled in a pretty design on it. A gift?

Her pleasant morning had just turned sour.

So he thought to shower her with gifts? Was this in hopes of her coming around to his way of thinking? She wanted to throw the token at the door. Admittedly, that would do her no good, especially if Rothburn couldn't see her fury.

She curled her fingers around the velvet-covered box. It did no harm to see what he thought a sufficient present for her enslavement. Pushing the golden latch through its hole, she lifted the simple satin-lined lid and frowned down at the token. She almost laughed. In fact, she might have in a different time, different place.

This gift seemed more insulting than giving her some sparkling jeweled bauble.

She should have known better. What a fool she was to think, even for a moment, that she was more than his sexual plaything. She slammed the lid shut and threw it at the looming wardrobe.

Where was Rothburn, anyhow? He hadn't left her alone in the few days she'd been here. If she hadn't lived in intimate quarters with her sisters for the past five years, she might have found it difficult having Rothburn ever present, even during her ablutions.

A knock sounded at the outer door, so she tiptoed

across the room and stood in the doorway of the bed-chamber. The maid who had helped wash her hair yesterday came in with towels and a bathing jug.

Did Rothburn think she'd find him a generous man and forgive him what he'd done by sending a woman to help her bathe? He was sadly mistaken. And she'd make him aware of that when next he made an appearance.

The maid curtsied awkwardly. Probably not sure if she should curtsy to a heathen such as Jinan.

The woman said something in Italian and then raised what was in her hands, an indication of her purpose since Jinan didn't understand the words uttered.

This might be her last chance to send word to Amir and Mr. Chisholm, so she asked slowly in English, "Do you speak something other than Italian?" Her words were stilted. She so rarely used English that her accent had twisted into something not altogether pleasant or familiar.

The maid looked at her and shook her head. "English not good for me."

Jinan tried again in French. The maid smiled. She understood at least some of the words.

There weren't many commonalities but enough that they could communicate. What Jinan needed most was someone feeling compassion toward her circumstances. They found words they both understood through the bath. The maid had the oils the slaves used in the harem. Something else Rothburn had gone to the trouble to procure.

When they finished, Rothburn still wasn't back, but she'd managed to relay to the maid that she needed a friend, someone to help her send a message. Perhaps the woman understood what it was to be all alone. Finally, Jinan had someone to confide in.

The maid spoke often with the man who delivered

some of the more exotic things his lordship had been buying and bringing to the villa. He spoke and read some French, and Donata thought maybe if she gave him a message on paper, he could get it to the appropriate eyes and ears. Jinan wrote out her message in French for the tradesman and another message for Mr. Chisholm in the Arabic scroll she'd learned from Laila. Her new confidante took the missives, tucking them into her bosom as she left. Insurance that Amir was notified of her circumstances. While Rothburn promised to retrieve her son, she would not depend solely upon him.

Jinan breathed a sigh of relief. One great worry out of the way. Would Amir come or would he send Mr. Chisholm in his stead?

"What is it she's doing?" Peters sneered, his lip curling slightly and his nose wrinkling in distaste.

"Praying."

She went down on hands and knees, her plump, ripe bottom in the air tempting him.

Donata had come out of his apartment not fifteen minutes ago. He thought Jinan would attempt a quick escape since he had asked the room not be locked. She hadn't left. Instead, she'd gone into the garden with a towel to kneel upon.

He wondered what she thought of the present he'd left for her.

Did she wear it now? Rothburn coughed into his hand and turned away from the pert buttocks begging for his attention.

"It's rather"—Peters gestured with his hand—"foreign."

Rothburn quirked his eyebrow. "I imagine she's

desperate to throw up as many differences between us as she can."

"Yes, but does she have to do that? You know the servants are talking."

"And what of it?" he asked, turning from the window that faced the garden and the earthly delight that was all Jinan. He sat on the settee in front of the banked fireplace and picked up his tumbler. He sniffed the liquor. Not ready to succumb to the amber fluid yet. He held it as a reminder.

"You know you couldn't keep them from discussing her. She's very—"

"Different?"

"Yes." Peters turned with a scowl and looked back to Jinan.

"It's what I find most appealing."

"Rothburn, as your friend I must advise against whatever attachment you have. Cut her loose while you're still sane."

Rothburn stood in sudden annoyance. "I never asked your opinion of her."

He didn't like to be under any scrutiny, especially by his most trusted man of affairs. It irked him that Peters was right. She'd cause even more problems when he brought her home. She'd be an overnight sensation; tongues would surely wag when he set her up in his household. They might expect peculiarity from him, but bringing Jinan home might become problematic for him in the House of Lords, and with some of the local tradesmen.

He didn't want a run-of-the-mill mistress. He wanted Jinan. And now that he had her again, he planned to keep her wings clipped so she couldn't fly from him. The only way to keep her at his side was to marry her.

"By all means, set her up in a cozy town house or even in this estate or in Florence."

"You know I won't do that."

Peters gave an exasperated sigh. "You cannot bring someone like her back to England. Look at you, man. You've been swirling the same swig of brandy nigh on ten minutes. You are playing with old habits, my friend."

Rothburn slammed the tumbler down on the marble mantel, the liquid sloshing over the side of the glass. At least he hadn't taken a drink. "I will not be *advised* in the matter of Jinan."

"You have enough problems with the gossipmongers. Consider leaving her here until you've wed."

Rubbing at his eyes and forehead, he thought carefully on his next words. Not that it mattered what Peters thought in the end since he had planned everything out so carefully regarding Jinan. "I'm not worried about the gossips. They can eat a flagon of crow for all I care. Jinan won't have trouble facing that lot. She's an accomplished actress."

"You can't mean to introduce her to society."

"I have every right to since she will be my wife."

Peters's mouth flapped in shock for a moment, then he took a step back and fell to the leather chair that was beside the window. "Rothburn."

Crossing his arms, he waited for Peters to rein in his shock. At least he'd shut the man up, but there would probably be a barrage of questions. Of course, Jinan would have to agree to marry him. That prospect seemed elusive, however.

"I'm not in the mood for this, Peters."

"You cannot marry her! She's a whore."

"You are walking a thin rope." He pointed a threatening finger at Peters. "Tread carefully."

"Think reasonably, Rothburn. You'll have financial backlash from this."

"I've plenty of money to live more than comfortably. You know this since you handle the books."

"But what of the business?"

"It's only natural for some vendors to find a problem with my foreign wife. I care not."

"Do you not care that you will be putting people out of work when business stops on some of our trade routes?"

He'd already considered this, but hadn't wanted to look at the problem too closely. He shrugged. Jinan was more important. "These things have a way of working themselves out. I'm not worried about it yet. She hasn't even agreed to be my wife."

"At least promise me you'll do something about her manners and her clothes." Peters pointed at Jinan's trousers and vest. "She can't continue to go about in that fashion. Especially in England."

Rothburn didn't care if she walked around in only her knickers and chemise so long as she was with him in the end.

Peters changed the subject. "I see you're of no mind to go over the accounts."

He stopped himself from giving Peters the caustic remark he deserved. "I need to deal with her first."

"She's been eating up a lot of your time. Your pockets have a limit, Rothburn. You can't keep going on pretending the rest of the world will stop on its axis while you sort *her* out. You have clients wondering when the hell you're going to call on them, and you need to negotiate new contracts with your traders."

"Just give me a month to sort her out. That's all I'm asking. You know full well the business can continue in your stead. You helped me build the bloody thing from the ground up."

"Doesn't matter. It's not *my* association your clients want. I'm not good *ton*."

"It's arguable that I am." He looked at Peters a long moment, thinking carefully on what he asked of him. "I have a favor to ask of you."

Peters raised a brow. "A favor? I don't think you've ever asked for a favor." The man's gaze slipped beyond him and toward the window facing the garden. "It has to do with her, doesn't it?"

"Yes. It seems I've left something important behind in the harem."

Peters's eyes met his again.

"A son. More specifically, Jinan's son."

Peters hissed in a breath. "Tell me you don't want me to retrieve the son. It's suicide. The prince will have me slung up by the balls for setting foot near his island. Rothburn, we've been in this business, dealt with all types, you know better than anyone you don't cross the bloody Turks."

"I don't want you dealing with him. I want you to send a note through channels that cannot be traced to this villa. I want the prince to consider a sum of money in exchange for the child and for Jinan, even though he has no way of finding her. Money, gold, jewels, part of my business, whatever it takes. I just want you to word the letter in a way that the prince knows I'm not going to give up till I have both in my custody. I'm sure he has a flock of children. He'll be able to part with one." He should ask Jinan who the father was. Somehow that didn't seem important.

Peters stood, crossed his arms over his chest, and walked toward the window. "I still think it's a mission that will be met at the point of a scimitar."

"Possibly. There is nothing to be done about it. I made a promise and I'll keep it even if it's the last thing I do."

"Consider it done. It shouldn't take more than a week to get word back."

"Now if you will excuse me, I have some things to attend to," he said with a pointed look toward Jinan.

Peters raised his hands to stall whatever else he might say about Jinan. "I don't want to know. I'll leave you, then. If anything dire comes up, I'll send a message from my lodgings."

"Thank you."

He could trust Peters to smooth out the ruffled feathers of vendors and buyers alike.

Right now, all he cared about, all he could think about, was pacing in the garden. When Peters left, he headed directly through the narrow corridor to the doors that were flung open into the sunny garden.

Jinan sat by the largest fountain where great golden koi swam. Her finger was circling above the water, calling the fish to her, but they darted away when they realized there was no food to be had.

He gave his trousers a tug at the knees and sat next to her.

She didn't bother to look at him. Why would she?

Rothburn cleared his throat. "I'm glad you found your way down to the garden."

She did not look up to him. "Have you sent word for my son?"

"I have."

"I thank you for that, but this game you play will not be good for you in the end. This is a waste of both our time and I fear you will meet your death from stealing Amir's property."

"You are not anyone's property. More than anything, I want you to at least understand that."

She made no response, so he changed the topic and asked, "Did you find the box this morning?"

He thought she would outright ignore him since she took so long to answer. "I did."

"I'll ask that we have the same arrangement here as we did in the Pleasure Gardens. You are to wear it at all times. At least until you are more comfortable with this life and the consequences of our unions."

"If I should refuse you?"

"Then we will have a repeat of the other night. I can't apologize, Jinan. You have enough power over me. I'll not give you more leverage."

Jinan scrunched her brows together, giving him a narrow look. "Whatever you wish, my lord."

He nodded, then scooted closer to her. It was time to take the damned veil from her face. As he lifted his hands to her face, she started to move away and finally looked him in the eye when his hand grasped her knee, stopping her escape. "What is it you want?"

"You have no need of the veil here. Few will see you, and any who do will remain loyal to your secrecy." Placing his hand over the pin at the back of her head, he waited for her protestations. None came, so he pulled the diamond-studded hairpiece slowly from its clasp. "Nothing between us, Jinan. I've seen you without it already."

The veil fluttered to her lap like a butterfly landing to perch in a sea of colorful flowers. She made no move to shield what was revealed.

He lowered his hand and ran the back of his fingers down her smooth cheek. Her skin was sun-darkened beneath the veil. She sat with her back straight but her eyes averted.

"Look at me, Jinan." His voice was hoarse with need.

"You want your house staff to see me? Is this it? You

want me humiliated by my position as a harem whore? You give them a means to identify me."

"I promise you my staff is discreet. No one will betray you in this household."

"You have betrayed me." Her eyes turned sad, as if all hope had leached from her heart. "Now you have removed the last shred of dignity I held."

He paused, not sure how to respond to that. "I have done no such thing, Jinan. You know I intend you no harm."

"Do I? I am no longer in the safety of the harem, and you cannot make me feel safe here."

"What if I asked you to be my wife? Would that give you any reassurance of my intentions?"

"Do you think I would so easily say yes? I won't. You've not proved your worth to me, Rothburn."

"Jinan." Griffin let out a sigh of frustration. His temper was quickly turning. "I have given you as much patience as a saint. I'm offering you something many women would beg for."

She snorted, then stood from the bench; her fists were clenched tight at her sides as she walked a few steps away and gave him her back. It was long moments before she spoke. "There is nothing between us. I'm not willing to surrender myself to you. Will you keep me locked up for the rest of my days?"

"You mean to tell me you loathe me so thoroughly?"

He had planned to counter her argument but couldn't seem to find the words to belittle what defenses she had left. Instead, he was on her in five quick strides, holding her in the circle of his arms. Tilting her chin up, he looked into her pain-stricken eyes.

"What can I do to secure your hand in marriage? What do I need to prove?"

Instead of answering, she averted her gaze once again.

It was answer enough that she was torn in her decision when her eyes filled to the rim with tears.

How tempting it was to call her Elena. She seemed so innocent, so lost.

Where are you, Elena? You must still exist somewhere in this woman before me.

His finger and thumb caressed the soft flesh beneath her chin. "I understand your hesitancy. I don't like seeing the pain in your eyes. For what reason do you reject me?"

"You do not understand my pain," she said, and gave him the full brunt of her tortured stare. There was something stronger than abhorrence, but he couldn't be sure it was directed toward him. What other secrets did she hide? What wasn't she telling him?

He lowered his mouth closer . . . not touching her lips, yet. God, how he yearned to touch them with his own.

"Jinan," he croaked out, the saliva gone from his mouth. "Are you really paradise?"

Then he pushed his hands through the long dark locks of her hair and laid his mouth upon hers. Her lips were soft against his. It was an innocent kiss that quickly became a devouring of pent-up need between them.

This was different from the kisses they'd shared in the Pleasure Gardens, different from the kisses they'd shared ten years ago in the grand duchess's secluded garden. There was more feeling, a deeper knowledge and awareness of each other than the inexperienced mutual desire they'd felt mere weeks ago.

Her lips parted beneath his, warm breaths mingled and fused in the moment. Could she become lost in this? Would she surrender the last of herself to him? Would he still hold on to his belief that he had done right by her? In his actions, his words, the ones left unsaid?

His tongue touched hers in tender exploration, and

he wanted to consume her, inhale every last bit of her into his system. Wetted lips slipped and fused together as they each became bolder, greedier for something more. He didn't want to press her for more than she was willing to share or offer. He'd already pushed her too far. This was not a one-sided kiss.

How had they ended up against the wall? They were conveniently there now. Then thought escaped him when her arms wrapped around his neck. She stood up taller, on the tips of her toes, he was sure, and her body pressed tight to his from thigh to chest. Her fingers curled through his hair, holding on with all her might as their bodies entwined and joined.

It was the kiss of kisses.

It was definitely pent-up need.

God, her kiss was paradise.

Bending his knees, he brought their groins together and thrust her against the wall in his desire for more. Moaning into his mouth, she wrapped herself more tightly around him. His hands cupped her buttocks, and he couldn't stop himself from indulging more of their senses. Their tongues still delved and sought a completion that could only be found by lowering them to the ground.

Once on his knees, he ground up into the damp center of her body, wanting her to ride out to her climax. Never had a kiss been so intoxicating. Never had he thought he could lose himself to a woman so that he forgot about who watched them . . . who could see them . . . hear them.

He didn't care about anything but kissing her. Her tongue was soft, smooth, and welcoming. She kissed like any experienced harlot.

But this was different.

There was a passion burning beneath the disguise of

Jinan. She'd longed for this as much as he. Perhaps as long as he'd wanted it. He pulled more roughly at her hair as he gained a grip, hauling her down on his body. He thrust up as she pushed harder against him, and just like that they found a rhythm that could satisfy them both.

His cock swelled in the confines of his trousers. He wanted to release his hold on her long enough to free his raging hard-on and fuck her right there, but he didn't want to distract her from the kiss.

It was too soon. He needed to ease her into this. He needed her to want him as badly as he needed her. He didn't ever want this tasting of each other's mouths to end. Her tongue swirled around his, and her lips pulled at his intermittently, taking the lower lip, then the upper one as she licked and nipped at them before driving her tongue back into his mouth in a tangle of need.

They both broke apart from each other, their breathing labored, and he couldn't bear for her to see the conflicting emotions running rampant in his mind, the feelings that were almost certainly reflected in his gaze. Whatever she asked for in this moment, he would give her. He'd deny her nothing right now.

"Shitfire." His forehead pressed to hers as her smaller body still rode out to a completion that could very well free her mind from what he'd done to her the last time they were together.

When her neck arched back, he licked then bit at her exposed throat. She tasted of woman, a light musty saltiness that had his tongue searching more of her skin. He was harder than hell, and he knew he'd get off soon in his trousers. It didn't matter. Like their first night together, this was about her letting loose her desire, her need, her emotions. This was about cracking through that barely penetrable façade to the real woman hiding behind the charade she played so well.

Her hips jerked out of rhythm between his hands, and her slick center rode hard over his bulging groin as she mewed out her orgasm. Her fingers were rough, pulling at his hair as she held herself above him, her breath coming in pants.

And because he couldn't end like this, he grasped her hips tight and rode up into her. In three hard strokes, his balls tightened up so much that the come spouting out of the head of his cock strained painfully against the binding material.

He let out a sound that could not be mistaken for anything but unbridled animalistic pleasure. Wrapping his arms around her back and placing his hands on her shoulders, he pulled her in tight, burying his face in her neck as he slowly gained control over his breathing. The heat of their wet groins spurred him on for an encore. But not out in the open where his staff could spy him at any moment. If they hadn't already.

What had he done?

It always came back to this. Damn it. He had come to talk to her, to apologize as best he could, and here he was fucking her where anyone could happen upon them. Damn it to hell, too, if he wouldn't do it all over again given the choice.

Lifting her from his lap and to her feet, he stood. As though embarrassed by what they'd just done, she looked down at her feet. Chucking her chin, he made her meet his gaze. Still the dark, bottomless brown he remembered. Now he had the rest of her face to soak up since the veil was gone—for a second and final time between them.

It was on the tip of his tongue to call her Elena and

ask her for only truths between them when, in thick Persian, she said, "I will make myself ready for you, my lord. I apologize for not wearing your gift."

Hell and damnation if he could say anything about their past—their future—when she threw up a solid wall between them with such ease after earth-shattering, mutual come-offs. There was nothing to say in the moment that wouldn't have her wishing him ten kinds of bloody death, so he spun on his heel and walked away.

It was most likely a mistake to give her the upper hand. He needed to break down these coldhearted walls she was so insistent upon erecting. There was a weakness somewhere and once he found that chink, he'd plow right through to the very core of the matter.

Stepping back in his office, he left the door open and watched Jinan through the window. She paced a short path on the cobbles that lined the fountain. In her hand she held the silken veil. Would she put it back in place? Would she still try to hide from him? He didn't believe she would.

After a few minutes of constant pacing, she headed inside. He turned as she walked past him toward the stairs that led to his rooms. She wasn't going to attempt leaving. That surprised him for some reason.

Should that not be worrisome? It wasn't as though she could escape him anyway. She couldn't find her way easily around Italy dressed in the garb she seemed so accustomed to wearing. Though he didn't mind that in the least.

He shook his head at his wayward thoughts. It was time to join Jinan, and hopefully she would be quick to don his gift.

He'd taken the last of her identity when the veil had fallen between them. It didn't matter that she'd already given him that gift in the harem. Now he wanted her to turn her back on the ways she'd become so familiar with over the last five years. She wanted to continue to play at being the hidden beauty; it helped to keep her patrons at arm's length. To keep him at arm's length. He was done with secrecy, with pretense. It didn't matter. It was a piece of cloth. The princess was no more.

The heavy footfalls coming from the hall were a sure indication he had followed. She had thought that he would do so as she passed his open study. As swiftly as she could, she retrieved the box she'd thrown aside earlier and sequestered herself in the bathing room.

There were glass jars with cork stoppers lined against the wall farthest from the tub. She started pulling them out, hoping she'd find what she needed. It wasn't long before the sharp scent of vinegar burned through her nose and down her throat. Tossing the stopper to the floor, she opened the box that contained the sponge and soaked it generously. Pulling the trousers down, she kicked them aside and lifted her leg to the edge of the tub.

No more fear of pregnancy. If he did touch her, at least she'd be prepared—like any good courtesan, she thought ruefully. Spreading the lips of her sex, she pushed the cool sponge deep into her sheath and made sure the string dangled free at the opening. With a pop of the stopper from the tub, she turned the water on to rinse the vinegar from her hands.

In a few days, her menses would come and Rothburn would let her be. Not that she reviled his advances or his touch. She couldn't even find it in her to despise him.

How long would it take for the missive to reach Mr. Chisholm? How angry would Amir be with her? Hopefully he wouldn't keep her out of the harem, away from her sisters and her son. He wouldn't be so abominable. At least she hoped that to be the case. He hadn't asked her to grace his bed since she'd stood on the auction block for another lover.

Well, it did her no good standing here mulling it over. She'd have a few more weeks at the most, then she would know her fate. Hopefully she would regain the promise her life held five years ago. She prayed it would be so. She knew she could not live without her son gracing her days, her life.

With a tug of the door latch, she faced Rothburn's questioning gaze.

"I feared you'd never come out."

"You asked me to prepare myself. What else could a woman in my position do but abide by your request?"

He cocked his head to one side; his smile was one of amusement. Even though it was the truth, he didn't believe her for a second. She'd put the sponge in for her benefit, not his. "Have you no desire to run from me again? I am almost disappointed in your resignation. In fact, you seem rather docile since yesterday's attempt on the windows."

"I have no reason to find escape." She pulled herself up straight, tilted her chin up—a decidedly English mannerism—and met his gaze. "Amir will find me. I will be with my son soon. It does not matter that you keep me here against my will."

"Don't be too sure about that, love. My name is not attached to the property we reside in." His grin was smug as he crossed his arms, staring down at her with far too much amusement at having bettered her. "You are lost from your owner, little dove."

"You are mistaken. I am most valuable to Amir. He will put up a fight for what is rightfully his."

"I find your devotion leaves something to be desired."

"Then you should have left me in the harem."

"No. Definitely not something I am willing to do."

"You are a fool to face the wrath of my master."

With those words, his grin faded. His lips thinned; his arms, which were crossed in enjoyment of their repartee, dropped to his sides in renewed anger. His fists clenched, then unclenched. Did he know he'd revealed a weakness in his character? He hated any mention of Amir. Not that she knew quite how to exploit this discovery.

He strode forward; the flat of his hand slapped the wall behind her with enough force that she started and a small high-pitched cry of fear escaped her throat. Effectively, he'd boxed her in between his straining arms as both hands stretched to the wall on either side of her head. His face was but inches from hers.

"He is no longer your master!" His words were clipped and slow as though he didn't think she'd understand them without the drawling. "Say it again, and I'll be tempted to do more than tan your hide. Damaged goods don't hold nearly as much worth as a girl playing the browbeaten, docile princess."

She looked away from him, afraid to incur more of his fury. He'd never shown a temper of this magnitude. Never threatened once to hurt her. Not that the opportunity would have arisen with all the guards present in the Pleasure Gardens. She was precariously balanced on the sharp tip of his barely tempered rage. She didn't know who to fear more, Amir or Griffin? The question was, which man really held her life in his hands?

Extracting herself from his furious grasp was key to bringing the situation back to her favor. "Please,

Rothburn." Though she knew he was more show than bite, she averted her eyes and added quietly, "You are frightening me."

There was a silent pause.

The angry tempo of his breath continued to fan over her face. Perhaps she had said the wrong thing? She daren't chance a look. Instead of facing him, she backed against the wall, ready to retreat under his outstretched arms. She knew she wouldn't get far, but it would be worth the effort.

"Your fanciful tales," he said dangerously, "fall flat with me, my dear. Your games have never worked." Then he pushed away from the wall. She was glad to feel chill air in place of his body heat. "Look at me, damn it."

How she wanted to dash away from him, to escape him to a room full of servants where he wouldn't dare lift a finger to harm her. His temper was volatile and she was close to shattering his control. She did not want to face the rage so tightly held at bay. He'd never been like this with her before. Never. She looked at his face but did not make eye contact. He let out an annoyed sound, then walked toward the bed, pulling his shirt from his trousers.

"Get over here, Jinan. And disrobe. If you insist on playing the whore, I'm more than happy to oblige."

She flinched at his harsh words, but he was right. She was nothing more than a whore. First her husband's, then Amir's, and now Rothburn's. They all wanted to be her lord and master. She looked at him for a moment, then her heart shut off to him.

The tears that had threatened moments before dried up. Her trembling hands moved swiftly to pull the vest off and untie the scarves. At last she pushed her skirts down her hips to pool on the floor. His eyes watched her progress. She hated that his smile was genuine and cracking through his angry demeanor.

Then he met her eyes and his smile faded. His firm resolve slid back in place when he realized she did not want to play his games. Before he could demand anything of her, she walked past him, lay on her back, and spread her legs for him. She put her knees up high, to give him the view he desired. He'd see the string curled around the swell of her buttocks, and know that she'd obeyed his orders.

He did not remove his trousers. She waited for him to make use of her, but he just stood there for some minutes. Finally, he sat at the edge of the bed, coming into her line of sight, and removed his shoes.

"Close your legs, Jinan. You'll catch a draft, and I've no desire to make use of you tonight. I only wish to have a nap."

There was defeat in the timbre of his voice, and she didn't fail to notice the slight hunch to his shoulders. It shouldn't matter that he felt properly punished by her actions. He'd taken her from her home; she could have no sympathy for him. She closed her legs—leaving the sponge in place, in case he did make use of her—and rolled to face the side of the bed he did not occupy.

CHAPTER FOURTEEN

Revelation

A few days had come and gone now and Rothburn had left her to her own devices during that time. She wasn't sure if he was still fuming over their last confrontation. But he was either short with her or said nothing at all whenever they crossed paths.

Another blessing and curse between them.

It was better that way. She hoped, because she did still love him, despite his ill treatment of her, that he strategized and readied himself for Amir's imminent arrival. It couldn't be too far off. Another week at most. He'd be a fool to think Amir wouldn't find him. One did not steal the property of a prince; the consequences were often deadly.

Thoughts of Jonathan plagued her mind. She knew as the days went on that her chances of returning to the harem to welcoming arms were more and more unlikely. Would Amir listen to her apologies for everything that had happened these last ten days? Her thoughts were interrupted when Rothburn stepped into the bedchamber, hands laden with two silver breakfast trays.

"I passed Donata in the hall. She said you were up and about."

She nodded. Where had this charming man come from? Pretending to be sincere now when he hadn't said more than a handful of sentences in the last few days. She was here against her will; she shouldn't find him charming in the least.

She looked him over, wary and reserved, and waited for him to set the trays down. One was placed on her lap, the other he placed on the side table where he kept a decanter half filled with brandy. Never had she seen him take a drink from it.

He approached her and took the lid off the dinner tray with a flourish and set it aside.

"Fish. Thank you," she said, naturally and gratefully.

"Of course, I wouldn't feed you swine or unblessed meat. I haven't once offered it, because I thought that would be decidedly cruel. I promise you I'm not often cruel, at least not intentionally."

At her skeptical gaze he assured her, "It is all halal. Do not ask how I arranged it, but I found someone who would do that for me when I procured the necessities and toiletries I thought you might make use of here. I do not know if you had a strict diet in the harem. Whenever we dined together, it was light fare."

"We followed a strict diet. We kept many of the traditions of the Ottoman harems. This is very kind of you."

She ducked her head, embarrassed by the expression of gratitude. She hadn't had anything but tidbits of food now and then because she had assumed his kitchen was not prepared for a woman with her dietary restrictions. She reached for the fork he held out and looked down to the array of food. There was some sort of pilaf, spiced differently from what she was used to. The fish slid apart like a creamy cheese. Placing it in her mouth, she tasted a strong undercurrent of lemon and rosemary. It was delicious and the most appetizing thing she'd eaten in days. Savoring the fish, she closed her eyes. She was only aware she made a noise of contentment when Rothburn chuckled, then retrieved his own tray.

He sat in the chair diagonally across from her, and they ate in pleasant silence. She never thought this could happen so easily after their last altercation.

When she picked up the last of the peas and popped it into her mouth, Rothburn asked her solicitously, "Would you like another helping?"

She shook her head no and handed the plate to him. He took it without comment. What moments before had been easy and comfortable now felt awkward and strange. He didn't sit in the chair to her left. He perched himself on the window seat facing her, so she couldn't stare out at the garden to avoid his gaze.

"We cannot go on like this, Jinan."

"Do you wish to resume your contract with me now that my menses have passed?" She knew that wasn't what he referred to, but she'd be damned if she would give him an inch. He deserved no kindness from her after his brutality.

"We do not have a contract. I'll not reiterate that again. I'm being sincere. I wish you believed my words. I've set you free from the servitude that island sanctioned. Is that not enough for you to feel at least a little grateful toward me?"

"You have taken me from the only home I know."

"Then you can stay with me. Call this place a home. Is it not obvious to you that I want more than a bloody contract between us? I should hear from Amir any day now with regard to your son."

"You speak as though you think you've won a hand of cards. This is not the case. I know Amir better than you ever will. When will you see that for the truth?"

"Do you want to know what I see, Jinan?" He did not wait for her to say anything, and he continued. "I see a woman who is afraid to embrace freedom when it's been offered to her. Damn well nearly on a silver platter." His voice was steady, but she heard the upset in it.

"You have no understanding of my life before now, so do not base your judgment of me on what you think you know and what you think you remember. I am not free here. I am not fool enough to believe your words for they are hypocrisy. You have caged me as well as a songbird. This cage might look and feel bigger because of the false freedom you've offered, but this design is no less obvious. I take it for what it is—my prison."

"I have given you the freedom of my home. I want you to feel comfortable here."

"Is this what you tell yourself? Are you so blind to your own deviousness? If this is not a golden cage symbolizing further repression, why do you refuse me what I want most?"

There was a long pause from Rothburn. He rubbed at the beard stubble along his jaw. "I wish you could see the truth of what I offer. If I sent you *home* you might never come back to me."

She sat up in her chair, unsure what she should say to that. Because that was the truth. If she went back to the harem, she'd never see him again. She could not choose to come back to him. So he was right. Leaving meant an end to everything between them. It wasn't something she wanted to think about. "What you do is not better than what Amir did. You cage me to act as your whore."

He must have misread her expression, her tone. His

hands brushed through his hair in a jerky displaced movement of frustration—a habit of his. "I will get nowhere with you, will I? I do not want you playing the whore. I never did. But you sit there pretty as can be playing the damned part so well, I wonder if I've dreamed you half my damned life. Made you something more in my head, in my thoughts, over the years we were separated."

"I'm not sure what you mean." Did he really want to acknowledge their past now? It seemed pointless, a lifetime ago. They'd both mentioned things that hinted at their past engagement, but they'd not once talked about it.

He stood quickly, glaring down at her. The words all but poured out of him. "Jesus, you are impossible. Do you think me a fool? I've wanted you practically half my life. I would have been content knowing I had lost you but could always return to you in my dreams. Instead I find you, and now I can never let you go." He sat back down with a huff; the words seemed to have drained him. He turned his back to the wall and brought one knee up to rest his arm upon. "Do you know that you've ruined me for all others?"

He didn't look at her, and she was glad for it. What could she say to a man who had wanted her for so long? Did he exaggerate? She'd known many a man to do just that. No, she knew he did not refer to some hypothetical beauty of the night. He spoke of *their* past. She knew it as surely as she knew her own heart where he was concerned. Life was so much easier when you closed yourself off from your past. She'd learned to do that when she'd married Robert, and had continued to forget the innocent girl she once was, as her life turned down more and more paths too dark to navigate with a light heart.

"I'm not the person you have dreamed of all these years." She looked away from him, unable to meet his eyes should he turn to face her. Her words were not a lie, but a truth made real by the path her life had taken. "I'm not the person you want me to be."

"Damn it, Jinan. Can we lose the deceit for once? Just once—once!—give me the truth." He didn't turn when he said the words. Just stared out over the garden she'd enjoyed looking at moments ago. His fingers stretched and cracked as he sat there, such a small movement, but one clearly derived from his agitation.

"What do you want of me? Maybe that is the only thing that needs to be clear between us?"

"I want the truth. It's what I've always wanted from you . . . between us. Just the truth."

"And what truth is that?" she asked, because she would not be forced to admit anything.

"Your games were pleasant during our reacquaintance. Did you find them to be so, too? Do you think I propose to just anyone I happen to fancy at a given moment? That I would spend so much money on a woman for the hell of it?"

If the proposal hadn't been a whim . . . a foolish puppy love between them, then why had he walked away from her, left her? That time in her life now was hazy. She'd fallen head over heels in love with this man in a whirlwind two weeks, then he'd disappeared. After that, the vapid Baron Shepley had courted her. She'd been forced into a marriage with the bounder when he'd ruined her reputation—quite intentionally, she was sure.

When she didn't answer, he turned to look at her. She could see the raw hurt in his eyes. She saw in his gaze that he wanted her to admit to their past.

But she couldn't.

"Do you need a refresher, *Elena*?" He still stared at her, daring her to lie now that he had called her by her real name.

Or perhaps to gauge her reaction to the one name she never wanted to hear again.

She made to speak when he held up his hand to silence her. "Hear me out."

"Rothburn, you do not understand my position in all this."

"Don't I? Let me fill in the blanks then, my dear. We met some ten years ago. I think you should take a moment to recall the Duchess of Glenmoore's ball. There was a proposal in the gardens at the aforementioned party." Those penetrating eyes of his landed on hers again—hurt lay in their depths. "Is this beginning to fall in place for you yet? Are you remembering?"

"I don't understand what you are getting at."

Rothburn took a deep breath, the only sound to fill the distance between them. It was clear he'd been waiting for her confession for some time, maybe from the moment he took her from the auction block.

"I remember our courtship, of course. Those were, at that point, the happiest days of my life. Then after proposing to me, you left the very next day, so I didn't think it had meant anything to you." She couldn't say more than that, and stared into her lap where she entwined her fingers to still their nervous tremble.

"I understand better than anyone why you married that scoundrel, you know. The man is dead, is he not?"

She did not delay her answer. "My husband is dead."

"I did look into his whereabouts. More specifically, your whereabouts. He shouldn't have been a hard man to find given his proclivity for gambling; I'd hoped to find men claiming he owed them money. Both of you proved impossible to locate once you moved abroad."

"He did not die well or with any honor. We did not have friends to turn to anymore."

"Had I known, I would have done more, Elena."

"Please do not call me by my birth name."

"And why not? It *is* your birth name. There is no reason not to use it now. I'd like to think there are few things we don't know about each other at this point."

"I implore you not to." Her eyes flooded with tears. She tried to hold them back, but she knew they would fall soon. This was too much, rehashing her sordid, awful life.

"For a long time I was angry with you. I thought you had only been interested in finding the next available suitor."

His words were more caustic, more detached, the longer he went on. She wasn't sure if his apparent anger was directed at her or at himself. It was in her best interest now to set him straight on the matter of her downfall.

"You can never understand the trials I have been through, Rothburn."

"I can imagine it was no hardship. I doubt you would have embraced that life so easily if it had been a hardship. I've never seen reserve in you, nor guilt. Not once did you ask for my help in taking you away from that place. How many men have you warmed? Have you enjoyed them all as much as you seemed to enjoy my company?" The whip of his words shattered her heart like shards of cold ice. She lifted her head, tears trailing a path down both her cheeks with the motion.

"Stop this." He must have been caught off guard by her raised voice. Mouth clamped shut, he allowed her to continue. "I was given no choice about that life. Amir has been most kind to me. He would never abuse me or neglect me. He has been above reproach in his care and generosity."

"I fear your faith is placed in the wrong sort of man." He snorted his disgust. "He's no more morally incorrupt than the people that visit his bawdy island."

"I do not mistake his generosity. He's been most kind, and I know you will never understand such a thing. You cannot understand the lengths he went to to save me from a death too cruel to repeat. I bear great respect for the only man to show me kindness in all my life."

She revealed too much with the last; she spoke strongly. She'd kept her past so deeply buried that once she started digging, the heart of the matter seemed to raise to the surface on its own, demanding she delve to the very core of her secrets. It was a strange personal revelation, too. For the first time in five years, she actually hated the fact that Amir's kindness had won her over so easily. It made her an unworthy woman and mother to not fight harder for her freedom.

"Elena."

His tone was low, soothing the frightened doe. Did he understand the significance of her words?

"Stop calling me by that name. *Elena* is dead! Do you understand?" She pounded her fist to her heart and choked back a sob. "She died in here five years ago. She *died*. She is no more. I cannot explain it to you, but she is no longer who I am. I am Jinan. It is not an act. It is not a way to hide. This is who I am. Not the whore as you so aptly wish to name me, but a woman who was reborn with the help of her master and the love of her sisters. Elena is dead and you need to forget she ever existed. Because it would destroy a part of me to remember what I once was."

She swiped the tears off her face, turning away from him.

This was a better silence they shared. She no longer felt awkward in it. She'd said what needed to be said. It was up to him and his goodwill to leave her be. It was up to him to take pity on her and bring her back home. Give her back to her son.

"I'll never forget Elena. Or the wrong my uncle committed against her."

She looked up at him, wondering what he meant. "Your uncle has nothing to do with me."

"Don't be so sure. There were letters found upon his death—enough to condemn him in the eyes of his peers for so many wrongs against people he acknowledged as friends. He was a deceitful bastard. He made sure I knew you'd been sold off to that bastard Lord Shepley."

Silence fell between them as the implication of his words took root in her mind.

What did he mean? She barely knew his uncle; they'd never been formally introduced. Although she'd had reason to distrust her husband's machinations in securing her hand in marriage.

"Did you think me so coldhearted as to attempt the seduction of a debutante and not offer marriage? I know my reputation precedes me on occasion, but I thought we had an understanding even if we hadn't announced it to the world. I thought we would marry."

"I had hoped, but you were so far above my station. I assumed when you did not dance attendance upon me after the Glenmoores' ball that you'd moved on. Please forgive me my ignorance. You will have to enlighten me in regard to your uncle."

"Come now, Jinan. Did you never wonder how you married a man without prospects? Your beauty alone could have ensnared a man of better standing than Lord Shepley."

"I still don't understand what your point is."

"Then listen carefully, for I do not want to repeat

myself as it is against my own soul that you've suffered this life.

"My uncle was nothing but ruthless and scheming. He wished me to marry someone of his choosing. You, my dear, unknowingly foiled his plans. Perhaps if naïveté were not a common folly in youth, I would have whisked you away from London to Gretna Green. But such *is* the folly of youth that I never saw any danger in courting you."

"Robert would never have mingled in the same circles as the *ton*." And because he gave her honesty, she could do no less. "I realized, after that night, that I couldn't expect you to indulge in anything aside from a flirtation with me. I knew my prospects were few with my lack of dowry. My sponsor was most kind to even allow me a season in London. It was to be my only season for she thought my beauty would land me a husband. She was right, of course."

"Jinan, please come sit with me."

He held his hand out in invitation. She didn't take it but rose and sat opposite him on the cushioned seat. The sun was high in the sky and warmed the cubbyhole. Folding her legs under her, she placed her hands in her lap and waited for him to continue with his tale.

"My uncle was more cunning then I ever gave him credit for. He paid a portion of Shepley's chits on the condition he petition for your hand in marriage. The wedding, though small according to the letters I found, was also paid for at my uncle's expense. My uncle knew what he was doing when he set that desperate jackal loose in your direction. Anything to keep me from marrying you. He promised Lord Alderly that I'd marry his middle child, knowing I'd flee to Europe till things settled down."

"This explains a lot. Fills in a lot of the puzzle pieces

I'd been trying to figure out. Actually, it doesn't surprise me that Robert was paid to do what he did."

"I cannot imagine he kept you in high standing, nor do I expect there was an abundance of love lost between you—" He paused, brushed his hand through his hair, and leaned his head back against the wall. "You do not show any kindness in your words toward him. Did you love him?"

She didn't respond, just turned her head to the side so he couldn't read the truth in her eyes. No, she'd never loved her husband. As much as she'd tried to build a life for them, he'd refused her sympathy. They'd learned to live with each other in the end, but only on cordial terms. Rothburn sat up and shrugged out of his jacket. She didn't look when he tossed it over to the chair she'd just vacated.

What was the use of him telling this story? It was so long ago. It didn't matter—not now.

Besides all that, rehashing it changed nothing. She needed to go back to the harem whether he wanted her to leave or not. That was her rightful place. Not playing house with this lord of the realm, who was bound to leave her when duty demanded he produce an heir.

Her place was with her son. It always had been and would be.

Was he trying to soften her heart? If he looked carefully, he'd see she'd always held him in the highest regard, but kept a safe distance out of necessity.

His hand wrapped around both of hers and lifted her chin toward him.

"Do you despise me so much?"

Taking a deep breath, she closed her eyes, and turned away from him. "No," she whispered.

"Then stay here with me, Jinan. You'll never want

for anything. I'll always look after you. I'll care for you as your husband never could."

"It will never be possible."

"And why not?"

Did he understand nothing she said? Turning her head, she stared at a bird flitting from branch to branch on the lone olive tree. Sliding one of her hands free of his grasp, she traced her finger over the edge of the cushioned seat. His hand was suddenly gone as his arms slipped around her shoulders and under her folded legs.

Telling herself she only wrapped her arms securely around his wide shoulders because she didn't want to fall, she stared at his neck. Maybe he'd said everything that needed saying between them, she wasn't sure. Not another word was spoken, not even when he laid her on the bed and made quick work of removing her silk trousers, vest, and scarves.

When she was naked, he stared down at her. His expression was so intense and full of unsaid feelings between them that she wanted to cover herself. He saw too much of her right now. Retrieving the box with her sponge from the nightstand, he went into the bathing room. She heard the pop of the cork and the clank of the bottle. It should strike her as odd that he knew how to do this, but then he had bought her the sponge to begin with.

When he came through the door opposite the bed-chamber, his shirt and shoes were gone. He wore only his trousers. The sponge he held aloft as he knelt at her side. "Say yes. I'll not take you unwillingly."

"Yes," she whispered.

Not once did he look her in the eyes as she reached for the sponge, knowing what he wanted from her. He shook his head, pushing one of her knees out. Warm fingers of his free hand spread the folds of her sex that bloomed out toward him. There was some type of oil on his fingers that he used to ease his fingers deep inside her. Biting her lip so she didn't groan, she spread her other leg out to make it easier for him to insert the sponge.

What a strange intimacy they shared by him doing this.

Fingers twisting and massaging her inner passage, he readied her body. Chancing a look at him, she saw his eyes were closed, his nostrils flared as his fingers explored and titillated. Eyes snapping open, they ensnared her in their liquid depths and prevented her from breaking away.

The cool slickness of the sponge was placed at the entrance of her sheath; his fingers moved slowly and methodically as he pushed it up inside, till his palm was flush to the mound. Leaning over her, he brushed his lips over hers, he parted them gently but did not invade her mouth with his tongue. No, he seemed content with the rubbing of their lips together, and a low groan escaped, the only indication he was pleased with the act. Just as quickly as his warmth had surrounded her it disappeared. His hand pulled away, his soft lips were gone.

She opened her eyes. He stood at the edge of the bed, pushing his trousers beneath his hips. His cock lay in the blond curls at his center. Not quite flaccid or hard, but filling and thickening the longer she stared.

What devil whispered in her ear, she did not know. But she sat up on hands and knees and took that growing piece of fevered ecstasy in hand and placed her lips to the tip, giving it a delicate kiss. His hand came round and threaded tightly through her hair. His pelvis thrust forward at the same time he released another groan.

She'd only ever done this to one other man, and it didn't bear comparison. There had never been any feeling in doing it before. She did it now to please him, to please herself. He held her heart and would never know it; his very being was imprinted deep in her mind . . . and he could never understand the true depth of it.

Love was not free to her. She would go back to the harem and never see Griffin again.

She opened her mouth to him and took him in deep. Her fingers lifted the weight of his sac, enfolding the soft tissue, squeezing and rolling the marbles within.

Some expletive she didn't catch escaped his lips as he thrust harder—deeper—into her mouth. He climbed onto the bed, allowing her to sit on her heels and her free hand to wrap around his firm buttocks to encourage the flexing of his hips forward. A low hum of appreciation filled her throat, vibrating down the length of his rod. Her finger slipped behind the scrotum to massage the soft flesh behind. His fingers gripped her hair, pulling taut, but she didn't mind. Tongue rolling around the soft purple head of his uncapped rod, she took all of him in her mouth, riding along his length.

When she started to roll the testicles in her palm, he pulled her forcibly from his cock and off the bed till she was level with his face. He stared at her a moment, then drove his tongue, with a force that stole her breath, into her mouth and thrust his hard, now damp, cock against her soft belly. His body was unforgiving as it took. Took everything she'd denied him before now. Her heart leaped furiously against his, her thighs grew slick with the fluids from her cunt. Sweat dripped between the valley of her breasts, collecting in the heavy crease above her ribs. Both his hands tangled tight in her hair as though he feared she'd escape him now.

That was the furthest thing from her mind.

But pleasure. Pleasure she could give him in spades.

By intuition alone, she felt this was her last chance with him. This was the last impression she could make on his soul.

Snaking her arms around his shoulders, she pressed her breasts tightly to his chest and tried to inch up his body until his cock thrust between the folds of her sex. She was tall enough for that, but he didn't seem to grasp what she was about.

Their teeth clanked painfully together as their kisses grew feverish. That didn't stop them from delving their tongues farther, tangling and tasting as she surrendered her body completely to him. Something she'd not done before with him or any other man. Not in all her life.

Would he understand the significance of this gift?

Who did she think she fooled? The passion he'd been dying to unleash finally burned bright and strong beneath his hands. The jut of her breasts on his chest made him hard as all hell. It was a challenge not to bend her over and fuck her as hard and furious as the blood pumping through his body.

She'd finally given him the truth. The only truth he needed to seal his heart to her completely. He was wrapped around that pretty little finger of hers. And the talent she'd shown with that finger not a minute ago had almost made him come off in her hot mouth.

The taste of lemon from their lunch lingered on her lip as well as the male muskiness from her sucking him off. He pushed her back on the bed, following her down, tasting ever deeper of her sweet, intoxicating mouth. He took his fill of the elixir of her mouth, filling, then retreating, tonguing and dueling for supremacy in this intimacy. She gave as good as she got, matching his pace, lingering as he did, indulging completely in the raw intimacy of the moment.

Untangling his hands from her hair, he slid them down to her thighs, grasped them and pushed her legs back so her ankles wrapped around his neck. With a deft hand, he positioned his cock and filled her in one smooth stroke.

The sound he made wasn't quite a growl or groan but all pleasure as he pulled away from her mouth and pressed his forehead to hers. Panting, because he *was* bloody well panting as he held himself above her, he closed his eyes and breathed in deep. He was so close to losing his seed. They wouldn't leave this bed for the next week if he had his way. What was sprouting a little seed prematurely in their joining when he could last longer in a second tangle between her sweet thighs?

Hands framing her face, he pulled up enough that he could look at her eyes. Was it possible he'd cracked fully through that tough exterior she wore like the strongest armor?

"Jinan," he whispered against her parted lips.

It was all he could say once her pelvis tilted upward, lodging his cock deeper into the hugging warmth of her velvet-lined sheath.

Her hands cupped his face, her fingers rubbing over the stubble as she stared at him with an open heart. It was at once the most erotic, sensual, and humbling sight he'd ever had in his life.

What would it take to make her his? What did he have to do to prove his worth? To make her stay?

God, it pierced his heart to get that look of longing when she continually refused to even think of sharing a life with him.

Reaching behind him and unhooking her ankles, he drew her legs down to clasp around his hips. Then he pulled out and thrust back inside her. He closed his eyes, remembering everything about her—her soft plump flesh, full heavy breasts, and strong feminine legs. Her hand so lightly touching the contours of his face as she explored his features with an innocence ironic to the circumstances.

He was so close; he didn't want to finish. Couldn't he stay in her perfect body for the rest of his life? Why wasn't it possible to build a life on this simplicity?

"Jinan," he tried again. There were so many words still not said between them.

His mouth was dry, breath ragged, voice hoarse. He stole into her mouth since words escaped him. Did she feel the longing and passion unfurling in him as he took her hard and kissed her with every ounce of affection he harbored for her?

With her ankles clasped around his buttocks, heels digging into his backside, she urged him on when he wanted to indulge in slow pleasure. She broke away from his kiss. Her breath came fast and hard as she sucked in as much air as she could with him crushing her.

"Love me," she said, and sucked in her bottom lip as her body arched in demanding supplication against his.

Was it his imagination? The words were so low and maybe he mistook them for words of bliss, not words from the heart. It was too much to resist what she offered. He'd love her any way he could.

Pulling from the warmth of her body, he flipped their positions and put his back to the head of his bed. She mounted and slid down his length slowly, a hush of air escaping her parted lips. This wasn't any better, he decided. He'd spill his seed quicker. She knew exactly how to fulfill their needs.

With his hands tight on her hips, he stopped the rise

of her body. She let out a mewl of frustration and rocked her mound against him instead. He did the only thing he could think of when all he wanted more than anything in the world was to indulge in something she'd denied him since they'd first met. He would not let her cheat him now. Pulling her head back with a grasp to the hair at her nape, he arched it back until she could no longer move.

"I like that you trust me . . . that you don't fight me when I take this kind of control."

The groan she released was half squeal, half moan, and it had him bucking his hips up hard so he could hear it again. She did not disappoint. Before he could rein in his end, his excess of emotion, he came to his finale, squirting inside her tight sheath. His hips thrusting so hard she had to wrap her arms around his shoulders and hold on tight as he pumped his seed deep inside her.

She collapsed atop him when his cock jerked a final spurt of milk. Breath ragged, mouth dry, he rolled into her center, never wanting to leave her heavenly warmth. Kissing her forehead, cheek, lingering at her mouth, he finally slipped his softening cock from her, a rush of fluid following his retreat. As much as he didn't want to leave her, she needed to be cleaned.

Retrieving a dampened cloth from the water closet, he made quick work of cleaning his seed, which mingled with her fluids, from her mound and bottom. The motion brought his cock back to semi-life, but he ignored it. Now, he just wanted to hold her and help her find her own crisis—but sleep was inevitable at the moment.

Tossing the cloth in the direction of the water closet, he climbed into bed, and pulled her soft body flush to his, aligning their pelvises. Arms wrapped tightly around her, he squeezed her close.

"You are my heart, Jinan. Don't leave me."

The words were lost, though; her breaths were deep and even in sleep.

CHAPTER FIFTEEN

Found

Raised voices. More than one. Dread filled the pit of her belly, she had so many conflicting feelings. It might be Amir. Which meant she'd be taken away. There was no hope of Amir releasing her son. Not to one who had stolen his property right from under his nose. She hoped Rothburn would not be hurt in the process. That thought was as bad as being separated from her son.

The shouting resumed. She was sure the deep booming baritone came from Rothburn. The words were too far away and spoken too fast for her to make any sense of them.

Racing to the door, she tugged at it. It didn't budge. She tugged harder, twisting the latch, but it held fast. She was locked in. Why had he done that? She shook the handle; the door wasn't going to open. Raising her palms, pounding against the door, she shouted, "Rothburn, let me out of here right now! Don't do this to me."

She heard the dull thud of running feet, pounding toward her. The sound of a scabbard unsheathing and the shush of the soft trousers the eunuchs wore caught her ear.

There had been no response to her angry outburst, but she didn't expect one from the eunuchs. Did they think they walked into danger? Was Rothburn even alive? God, please let him live.

She backed away from the door and called again in Turkish. "Please, unlock the door."

Thump.

She jumped back a step, unprepared for the door to groan in the frame.

Thump, thump.

The frame split and the palace guards came through, forming a protective circle around her. She slumped her shoulders in relief and regret, her heart beating furiously in her chest as her mind tried to sort out everything that was happening.

There was so much dread mixed with sadness that she didn't know if she wanted to scream or cry. Her interlude at Rothburn's estate was over. It felt as if her heart were shattering, splintering, never to be put back together again.

She was going back to the harem. Provided Amir didn't banish her for Rothburn's actions. As much as she hated to admit it, she didn't want to go back. She wanted her son handed over, and she wanted to live out her days as Rothburn's mistress. Chattel couldn't voice opinions, though. It wasn't her place to ask for anything. Either Amir would listen to Rothburn or he wouldn't. Nothing she said would change that.

At least Peters had made it out of the estate before it was stormed by the bloody Turks.

A dagger was held tight against the pounding life vein at his throat, but he refused to believe Amir would kill him over Jinan. How the hell had Amir found this estate? The ownership was well guarded, had been even in his uncle's time.

"You go surprisingly far for a whore, Amir."

Griffin would not reveal the depth of his feelings for said *whore*. He wanted to spit as the word repeated in his mind. It was necessary to talk this way while dealing with a man who sold women's favors—Jinan's favors. *Don't show any weakness*. Jinan was his greatest weakness.

"You think me so foolish. I am not blind to the goings-on in my own home. You underestimated my ability to track down your property. You steal from a prince of the Ottoman Empire, English. This is punishable however I see fit. She has not much more worth than a horse, but you've risked my wrath regardless."

"We are not in your homeland for you to exact punishment in your preferred fashion." The blade nicked deeper. Griffin had to angle his head back to keep it from cutting too deep. It was hard to keep his eye on Amir in this awkward position. "Let us be gentlemen and discuss this."

Amir pulled the blade away with a laugh. "You think me so unintelligent? You are dim-witted. Let us do this your English way, English. Shall we swill some liquids and shake hands on a *gentleman*'s honor?"

"I won't release her so easily."

"You are mistaken if you think that this is up for negotiation. I have not given you a choice in the matter. Your home is surrounded by my guards."

"I can pay you whatever it is she owes you."

Amir let out another guffaw. Griffin was unimpressed but what else could he say? This man was not simple to deal with. One could never be sure if they should cover their groins or laugh along at the prince's jokes. Unnerving but most likely he did this intentionally to throw off enemies. The unpredictability of this prince kept his adversary unprepared.

"Surely we can come to some sort of arrangement."

"I think I will take what is mine back." He raised his brow with interest. "I would like your version of the heist, though."

"Perhaps the exchange of information will help with the negotiations." Griffin motioned to the leather chairs. The eunuchs made no move; every one of them had their hands clasped over swords and scimitars.

Amir moved to sit, setting his dagger across his lap. "You made it out of the palace with the help of a slave. He has been beheaded for the transgression."

Griffin nodded, but cringed inwardly. He needed to turn the talk around so they discussed Jinan and the child. A direct approach was best. "I would like to discuss a price for Jinan." First her, then the boy.

"She is not for you. What do you want with a harem girl? You cannot marry her, for she belongs to me."

"But you are not married to Jinan." At least he didn't think she was. She couldn't be, could she? Amir wouldn't sell his wives' favors. There was the child tangled up in this mess. Perhaps she was one of his wives, because she'd given him a child. Doubt assailed him as Amir let the moment stretch out in silence.

"No. But she is still mine." So the child wasn't Amir's. Not that it mattered to Griffin. If she wanted the boy, he'd negotiate for him.

Griffin breathed a sigh of relief. "I beg to differ."

"Yes, you may do so at your will . . . but it does not change the fact that she is mine. I own her." Amir's gaze wandered around the room, a sneer lingering on his lips. "I can't imagine she wants to stay here."

"I assure you she does," he countered, eyes never leaving the prince's. "I've given her no reason to want to leave. She is not a slave here, forced to share her favors to fill your coffers."

"Ah." Amir's smile was slow as he leaned back in the chair, looking for all the world at ease. Well, he had a right to feel at ease when his guards watched Griffin with hawk eyes and daggers at the ready. There was no threat in this room to Amir. "You are mistaken there. I treat my girls better than most husbands do."

The silence stretched for some minutes. Amir seemed to relish it, his fingers drumming along the arm of the chair. The only other sound was the chime of the clock on the noon hour, then *tick, tick, tick*.

"I'm willing to pay generously. Whatever it is she's indebted to you for and more to keep you happy."

"This is where we have a problem. How many times must I say she is not for sale?"

Griffin stood but kept his voice level. "She doesn't want to go back." At least he hoped he'd convinced Jinan that it was better for her to stay here with him.

Amir stood, nodding to the guards who flanked the door. "Retrieve her."

"You surround her with armed guards and expect her to answer you truthfully?" He thought the man would be more reasonable. "I am willing to pay you more than the original contract. She cannot owe you more than that."

How had Jinan become so indebted to this man? Surely his last contract had paid whatever she was indebted for. This should be an easy negotiation. Amir liked his money more than his girls. At least that was the impression Griffin had after seeing all the harem girls wantonly displayed for the richest men in the world.

"There is no negotiation. She belongs to me. A gift from my brother."

"Given her past, I find that hard to believe." He had nothing to lose. That was the only reason he risked mentioning his past association with Jinan. He wasn't on even ground and to find his footing, he needed something to connect him to her. God, this was not how he had envisioned the conversation with Amir. "Name your price, man."

"There is no price. For her or the child." Amir raised one thick black brow and crossed his arms, assessing him. "Her past is her own. She belongs to me now. Ah, here she comes." His hand, palm up, stretched toward the door.

She stood frozen for a moment, looking Griffin over, tears filling her eyes. Then she turned away from him. And damn it all to hell, Jinan ran to Amir, dropped to her knees, and kissed his damned feet. They spoke in a fast succession of Turkish. He understood most of it, and he did not like what he heard. Jinan slavering her damned tears all over Amir's shirt, apologizing for her disobedience and hoping that her son was well— though he couldn't fault her for the last part. She swore of her duty and gratitude to Amir, saying she had wanted to go home but did not know the way to the island, asking forgiveness over and over.

Had he made no headway with her? What of their shared secrets and confessions? What of the passion that had brought them even closer?

"Jinan—" He could say no more than her name, and hated that his voice sounded gravelly, strained with too much emotion.

She turned to him, her face full of tears, and he was sure they were for more than sadness for her *wrongs* to her master. He stifled any emotion and cleared his throat. Now was not the time to reveal his weakness.

Her eyes filled anew as she walked toward him and ran her knuckles lightly down his jaw, stopping at his chin. In English, she said, "My love is yours for safe-keeping. But my heart lies in my master's hands, as you know. This is all I can give you. It was all I could ever give you, Rothburn. I tried to tell you I could not leave him." Fresh tears fell from her eyes as Amir pulled her away with a look of pure venom in Griffin's direction. The guards flanked her, and they pushed her from the room, barely giving her the opportunity to look back at him.

He frowned after her, wondering how to stop this from happening.

Amir intruded into his thoughts. "You see, Jinan will not contest this. She knows her rightful place."

"She does not want to go with you! I will not rest until she is mine."

He'd give Amir points for thinking fast. Before Griffin could take his next breath, there was a scimitar at his throat and a dagger pressed to his kidney. "You would do well to forget *my* little bird. She has chosen her place for reasons of her own. She cannot make any decision under your watchfulness. I do not like you, English. Stay away for the time being."

"I'll not let this rest."

Amir removed the scimitar, scowling at him. He tucked the blade into the sash at his waist. "Stay away from the palace, English. It is forever closed to you. Should you disobey me, I will not be so forgiving. You will not leave unless you can carry your innards with you." Then he turned and motioned half the guards out of the room; three of them encircled the prince.

Amir walked to Rothburn's desk, pulling out something from his shirt.

The letter Peters had penned, and then came the

green emerald, winking at him in mockery as the prince placed it on the mahogany surface next to the white parchment. The man who'd helped him escape the harem with Jinan had, indeed, been found out.

He did not betray his anger by staring at the jewel. He focused on Amir.

Could there be a solution to this? Amir's guards sorely outnumbered him, so he could not take back Jinan by force. He could be persistent, though. The fight for her would not end here.

He'd follow their entourage out to the docks. Perhaps if she saw him again, she'd stay. Racing to the garden entrance, he took a right to the stables. Odin, his Arabian, was housed here. His horse had a sixth sense about Griffin. A whinny and kick at the stall door could be heard before Griffin came into view. The stablehand stood at the stable entrace, face white in what Griffin could only describe as fear.

"My lord. Peters is on his way with help."

"I can't wait, Gian. Ready Odin and be hasty about it." The boy went off to retrieve his saddle, and Griffin walked toward Odin. "Good day to you, old fellow. Do you feel like a race to the docks?" He rubbed the fine white stripe between the animal's eyes, the only other color on Odin's black coat. Odin bobbed his head in eagerness.

Once the horse was saddled and mounted, Griffin urged Odin onward. Jinan would not escape him so easily.

He traveled at a safe distance behind the entourage traveling with Jinan. The prince must have hired every horse at the lodging inns near the docks. They made a colorful sight racing in their foreign gear toward their ship. Had the road been wide enough, Griffin was sure they would have ridden in war formation. Not that they needed to present more of a threat. Lords, ladies, and people running errands about town fled at the murderous sound of clomping hooves. Griffin remained on their tail. The prince had to know he followed, but apparently he found him unthreatening for no one tried to stop his progress.

Jinan sat behind Amir, her orange silk skirts and scarves flowing behind her, and a scrap of material tied about the lower part of her face.

At the dock, Amir turned his horse, looking for all the world like a sheik stealing his virgin bride. Griffin slowed his horse to a canter, his jaw clenched as he walked his horse toward the enemy, for surely that was what the man was.

Jinan belonged here with Griffin. What did she think to accomplish by staying with Amir? Amir could not give her the freedom he could. She could be Jinan and not some whore playing a tune for the next patron to afford her favors. No, she would be free to express herself as she wished.

Her dark eyes didn't meet his, but he wasn't so far away that he couldn't see that they were still flooded with tears.

Amir's hand rose, motioning for the royal guard to fan out. Griffin wasn't such a fool as not to understand the meaning behind this. Still he pushed Odin forward, ignoring the scowl on Amir's face and the crowd on the dock, whose attention they had captured.

"Jinan," he said, hoping she could hear the pleading in his tone. "Don't leave what I have to offer you. I know you do not want to go back."

His only response was for her to turn her gaze away. A eunuch—damn it, it was the same man he'd bribed—helped her from the back of Amir's horse and urged her up the plank. He'd been bloody well duped. The man was not dead. It didn't make sense. Amir had let him escape. But why?

Half the eunuchs dismounted, while one took the reins of the horses to return them from whence they came.

He met the prince's gaze, the question clear in his eyes. If he'd allowed Griffin to escape with Jinan, why had he come for her now and refused negotiation?

Odin, sensing his agitation in the squeeze of Griffin's thighs, stepped forward. Like the synced rings of the Saracens' spellbinding bell dance, scimitars were slid from sheaths as the last fall of Odin's hoof hit the cobblestone. Griffin reined him in.

"If you are smart, you will stop where you are, my lord."

Such formalities from a man who, not a half hour ago, had threatened to gut him.

"Bey Amir, I implore you to do the right thing."

"Never fear, good man"—Amir dismounted with fluid grace, a man born to the saddle—"I am."

Turning, Amir walked away as three guards stayed mounted, scimitars still threatening Griffin if he should move toward the prince. Griffin was not so foolish as to move forward, nor foolish enough to leave. There was hope still, he thought, as he saw her standing at the stern, face masked and impossible to read. She watched him intently, though, ensnaring him with those brown eyes of hers.

The guards finally dismounted, their backs to the ship as they watched him with weariness. Did they think an unarmed man would attempt to overthrow them?

In the next moment, the plank was gone, the boat steering out of dock. How long did he stand there? Jinan pressed her fingers to her lips, then raised them in farewell. He could see the dots of henna from her palm down to her wrist and forearm. Her palms came together, and she bowed her head to him for long minutes.

When she rose, she turned, the wind catching the silk of her scarves and leaving a shimmering fiery trail in her wake.

Then she was gone.

CHAPTER SIXTEEN

Love Lost

"Peters." Rothburn nodded at his friend's arrival.

"You look like you're about to stand before the executioner."

"I thank you for your honesty. What are you here for? Good news, I hope."

"Afraid not. Amir refuses to hear your suit once again. Here"—he placed a crinkled but sealed envelope on the desk, addressed to "The Most Honorable, the Marquess of Rothburn"—"read his demands for yourself. I'm sure he's not written more than he relayed, most direct, to me."

"What did he say when you went to the palace?" He fingered the gilt edge of the paper.

"I think he's reiterated it in the letter. I'm sure he thought I'd not relay the full message to you in person."

"I offered him a fair price. More than fair." He tightened his hold, angry at Amir's refusal to cooperate.

"He insisted that she was not for sale."

His jaw clenched. "I can't see why not."

"Can't you? I say, Rothburn, it's obvious he adores her."

"So do I!" he shouted. Clamping his mouth shut, he

brushed his hand through his already disheveled hair. He pressed out the crinkled letter, and read:

Dear Lord Rothburn,

Your man of affairs is most relentless and resilient to my continued objections. He's sought out Mr. Chisholm and now he has the impudence to come directly to me. Leave off with this mad pursuit of yours. I assure you, your man will not live to bring you another letter if you disobey my direct order. Jinan is mine. She has always been mine. You make her life more difficult if you pursue her this way. You have the other patrons most curious. It seems gossip has escaped of how you abducted one of my lovely girls. She will not be safe if you continue with this foolhardiness. Let her go—she was never yours to release, yet I ask in benevolence, this once, to let her go. No good can come of your maddening persistence.

Humbly yours, Prince Amir Yussuf

Rothburn crumpled up the letter and tossed it toward the fireplace. It rolled to the poker just short of where logs would burn. "Damn that insufferable oaf of a heathen." He picked up his tumbler, half filled with brandy, and threw it in the fireplace, too.

"Yes, well, your cursing is lost on me. Listen to me, Rothburn. It's time to move on, and as your friend, I'm telling you, you must stop this pursuit. You've neglected the business and your duties to your title."

"It's not easily forgotten. If I wasn't titled I wouldn't have this problem right now. I won't let her go again." His hand smacked hard against the surface of his mahogany desk. *And if I can't have her, I want no other.* Yet he couldn't put voice to those words; to say it aloud seemed too final.

"Good God, man! You'll end up dead or tossed into one of their damned cellars if you continue with this."

Griffin pushed all the paperwork on his desk out of his way, not caring that half of it landed on the floor. "This can't be the end of it."

"It is—"

"I don't want it finished. I know I cannot make it to the island and survive entering the palace. Stop your lectures, Peters. You're only angering me more."

"I hope you aren't planning anything drastic or foolhardy."

Rothburn pushed his chair back; it toppled over in his haste to get up. He scooted out from behind the desk, shoved his fists in his pockets, and started for the open study door. He'd had enough of lecturing. He'd had enough of life in general. Pausing at the threshold, he turned to Peters. "Close up the house. You leave for Florence in two days."

He felt consumed. By her.

Every goddamned waking moment.

"What of you, Rothburn?"

"It's not your place to question me."

"Someone has to if you are planning something unwise."

"It is unwise because you don't understand why I'm going to do this."

"Don't go back to the palace."

"You have no say in the matter."

It was *her* in his head, in his heart, in his goddamned thoughts. It never stopped. It would never stop. There was only one solution left.

* * *

Rothburn refused to tug at his cravat. It was damnably hot today. Sweat trickled down his temple, down his back, from his underarms. The man sitting across from him didn't have so much as a hair misplaced by the heat swamping the island.

"I advised you not to come," he said.

"Yet you've proved your previous words false by letting me pass the threshold of your home without maiming me."

"This is true, English." He waved to a slave holding a pitcher of cool liquid. Two glasses were poured. Rothburn did not take his.

"I assume you will hear me out on the negotiations."

"Listen, yes; accept, probably not," he responded, taking a deep drink of the water.

"You cannot offer her more than I can. I promised to keep her safe, to give her the life she was always deserving of."

"What of the boy?" Amir questioned.

"I've promised her son a life with us, away from the depravities of this place." It did not hurt to give the truth in this. Surely Amir understood that this place was no better than any other whorehouse catering to the wealthy around the world.

"You come here to negotiate, and while hoping I will listen to what you say, you insult me."

"It is the truth of the matter. I'll not sugarcoat anything for you. You've allowed me to come this far, so I know you want to hear my offer. Otherwise you would have had me gutted the moment I stepped from the safety of my boat."

Amir only raised a brow. Perhaps it was not a good idea to give the man any ideas that would mean his demise. "What more can you offer her? I've given her a life that she can live without shame. A life where her child is protected from the evils in this world."

"You have turned her into a prostitute, forced to sell her favors to the highest bidder. This is not the life a woman would choose for herself."

"Are you so sure of that?"

"Yes."

"I assume you know her. Knew her before the auction."

It was not a question, but an observation, so he did not answer the prince. "While I respect your wish to keep your property, especially after the way I relieved you of her, I am not a man you want to cross."

"You are not in a position to threaten me. I hold what you deem most precious. It would be a shame should something happen to her because of your own foolishness."

"If so much as a hair is pulled from her head, I'll set a legion of mercenaries your way."

"You are a worthy opponent, Lord Rothburn."

"I'm glad you think so."

Amir stood; Griffin followed suit. "I will think on this. You are not a thorn easily plucked and so I must think carefully on your proper extraction." Interestingly put. "Of course, you are invited to stay in the gentlemen's quarters in the meantime. I will send a note to you once we've talked."

Griffin bowed. "You will understand if I stay aboard my ship till you've come to some sort of decision."

Six hours later, a missive did come to his clipper. It read simply: "Fifty thousand pounds, and one month. Leave my shores and have arrangements made. I do not wish to see you again. A.Y."

He had a feeling Amir was a man of his word. So he had the captain raise the sails and did as he was bid for the first time in his life. A month wasn't so long to wait.

CHAPTER SEVENTEEN

Home . . . Condemnation

"Little bird."

Jinan glanced up at Amir. Arms sturdily crossed and one dark brow raised, he stood in the arched entry of her room. He wanted a moment alone with her, but she wasn't ready to face him alone; she hadn't been since they'd come back to the palace.

"The girls say you haven't been eating."

"Amir." She looked back down to the children's fairy-tale book about princes and princesses who got their happily-ever-afters. Jonathan was sounding out some simple English words with her, showing his growth every day in his learning.

He looked up at Amir, a smile lighting his face and his eyes.

Amir smiled back, but did not come forward. "Let Reema take the boy."

Her head whipped up in alarm. "No."

"He'll be fine," he said calmly, "it's only for a few moments."

It wasn't as though she had a choice. His fingers snapped and Reema came solemnly into the room, head downcast as she took Jonathan's hand and walked him from the room.

She hadn't once been lectured or asked about her time with Rothburn.

She'd seen Amir watching her from time to time, his gaze filled with questions. Questions she didn't want to answer. "Are you here to lecture me? I only ask that you do not talk about *him*." Her voice was harsh. Amir was right, she wasn't herself—not since coming back from Rothburn's.

"I cannot put you on the auction block when you talk like this, Jinan. Do you see the position you've put me in?"

"I apologize." She bowed as if she were the perfect supplicant. In reality, she couldn't look him in the eye. He read her too well and would know soon enough where her heart belonged. That she did not want to be here anymore. She hated her life here, now.

"Are the other girls very mad?" Her voice was small. She'd been cruel to her sisters, often ignoring them when she went about her daily routines. But she couldn't face their questioning gazes, either. They wanted to know why Rothburn had stolen her away.

What he was to her.

Rothburn meant too much to her, that was the answer.

Amir could attest to that after hearing her parting words to her lover.

"If you took but a moment to talk to them, you would know. You have all but forgotten them since you've been back."

Her head snapped up in protest. "I have not. I've done my duty as I was taught."

"You know as well as anyone that if your heart is not in it, it is all for nothing. Your fire and your passion are no longer visible. You walk around here, hanging your head in shame, when you should be happy to be back in the home that has cared for and honored you these last five years."

"I'm sorry, Amir," she said, crawling to him on hands and knees and kissing his feet. "Please forgive me. I will stop my nonsense. I will talk to Laila at first light."

He knelt and grasped her arms to pull her to her knees. "Bowing and scraping before me does not prove the strength and truth of your words."

She didn't know what else to do. This melancholy was unlike her. Not once had she been this miserable since she'd accepted her fate as a harem girl. Why was it so hard to embrace with an open heart again?

Because she'd left her heart in Rothburn's hands, whether she wanted to admit it to herself or not.

"Little bird, what am I to do with you?" His thumb brushed under her eye, swiping the one tear that spilled over. A whole flood more came as if his touch were permission to release her hurt. She buried her face in his shirt, her fists clasping the material so he couldn't let her go.

"Shh, tell me what has you in this state."

"I do not want to be sold again. Release me, Amir. Release me." Finally, she said it. "I—I feel—I can't do it, Amir. Please don't make me stand up there again. I will do anything. Just—just let me stay in the harem without seeing any of the patrons. Let me keep you company, if I must . . . *anything*." She tightened her hold on his shirt. "Do not sell me again. I couldn't bear it. I couldn't survive it."

"Shh"—his hand caressed her hair, a soothing reassurance—"you know I will not let you fly from the coop. Your wings are clipped by my decree, remember?"

He tilted her chin up with his knuckle, forcing her to meet his eyes. She felt the dampness of her tears staining the whole of her face. She probably looked a terrible, unfit mess.

She felt like a terrible, unfit mess.

"Amir, what am I going to do? I can't do this, I just can't."

"Don't you know, little bird?"

"No," she said, bowing her head. She inhaled deeply of his masculine scent. Mumbling into his shirt, she said "I know naught anymore."

"Such sadness from you. Come, we'll walk in the fresh evening air. It will refresh your constitution, or so the English are wont to say."

That got a small smile from her. The dried tears on her face made it feel stiff, though. The tears hadn't been enough to erase the pain she felt with every beat of her heart. She hated herself with every bone-chilling pump of blood through her body. She wanted nothing more than to throw herself at the mercy of Rothburn when she should be thinking of the welfare of her child.

They made their way from her quarters, down the long white hall to the harem garden. The scent of jasmine rushed over her, enclosing her. They walked under a pear tree and onward to the great fountain that lay at the heart of the harem quarters. Nightingales cried their mating song above, their last cry before day's end.

Amir did not fill the peaceful hum around them with nonsensical conversation. He knew she wasn't herself—knew her heart was torn.

"What if I freed you, Jinan?" Quiet condemnation lay in the timbre of those words.

Did he want her to confess her greatest sin? That of falling in love?

"Amir . . ."

"Hmm?"

"You are older—perhaps wiser—than I. Have you ever loved?" she asked.

"Such a question from you, Jinan. I've loved all my girls."

Not the answer she wanted. She'd been born and raised to marry one man, to accept the sexual attentions of one man. Had those traits not been bred into her so strongly she might have understood the freedom of Amir's love.

She pulled him to a stop, wheeled around so she faced him and looked him in the eye, although it was too dark to look upon his bearded face even in the glow of the lanterns. She cupped her hand to his jaw and studied him for as long as he held her gaze.

"Why do you love me?"

He gave her that devilish grin she'd become acquainted with in their first weeks together.

"You doubt me?" he asked with a tilt of his head, moving away from the gentle hold of her hand.

Yes, she doubted he loved her or loved any of the women here. Of course, she could not put voice to those words. She turned away, sliding her hand from his arm, and walked toward the great fountain. Smoothing out the silk wrap tied about her waist, she sat on the edge. Amir made no move to join her so she raised her hand to him, face averted.

"Come, Amir. I won't ask more questions if you do not wish to answer."

"I will answer you. I am just surprised that in all my years on this island not one of my girls has ever asked me such a thing."

"Never? Not even Laila?"

"No. We grew up together and have come to a point of being able to read each other without words."

"Laila has an effect on all of us here. I did not tell you, but without her I never would have felt welcome. She is a good sister."

Silence fell between them again. Amir sat at her side, his finger dipped into the pond to attract the koi to the surface. Their golden backs broke the surface, then retreated to the bleak dark bottom.

"Jinan . . . the only way for you to come out of this state is to stand upon the auction block."

She gave a heavy sigh and closed her eyes as the axe fell upon her dreams, opening her mind to reality.

"It hasn't been a year. You always give us time between auctions."

"This is the only way for you to stop thinking of your Rothburn."

"It's not the way, Amir. You need to let me go, whether you believe it or not."

"I have told you this is not something I'm willing to do."

She bowed her head, threaded her fingers together, and asked the only question left to her . . . "When?"

"Tomorrow."

Her head snapped up. "Amir. It's too soon—"

"No, it's not." He took her face in his hands and his black eyes stared deeply into hers. "You will do this. I am not giving you a choice, *Elena*."

A great sob of distress, of objection, escaped her. "I am not she."

"Then stop this sadness, this dismal moping, Jinan." His voice was harsh. Harsher than she'd ever heard it. He'd always been such an easy man to talk to. Until now.

"I'm sorry," she said pathetically.

"Are you?" His hands tightened to a vise on either side of her face; his mouth lowered to hers, coaxing a reaction to prove her undying servitude. "Are you?"

She couldn't do it, tried without success to pull away, gave a short whimper of objection before his lips met hers. She clenched her mouth tight, and her eyes welled up and flowed in a stream of shame down her face. She closed her eyes, nostrils flaring, and tried to hold back her sobs of heart-wrenching pain.

He shoved her away from him with a growl of frustration. She fell to the side, off the ledge of the fountain, and her knees landed hard in the packed sand. She pulled herself together as quickly as she could, wiped the tears from her face, and bowed to the ground in apology to her master.

She could hear the soft shush of his slippers as he paced.

"You'll stand before the patrons tomorrow. You've no choice in the matter," he shouted, startling her. He never shouted.

She crawled to him again. "Please don't do this to me. I beg of you, Amir."

She clasped onto his ankle and laid her gratitude at his feet in sobbing, salty kisses. He kicked her away as gently as he could, but dislodged her with enough force that her palms landed sharply on a bed of rocks. She would not beg any further for he'd not be so kind a second time.

Keeping her head and body bowed to the ground, she waited for his anger to lessen.

For long moments he said nothing. Then the swish of his feet receded as Amir left her bowing alone in the gardens around her. She didn't know why she was so sad or why she couldn't find it in her to rise. Instead she sobbed into the earth that held her in this world of hell and eternal sadness. Would standing on the auction block wash her heart of love? It had to for her to endure this life again.

The auction was to be a cure for this madness.

She sobbed harder, her body shaking uncontrollably, her fingers digging between the stones that made the walkway here. She felt no pain and desperately wanted to.

Arms came around her. More than one pair. They held her without words, caressing her back, warming her chilled skin where the silk did not cover her. They comforted without questions.

Her sisters.

The women she'd neglected this past month.

How foolish of her to deny the love of her sisters. Had she forgotten so easily that they'd sustained her since she'd first arrived here? Had she forgotten that they'd always made the day more pleasant, more bearable? They gave her reason to go on, to never falter in her life as Jinan.

When her distressed sobs ceased, she was led to her room. She paid no heed; she cared not about the material things surrounding her. Someone stripped off her outer skirts and placed a light blanket over her. She stared at nothing in particular—unable to close her eyes, unable to sleep even though her body was so worn out.

One sister climbed in behind her and wrapped a comforting arm about her middle and brushed her fingers through Jinan's hair.

Still she did not close her eyes. "I can't—"

"Shh. I know, sister. Sleep. We will work it out tomorrow."

"It'll be too late, Laila."

"No, it will not. Sleep or you'll be in no state to defend yourself, little sister."

Jinan was too tired even to cry. Simply put, she was too worn down. Tears silently slipped down the side of her face, running down her cheeks onto the pillow.

"Why can't I do this, Laila? Why?"

"Don't worry on it now. I'll talk to Amir in the morning. Just sleep."

"I can't find myself again. Do you understand that?"

"I know what you must feel. You loved him, didn't you? Is that why he took you away?"

"Yes. He loves me."

"You cannot always trust a man's words."

"He did not need to speak for me to know the truth and depth of his emotions."

Laila gave a soft chuckle. "It is always the quiet ones we must be careful of."

"I knew him, Laila. From before . . ."

"Ah, you see, this makes sense to me now."

"I don't think it does. I never aspired to marry him. He was so far above my station and rank. Now more so—"

"Let go, Jinan. It does you no good to hold on to this past. You cannot have a future with him. You should understand this more than most, hmmm? This is your life, little sister. This is our life."

She curled into a ball to ease the pains building in her stomach from all the crying. Laila wrapped herself around her back, attempting to comfort her.

"I know. I'm trying to forget . . ." She sobbed again. "I'm trying so hard to forget."

But how did one forget her first love? Her only love? Forget the person who captured your heart and made you want so much more?

"My eyes are red and swollen."

"Maram has gone to get cold water. It will help. You must trust me in this."

"Look at me, Laila. I look the mess I feel inside."

"Trust yourself. You will get through this night."

Jinan stared at her sister in the looking glass. It did no good to argue. Amir had come down after morning prayer to make sure she knew her duty. She was not foolish enough to think she could have any life aside from this. There was no choice other than the one Amir had given her. It was his will that she be sold on the auction block.

She'd given him a succinct nod, and gone on to the bathing house for the remainder of the morning. Maram had threaded the hairs that had shown themselves in the last few weeks of neglecting her body. She felt a new woman . . . almost.

Almost.

Part of her was missing. A big part. She felt like an empty, pitiful . . . soulless husk.

Hopefully, in time, she would forget Rothburn. As unlikely as it seemed now, she could only hope time and distance would have mercy on her battered heart. Laila pulled up some curls and pinned them around the bauble that held the veil.

Forever hidden behind the veil she would remain.

What she needed to tell herself was that Rothburn had made this life worse for her. If not for him, she'd have no qualms about her place in the palace, or of her duties as a harem girl.

"Who is scheduled for the auction tonight?" Normal talk would help her focus on the task at hand.

"Amir said some members of the Russian embassy, Villieux and his lot, Asbury, I imagine. He said something about it being a small affair tonight with all the high bidders. All here for your charms, I believe. Don't look at me like that. I am telling you the truth so you will be better prepared. I think Amir is angry with himself for having let you slip away. He was livid when you escaped from the palace."

"I had no choice in the matter."

"I never said you did. But he still adores you, Jinan. Do you not see that?"

"If he adored me, he'd do as I begged him last night."

Laila raised one brow in question. "Do you really think he would let Rothburn keep his talons in you for the rest of your days here? He wants you to forget. This is the only way he knows to ensure you forget your time with that man. A man you obviously care for deeply, more so than your own master."

Put that way, it started to make more sense. Amir was angry she didn't hold him in as high a regard. How could he expect such a thing when he never gave her more than the security of this home? Laila pulled the laces closed at the back of her vest. The red and gold brocade cinched under her breasts, lifting them, putting them out on display for her observers. She sighed in disgust at the sight, and her resignation did not go unnoticed by Laila.

"It won't be so bad. There are no cruel masters here tonight."

"I feel ill with the thought of fucking with any of them."

Laila clucked her tongue at the use of so strong and foul a word. "Think of your Rothburn if you must, or even Amir. You know it's worked well for me when I've gotten a lord I do not find any attraction in."

"I doubt that will help me tonight." She lifted the diamond-and-ruby-studded hairpins for Laila to take. "Will you put these through the veil loops, please?"

"Of course. These are new? A gift from Amir, perhaps?"

Jinan nodded. "I think he feels guilty."

Laila chuckled and pulled the veil up around Jinan's face. "That would not surprise me. He hates to disappoint us." The pins slid through her hair, holding the yellow silk veil in place. Small golden bells lined the bottom, the weight keeping the veil in place like a yoke about her neck.

"Turn. We'll line your eyes now." Laila stuck the black kohl stick in the flame of the candle set beside her. Lifting it to her mouth, she blew on it to take the edge off the heat, then pulled Jinan's eye out from the corner, drawing a line thick enough to cover her upper and lower lash lines.

She closed her eyes, allowing Laila to fan her hand over the kohl. Closing her eyes was a mistake. She could only see Rothburn in her mind—it was such a strong, clear image. She was a coward not to have asked for her freedom when Amir had first taken her from Rothburn's villa.

Laila's hands stopped fanning and Jinan opened her eyes. Her friend stared back at her, worry evident in the depths of her brown eyes. Laila cupped her cheek. "You will be fine. Once you get through this, it'll all start to feel normal."

Jinan shut her eyes again so she didn't cry away all the black lining that gave her the damnable sham Turkish look.

"You can do this, sister." Laila used her calming tone, but it did nothing to soothe her. Her palms were sticky with sweat; they hadn't had time to henna them. Her heart beat erratically against the wall of her chest, *thumpity-thump-thump-thump. Thump.* And then it started all over again. It raced for no other reason than dread.

Laila took her hands and pulled her to her feet. She

fussed with the red and yellow skirt. She would remain dressed, mingle with her sisters or on Amir's arm, and then be stripped and placed on the auction block like some sacrificial lamb. What she would sacrifice was her sanity if she continued in this vein. But she had no other choice.

With her mind occupied, she'd forgotten the main reason she was here. Why it could be no other way for her.

This was not only about her life. Without this opportunity or the generosity of Amir, her son had no future.

She could never forget that.

Taking a deep breath, she squeezed Laila's hands in her own, then gave her friend a great hug. "I'm well enough to go on. Let us go before my nerves fail me entirely."

I can do this . . . I can. *God, give me strength to sell my body to another. After all the love I've known and lost. Give me strength.*

"Jinan, it's good to see you grace our presence again. Such a lovely sight you make, *ma petite*." This from Villieux, not currently wrapped around another harem girl. So strange that he came to talk to her. He must be planning on bidding. It had been so long since she'd been up for auction that the men seemed most eager to chat with her.

As Amir stood at her side, she leaned toward the young count and, because it was expected of her, whispered in French, "It is good to have the grace of your presence, Master Villieux." He turned, looking her directly in the eye, and smiled. Definitely, he planned to bid. She swallowed back the lump in her throat and held his gaze.

The heat of Amir's hand was a constant presence at

the base of her spine. A tangible reminder that she should not stray from his side.

Not that she planned on it. At least not this night. Her nerves were on edge at the prospect of giving her body to another man.

The dancers entered the room as the musicians pounded out an enticing beat. They fanned out in a rainbow of rich color; their brown skin gleamed under the weight of gold chains and jewels. Amir grasped her hips, walking her backward, away from the patrons and to the farthest corner of the room.

"Jinan," he said for her ears alone. "Do you feel more yourself? You look better today than you did when we last spoke."

There was no permissible response because she did not feel herself. She pushed back into the evidence of his desire. She arched her back and threw her head over her shoulder. "Do what you will." She could commit her body, but not her heart, to this. If he wanted to display her carnal wares to the lords, so be it.

His hand spanned between her breasts. Amir was well versed in teasing. It would be so much easier to forget her past if he would take her. Instead, he wished to arouse her senses and her emotions. Though she would never betray her love—there was only one person that belonged to.

"Why do you do this, Amir? Let me go. Let the other lords view me before I am stripped down and studied upon the auction block."

"As you wish."

His hand fell away then. She turned and faced him, studying his unchanged expression. The man never showed any true feelings toward his girls. He taught them the trade he sold them for, lavished them with pretty baubles, but never had she seen love reflected in his eyes. Why she expected to see it now, she wasn't sure. Nothing ever changed here. Forever she'd remain his whore. Forever in his debt because of his generosity in the rearing of her child. She was a fool to have thought otherwise.

A bloody fool for falling in love with Rothburn.

She was supposed to protect her heart, not hand it to a man on a silver platter along with a knife for him to do his will.

She looked away from the intense gaze she could not read, and walked over to Laila. Another hour. Then she'd be another man's whore.

Another man's plaything.

What did it matter? This was her life and would forever be.

Laila stood at her side, collecting the scarves that were pulled off her body. Wearing her veil, and a series of gold filigree bands about her wrists and ankles, she stepped up on the podium.

Mr. Chisholm tapped the side of the dais and called attention to her voluptuous form so wantonly displayed. The men were eager to assess her after so long and milled closer. The fantasy was clear in their eyes. Amir had brought only those who would bid this eve.

"Gentlemen," he began, "it is my greatest pleasure to sell off the beautiful Jinan for your lavish attentions. I know many of you have been waiting to steal her away from her previous lord for some months now. Never fear. Here she stands, eager to please the next gentleman to win her favors." He strategically paused in his speech, letting it sink in that she was back in the game, and it was anyone's win. "I do not think it fortuitous to start bidding at five thousand."

She watched two patrons step back into the shadows. They might have money to spend but would not play for stakes so high. Among the faces standing close, she saw Villieux smirking, Asbury leering, staunch Montgomery all red-faced with bemusement, the gangly Chekhov sneering at the others, and a number of other familiar and unfamiliar men.

"Five and a half," from the rogue Villieux.

"Six."

"Eight." Asbury testing his luck again. She always went out of *his* price range. She didn't understand why he bid. Rivalry, that's what she'd forgotten. It was always about the rivalry between him and Villieux.

"Ten."

"Fourteen." Villieux really wanted her.

"Eighteen," the Russian yelled.

"Twenty."

"Twenty-two."

"Twenty-four."

For the first time in all his visits, the Russian had bid this high. She was sure Villieux had just met a worthy adversary. He scowled at the count. The count offered a tight smile in return.

The silence stretched; there appeared to be no other bidders—she hoped the price pleased Amir. She wished she had something to lean on for she felt rather faint now. Any minute, Villieux would take her down from the podium and test her wares. He was one for flaunting his prize, too. He'd probably fuck her right in the middle of the floor on the lion-skin rug.

She swallowed back the bad taste in her mouth convulsively. If she didn't faint, she might just throw up right here and disgrace herself. Disgrace Amir. She bit the inside of her cheeks and closed her eyes to find a calm equilibrium. She did not want to dishonor herself or her master. Not on her first auction day after what felt like a lifetime. If she faltered now, Amir might not hesitate to take away her privileges, take away everything he'd offered to her son.

She looked Villieux in the eye. That glint of satisfaction might have filled her with anticipation in the past, but it only sickened and repulsed her now. It appalled her that for the first time in five years she was looked upon, so obviously, as a whore. Silly of it to bother her. It was what she was and had been all these years.

She looked to Laila, grasping her sister's outstretched hand.

Someone cleared his throat, and a strong voice rang out amid the excited murmurs and congratulations to Villieux.

"Thirty thousand."

Jinan paused, hand clasped tight in Laila's. Her sister squeezed back.

What did this mean?

She looked to her sister, but she also looked puzzled. Mr. Chisholm observed the melee of men, mouth flapping as though he'd catch his voice back that way.

Not once had *he* ever bid on the harem girls.

Why would he?

He owned them all.

It didn't look as though she, her sisters, and Mr. Chisholm were the only ones confused by the proceedings. Indeed, no. Even the patrons seemed stupefied by the turn in bidding. Did they wait for him to withdraw his bid? To tell them all it was a good jest? But Amir was not the type to joke about money, about his women.

"Mr. Chisholm," he said, "have the guards bring Jinan to my private quarters."

She gulped again. His private quarters? He meant to bring her outside of the harem quarters. Not one of the girls had ever been to that part of the palace.

Did he plan to expel her? Why had he bid on her?

What would he do? Have her killed? As silly as the notion had seemed months ago when she'd said that very thing to Rothburn, more and more she was worried those words would come true.

Three eunuchs came forward, hands threateningly close to the handle of their scimitars. Perhaps they were as confused as she.

Amir clapped his hands, and she was whisked from the dais toward the one door she never had had the desire to leave through. The eunuchs did not gather her scarves before leading her onward. Proceedings resumed, and the dancers ran into the room—she could hear the sounds of their *kuchi* bells—to start a new number. The hush that had fallen at the conclusion of her auction returned to the noisy affair it had been before the bidding.

Looking over her shoulder, she saw Laila staring back, a sad expression on her face. Laila raised her hand in what could only be construed as farewell, tears fresh in her eyes. An urge to run back to her sister and hold on to her one last time washed through her system. She almost did, but Ahmed, the elder of the eunuchs, propelled her forward through the archway.

The dip in the bed told her she was no longer alone and her body stirred to bitter awareness.

She'd climbed under the covers of the great four-poster some hours ago. Amir did not join her immediately after the auction. She didn't even know if she'd see him again. Nothing made sense. A slave had brought in fresh water and instructed her to wash herself, which she did and stripped her veil off, leaving only her jewelry. Then after a nerve-racking hour and no sign of her master, she'd climbed into the bed.

The sheet she slept under swooshed away from her

overheated body. Goose bumps rose, her nipples tightened to peaks.

It was dark, the moon only a quarter full outside so there was very little light to see by.

She sat up and put her palm to Amir's bearded face.

"Amir," she whispered, "why have you done this?"

He covered her hand with his own and sighed. "You mean you have not figured it out? It should be obvious, little bird."

"Please, Amir. No games between us. You've scared me this eve. I no more know what to expect now than when you rescued me from Rothburn."

"Rescued you, did I? I thought you seemed rather sad to see me."

"How could you say such a thing? You make me for a harlot indulging in Rothburn while you were so far away. Do not twist the meaning of my words. You brought me home. I knew you would come for me, I trusted you to come. You never disappoint me."

He didn't respond. One hand was busy drawing an invisible pattern on her bent knee.

"I am only a means to an end for Jonathan."

"Please don't say such things. You are the only father my boy knows. Did you become his father figure to please me? We both know the truth of that. You did it of your own will because you adore him as much as I. I am yours to do with as you wish. You know how much I have always tried to please you."

"I do know your loyalty, but it is because I hold all the cards in this arrangement."

"Tell me what you want of me, Amir. You speak in riddles tonight."

He kissed her forehead before he answered, "Do you know, you were always my favorite?"

"Am I no longer?" Did this mean he would have her killed? Expelled?

"You are spoken for now." His voice seemed resigned.

Her eyes filled with tears. What did he plan?

"Why did you bid on me, Amir?" Her hand reached out, and stroked his linen-covered arm.

"It is a parting gift of your worth. Actually, to me you are worth a great deal more."

"I don't understand."

"I know you are more intelligent than this."

"Do not mock me. My nerves are on edge. I was afraid you planned—"

He silenced her with the press of his lips. Both his hands cupped her face as he deepened the caress of their mouths, his tongue making its way between. On impulse she tried to pull away, but he held her fast and growled his disapproval.

The tips of his fingers pressed into the back of her head painfully. Then he pushed her away, toppling her over on the bed. Jinan caught herself with her hands underneath. Did he plan to treat her with cruelty? In all their years together, she'd never feared him or been unsure of his treatment toward her. For the first time in more than five years, she was unsure and afraid of him.

He rose from the bed, pacing in front of her, the tread of his slippered feet soft and constant on the carpet underfoot. She did not dare move. She still felt unsure.

"Your wings are no longer clipped."

She turned her head to the side and stared at his form through the fall of her hair.

"Do you mean I am free?" she asked in a small voice.

"Exactly that."

"And my son?"

"Yours."

"So, you are throwing me out of the palace. I must find my own way now? After my obedience and respect to you?"

"Little bird." His voice was gentle, soothing the tense falcon. "When your heart was no longer mine for safe-keeping, I knew I had to let you go."

Her tears did fall now, not in sadness but in guilt.

"Amir . . . I'm so sorry." She crawled off the bed and threw her arms around his shoulders. "Don't throw me away. I will do better."

"It is not you who must do better. You leave at first light, Jinan. You won't see your sisters again." He yanked off the coin bracelets around her ankles. "I'm selfish enough to take that away from you. I don't want them to know what's become of you." His voice sounded strange, edged with emotion.

She cried harder. Just like that, he was tossing her away. Because he couldn't have her, she was no longer welcome here. Her sisters would be torn by her absence. It broke her heart to realize she would be without her family. She pulled herself out of his arms and stood tall.

"Where will you send us?"

He stepped forward, not willing to let her put a wall up between them, and wrapped his arms tight about her, squeezing the air from her lungs. "Home. You are going home, Jinan."

CHAPTER EIGHTEEN

Found

One Week Later

She turned her horse into the roundabout of the dirt drive-through. Amir's head eunuch had the other guards drop her trunks and then with a nod of farewell, he led them off.

Jonathan sat in her lap, looking around him in wonder. He'd never been out of the palace nor off the island, which she later found out was part of Greece, just off the coast of Corfu. Familiar yet not.

There had been questions throughout their entire trip. He was a curious little fellow, but she didn't mind.

"Mama . . . who lives here?"

"Lord Rothburn, my sweet." The shutters were closed, and the place seemed quiet. Was she too late? "But I do not know if he is in residence."

"Look, Mama, ducks! Can I go play with them?"

She slid off the side of the horse, her feet wobbling a bit in her heels as she lifted her son from the saddle and to the ground. "Off with you then."

He ran after the ducks, which fled at the sight of her

exuberant child. She wiped the sweat from her forehead; she was not accustomed to English clothes. Even though she had skipped the heavy binding layers beneath because it made her ill to lace the contraptions to fashionable tightness. These English clothes made her feel as though she wore too much. She still felt seasick. As with any boat ride, she'd been dreadfully nauseous on the trip here. At least she'd been given some horrible-tasting liquid that kept her sickness at bay. Once they'd docked, there had been no time to regain her strength before Ahmed had purchased horses for them to finish the journey. Well, rather, to finish *her* journey.

She left the horse standing in the drive, reins tossed over the saddle, and walked up to the front door, keeping an eye on her son the whole while.

The door swung open, and the butler seemed at a loss for words.

"Madam," he finally choked out.

"*Salaam*," she said before she could bite her tongue. Old habits were hard to quell.

"Rothburn is not here. The staff moved on early this morning."

"Oh, I see." Not exactly what she wanted to hear. Now what should she do? She had money enough to live wherever she chose. What had she hoped . . . that Rothburn would wait for her? It had been weeks since she saw him last. Anything could have happened in that time.

And a smart man would move on.

"You are English?" He seemed shocked at hearing English. Perhaps English was not common on this Italian coastal town.

"Yes." She bowed her head to hide the tears that formed. No sense in losing her head in front of the servants. "Apologies," she said, turning away from the door. Better not to shame herself.

So she was alone. It wasn't the first time she'd had to find her own way in life. There had always been a man leading or directing, but she could do this on her own. She had the means to do so.

"Madam," the man called out, "his lordship left a note for his solicitor. That's the reason I stayed on. Shall I give you direction? He rides for Florence, having left a few days ago. You were to meet him there, not here."

She wiped one gloved hand through her tears, and turned. She was to meet him there? Whatever did the man mean?

She said, "Your direction would be most welcome. I know this is a rather strange request, but is there a maid in the house I might employ as a travel companion?" Her English rolled off her tongue with more force than it should, but at least she wasn't speaking any *heathen* language for this good man. Not that she was ashamed . . . never would she be.

She motioned toward her son.

The butler stepped out of the doorway and followed the sound of laughter coming in the direction her son ran, chasing after quick, waddling ducks. He did not say anything, only scrunched his brow together before offering, "Come in and freshen up, madam."

She returned his smile. It was good to see a friendly face after having been in the company of eunuchs who all but ignored her these past few days.

"Do I know you, good sir?"

"No. But I do know you. One could say, you've been a thorn in my side."

"How so?" She halted her steps, not sure if she should go forward, or head back toward the docks where she could hire a carriage and horsemen for the journey north.

"You mean a great deal to his lordship." The man bowed. "Allow me to introduce myself, my manners have flown the coop with your miraculous arrival. I am Peters, Rothburn's man of affairs, and his closest friend."

"Come in, Peters. I see you've made ideal time."

His friend walked hesitantly into the room and sat in the high-backed chair across from him at the hearth.

"I arrived only moments ago. How long have you been here?"

"A couple of days. Didn't stop much except to switch out horses." He swilled the brandy in his hand. "Help yourself, man."

Peters raised his hand in objection. "Too early for me, friend."

"You seem rather distracted. Was the trip here not as smooth as you planned?" He grinned. "You always were a horrendous rider. Tell me you kept your seat all the way here. Mind you, you are looking a little pained."

Peters coughed into his hand and looked away. "I took the carriage. There is someone here to see you."

"You didn't bring Asbury with you? The bloody fool wanted to ship out his latest pickings from India. I told him I wouldn't do it. He's part of the problems brewing in the East." Griffin stood, clunking his glass down on the walnut side table.

"Come on then. Might as well send him on to Hayworth—that fool doesn't care about the Eastern demise. He'll look forward to sending the man's opiates through the East."

Peters was at his side in moments. "There is a lady

here to see you. An—an English lady. She was looking for you at the Cordenelli estate."

Griffin stopped in mid-thought. She'd gone to Brindisi, not Florence. "Which room did you situate her in?"

"She's in the music room. I didn't know where else to put her."

He clapped his friend on the back and hurried off.

The plunk of piano keys—sorely out of tune—met him halfway down the hall. A jovial gigue. Mozart, if he wasn't mistaken. Standing outside the music room, he pushed the door open a crack to see his fair lady. Her back was to him and he saw her dark hair heavily coiled about her head, a few wisps escaping and tickling the small amount of exposed skin beneath her sprigged muslin day dress. A child sat next to her, dressed in white short pants and shirt. His hair was as dark as his mother's.

The boy plunked away next to her; her tune was light, lively, his was a silly child's parody of the great composer. Neither heard the creak of the door as it swung open enough for him to step into the room. The mother bent her head down to her son, laughing in his ear, speaking in a singsong voice . . . speaking . . .

Turkish. It was indeed Jinan. The day had finally come.

The tumbler slipped from his suddenly slack hand and crashed to the hardwood. It bounced without breaking, then rolled lamely on its side, spinning through the spilled brandy. The boy jumped down from the bench and stood in front of his mother, fists clenched at his side as though he could ward off any wrongdoers. Green eyes stared back at him in shock—he was the very image of his mother, except for the eyes.

Her fingers froze above the keys, her head tilted, neck prettily turned to expose its long elegant line.

"Jinan."

She slid from the bench and stood. She took her time shaking out her skirts before she turned and faced him, head bowed.

"Jinan." He swallowed hard, at an utter loss for words.

"Mama." The boy glanced up at his mother, tugging at her English skirts.

She said something too low for Rothburn to make out. Her son turned and gave him an angry look before stepping outside to the verandah, which had an exquisite view of the vineyard below.

"I arrived with your man of affairs. You are shocked to see me?"

"You were to arrive here, with an entourage. Not in Brindisi." He took a step toward her.

She put a hand up between them. Did she not understand that he'd freed her? "I must be quick, Rothburn, as my son does not need to be exposed to indecencies."

"Jinan—"

"I'm free. Amir has given me leave and left me a great sum of money, so that I shall never find myself in dire straits again."

So that bastard hadn't told her the truth. Would Rothburn spoil it for her? Tell her he had paid to have her released?

He had her in his arms before she could say more, hugging her tightly to him. He dropped his face into her hair and inhaled the rose-water scent so familiar to him. "Jinan. My God. I've missed you."

She pushed him away, her skirts bumping into the keys on the piano. He broke apart from her with great reluctance but did not release her hands. Together they stared at their clasped hands. She did not wear the jewels and bracelets he was accustomed to seeing. Massaging her fingers a moment, he raised his hands to capture her face. With a light touching of their lips, he closed his eyes and rubbed their lips together. Nothing more than a need to touch her assailed his body. To hold her for an eternity now would not make up for all their time apart.

"Are you hungry? Can the staff prepare you or your son something to eat?"

"No, we are fine, Rothburn. We stopped at a lodging inn before coming here."

"At least let me call a maid to take your son down to the kitchens. We have a great deal to talk about. He can spend time with the kitchen maid's son and daughter."

"Thank you, that is most welcome. Jonathan is eager to meet boys his own age."

"A very English name." The very name she'd mentioned so long ago in her fevered state.

He rang for the maid, and before they knew it, they were alone.

Jinan walked out onto the verandah, resting her hands on the stone balustrade that wrapped around the terrace. "I don't know where I'm supposed to go from here."

"I realize now that Amir wanted you to have a means to escape me if you chose. He released you at my insistence, and at a price he named."

"You got me out of the harem?"

"Yes. You were supposed to meet me here. I see now that Amir was hoping you'd disappear from both our lives." He stepped behind her and wrapped his arms around her. How badly he just wanted to touch her. Resting his chin atop her head, he said, "Stay here, with me."

"And my son? What of him? Amir was kind enough

to let us go, but I'm at a loss for what to do with myself, let alone him. I've no connections to get him into the schools he should attend. Amir had all that."

He stepped away and turned her around to face him, her derrière resting on the balustrade.

"Tell me who the boy's father is. I know it can't be Amir's, he wouldn't have included the child in the bargain had he been his son."

Her brow furrowed, she seemed puzzled by the question. "I did not intentionally keep that from you. I assumed you'd guess. Jonathan was born in wedlock. He is Lord Shepley's heir."

He felt elated, that was the only way to describe it. She was not bound to Amir, to the harem, to any other man in the world. She was free, and it wasn't he who had given her her freedom from the gilded cage. He might have precipitated it, but she'd done it on her own by coming to him in the end, and she was here now. And he had so many questions he didn't know where to begin.

"How is it that Amir took in your son?"

"I fit the bill. Have you not noticed anything strikingly similar about all the harem girls?"

"I hadn't really noticed them . . . not once I recognized you."

"All the women are taught English. He has a fondness for English women. But more importantly, we all have dark skin to attract foreign lords. Surely that was obvious." She frowned. "It doesn't matter, though."

He lifted her chin with his knuckle. "How did you end up in his clutches?"

"He saved me."

She pulled out of his grasp and stepped around him. Why wouldn't she face him? "Jinan, you don't have to tell me anything if it makes you uncomfortable."

"You don't understand. You must know that this life was not of my choosing. I do not want you to think so poorly of me. It was not a vice I slipped easily into playing." She turned and faced him, a sad, determined look in her gaze. He nodded his understanding. "You see, you could not find out more about my husband because he died at the hands of a wealthy slave handler in Constantinople. He died shortly after he sold me to that man."

Without intending to, he gasped. She snapped her eyes back to his then. Because her husband had given her up so easily, she'd fallen into the worst life imaginable. "How long did this man own you?"

"Not long. Maybe a week. It was so long ago that I don't recall." She shook her head, maybe in an attempt to cleanse her mind of the memories. "I try not to remember it. I was chained there like some vile beast. I was beaten and was handled by so many men, though none ever violated me . . . I was still producing milk."

He walked toward her and pulled her into his arms, even as she tried to push away. "This is making you miserable. I believe everything you've ever told me, Jinan. You do not have to tell me."

She leaned back over his arm and gave him a long assessing look. Did she not believe his words? "There are no more horrors," she said. "Mr. Chisholm found me and made an offer I could not refuse if I agreed to harem life. Amir found my son and purchased him from the slave handler. Jonathan might not be alive today if someone hadn't taken notice of me."

Griffin thumbed the tears off her high cheekbones. "Shh," he said, hoping she was reassured in some way, and then he lowered his lips to where his thumbs had just pressed.

"I'm sorry." Her soft voice whispered out over his Adam's apple.

"You have nothing to be sorry about. I'm just sorry I didn't find you sooner. I should have tried harder to find you. But I didn't. I am the only one who should be sorry."

He pressed feather-light touches of his lips against her damp skin, up into her hairline. "I love you. Do you know that? I've loved you for as long as I can remember."

"Rothburn . . ."

"Say you will stay with me."

"And what of Jonathan?"

"He is yours, Jinan. I wouldn't ask you to part with him after all you've been through to keep him at your side. I never planned to separate you once I finally got you out of the harem. Had I known of your son initially I wouldn't have done what I did."

"I can't go back to England. I can't face the *ton* and the gossip. My husband was not well liked. He did not succeed in making friends. He had a great deal of enemies after his many bouts with unlucky gambling and carousing."

"I won't ask you to return there. Just stay with me here. With your son. I'll do whatever I can to name him my heir if you wish."

"That is not his place."

He put his finger over her lips. "We have the rest of our lives to figure that out. I'd say it's about time you called me Griffin."

Her lips trembled beneath his finger, then tilted up in a smile. "Griff . . . yes, I like this name."

He lowered his mouth to hers, capturing it in a kiss to seal their words. He tasted the plumpness of her lips, not going further, not wanting to stop whatever confessions she still must make to free her of her old life.

When she broke away, they both breathed hard for

air. His fingers were wrapped tightly in the coils of her hair, the pins loosening as he searched them out.

"Say you will stay with me, Jinan. Nothing else matters but that."

"I once thought you above my station, Griffin. Out of my reach. You are not. I know this now."

"Never have you been out of my reach. I'm sorry to have let you down. I'll never stop telling you that."

"I ask two things, as your mistress. Amir has given me provisions . . . I ask this: You must help my son inherit his rightful title because I can never reveal the truth of who I am, and you must remain faithful to me. This last one is a lot for me to ask because you are in need of an heir."

"Jinan . . ."

"You must hear me out. I cannot stay in your shadow and watch you raise a family."

"I do not want to marry another."

Whatever she was about to say was stopped in mid-word. Then, "What of an heir?"

"I have a cousin that will fill the seat just as well as I. Possibly better."

"So you promise me these things?"

"Of course I do. But I never wanted you as my mistress. I want you as my wife."

She pulled from his grasp, staring at him with her arms slack at her sides. "I cannot marry you. Not after everything I've done."

"We will marry. Any children from our union will have a right to my name! I do not care how we came to be together in the end or what hardships you've lived through. Just say you are mine. Please, Jinan."

She clenched her fist over her heart, and he held her hands tight. "Say yes, Jinan. Please say yes, I can't bear to let you go again. We can live here. Move somewhere else . . . anywhere but England, which has only scorned you. Just stay with me."

A gasp of surprise escaped her.

"I love you." And with that she flung herself into his open arms. She squeezed him as tightly as she could, holding him in a great hug. He held her just as tight. So this was it, the start of their life.

They'd found each other after being lost from each other for so long.

This was the beginning of paradise.

Epilogue

One year later

Griffin looked up when a soft knock landed on his study door. Jinan slipped into the room, giving him a pointed look, lips pouting for only a second before she hid it.

He smiled. "Peters, we'll resume this discussion tomorrow."

Peters turned around, seeing Griffin's wife, and bowed on his way out. "Felicitations, my lady."

He watched his sweet wife duck her head, a blush infusing her cheeks and neck. "Thank you, Peters."

She walked toward him and around to where he sat in his desk chair.

Griffin pushed his chair out and pulled her gently down into his lap. He lowered his head and kissed her distended belly. "What brings you here in the middle of the morning?"

"Jonathan went off to the pond with Ceci and Ally. It had me thinking. We're all alone *and* we have the house to ourselves before the baby comes in a few short months." She turned her head to him, pressing a light kiss against his cheek as her fingers pulled his necktie loose.

"If you start that, love, I'm going to keep you in bed for the rest of the day." He groaned into her mouth as her fingers slipped free the buttons of his shirt.

"Maybe I've been a little ill all day, and you need to nurse me in our bedchamber."

"That sounds decidedly delicious. I'm afraid we won't be able to leave this room with any decency now."

Her hand lowered to his raging stiffness. He picked her up, stalking over to the chaise in five quick strides. Setting her down carefully, he went to turn the key in the study doors. He disrobed as he walked back around to his wife, then helped her out of her loose shirt and trousers. "I like that you've pulled out some of your old clothes. So much easier to undress you."

She laughed, and the husky deepness had his cock jerking to attention. "I do not like English clothes when I'm so fattened by your baby. These are more comfortable."

"Mmm, I'm not complaining. Now lean back." He knelt between her open thighs, kissing her naked belly, her heavy, swollen breasts, and sucked the peaked tips into his mouth.

"Griff, I'm so over the moon I might find my crisis this way. Touch me." He lowered his hand to the bare folds of her sex, flicking his thumb over the distended pearl.

It pleased him that she still kept up this particular harem tradition, for he was loath to see the hair grow back—he loved her like this. They'd had to hire a companion who could meet her many needs, but Jinan had taken the woman under her wing, welcoming her like a long-lost sister. The two were damn near inseparable, unless Jinan was with him, of course.

When he looked up, it was to see her head thrown back, biting her plump lower lip, as she moaned something unintelligible. Her fingers dug into his shoulders. He stood and kissed her mouth. "Will you kneel over the bench?"

Her smile was sultry, seductive, and too damned much for his sanity. She pushed off the chaise, kneeling on the pillows he threw down on the floor. She gave him her rear and a look that said, *I dare you,* over her shoulder. He was on her in seconds, his cock slipping into the welcome warmth of her cunt. They both came within a few strokes. He liked how sensitive she was during this time of her pregnancy.

He pulled out of her and sat on his haunches, bringing her down onto his lap.

"Is that what you needed, love?"

"Yes," she said, trying to catch her breath, her breasts heaving in his grasp.

"How come you didn't go down to swim with Jonathan? There aren't any djinn this time of day." He gave a low chuckle as he said it, earning him an elbow in the ribs.

"I really do need you to attend me in bed . . . for the rest of the day, my lord."

"What did I say about the 'my lords,' my lady?"

She slid off his lap; the feel of her wet slit sliding down his thigh inflamed his cock to stand fully erect again. "God, woman, you're killing me."

"I can't help it. It's not as if I expected to have any relations in this state." She faced him on her knees. He didn't like her kneeling on the hard floor, so he gave her a hand up, retrieved her shirt and slipped it over her head.

"I like that you need me, Jinan. I've needed you all

my damned life and felt lost without you. I don't want you to feel that way."

He held the trousers out to her, but she didn't take them. Jinan stepped close enough to place a kiss on his lips, wrapping her arms around his shoulders, her belly a strange, welcome bulge between them.

"I've loved you all my life, Griff. Don't forget that. At least we found each other in the end. Now come to bed and nurse me for the rest of the day. I think the doctor prescribed a good gamahuche to relieve this excess feeling trembling through my veins."

He smiled at his wife, bending down so she could put her legs in her opened trousers. "I do recall something about that in the doctor's orders. Shall I carry you upstairs or are you able to flee before I can pounce again?"

She laughed and raced for the door. He gave her enough time to unlock it before he was hot on her trail. Life really couldn't be better than this. He had the wife he'd always wanted, a son, and another baby on the way. He caught her just as she reached the bedchamber, slipped in behind her, locked the door, and did exactly what the doctor had prescribed.

Turn the page for a sneak peek at

THE SEDUCTION OF HIS WIFE

by
Tiffany Clare

Coming February 2011

From St. Martin's Paperbacks

Richard watched Emma toss pieces of bread into the pond. A gaggle of geese and two pairs of swans swam forward to grab them before they sank to the bottom. A breeze tickled at her hair, lifting it in its cool embrace. She pulled her lace shawl up around her shoulders and looked skyward. He did, too.

Storm clouds were rolling in. Fast. When she stood, the birds honked at her sudden movement and swam away. Emma still hadn't noticed him watching her, standing beside a large birch tree not more than a dozen feet away. Tying her wrapper at her breast, she gathered up the papers she'd been sketching on.

This morning as he'd shaved, he had come to the conclusion that he had a strange notion to court his wife.

When they were younger, she was captivated by his every word. Alarming as that had been for a young man forced to spend company with a childlike girl, that kind of adoration could be used to his advantage. Given time, she'd find him charming again.

Without a doubt, she was the type of woman to come

around once she could call someone a friend. He would make sure he filled that role—he estimated that shouldn't take more than a couple days.

Struggling with her hat, she finally let the wind have it. The straw rim was tugged clear off her head with a violent stroke of the wind and lay wrapped about her neck, still tied by the pink satin ribbon. Head back, she looked to the sky. The sun was quickly disappearing. An electric charge hummed in the air as darkness enshrouded the countryside moments later.

He stepped forward, keeping one hand on the rim of his hat. The wind carried away the words he used to call her attention, so he walked toward her and turned her around to face him. She squealed as he spun her around.

"We need to find shelter!" He had to yell the words so they weren't lost in the howl of the wind.

She turned away with a scowl. Clutching her elbow, he pulled her along the dirt path with him. She yanked free after a few steps.

"Don't you dare pull me around." She glared at him for a long moment before she knelt down to the grass to pick up a pencil she'd dropped.

A crack of thunder sounded in the next instant and a downpour of rain let loose from the heavens. He looked skyward in exasperation. This was not how he wanted to spend his morning. It was at least a half hour walk to the manor in better weather. As it was, the dirt paths would fill with mud and be too slippery for his wife to traverse in her mass of skirts.

Grasping his wife's hand, he turned and yelled over the storm, "Pick up your skirts. We'll make a run for my father's old hunting cottage." She didn't hesitate to follow his lead this time, all her art things tucked against her bosom.

Running up to the front porch of the cottage, he lifted the latch and pushed the door open.

"Why are we stopping here?"

"Because it'll be a mud slide over the paths to the manor. It's the closest shelter from the fishing pond."

She looked at him, obviously piqued. It was an expression he was quickly getting used to seeing. He'd bet his finest cravat pin that she was annoyed that her plan to escape him this morning hadn't been successful.

She untied her shawl and shook some of the water from it in the open doorway. "I suppose we'll only stay long enough to wait out the storm."

She did not enter the cottage.

Taking his hat off, he wiped the water from the top and brim and set it on the worktable to dry.

"Come inside and close the door. I'll start a fire so we can dry out our clothes."

"We won't be here long. The storm will leave as fast as it arrived."

Richard looked beyond the sodden, dripping frame of Emma to the roiling black clouds shot through with flashes of white lightning. It was not going to pass anytime soon. The weather had been building in this direction all morning.

Was his company so detestable? He sighed out his frustration, and ground his teeth together. This attitude of hers was starting to grate on his nerves. She *had* locked him out of her room. Did he really expect her to act warmly toward him?

"While we're here, we can discuss the course of last evening."

She didn't turn to face him as she addressed his question. "I see no reason to discuss anything."

Smiling tightly at her audacity, he threw some peat into the hearth, struck a flint, and then lit the moss.

The wind was picking up outdoors, sweeping away any warmth the fire gave off. "Come inside, Emma. We'll probably be here another hour."

"I certainly hope not."

He clenched his fists at his sides. Her penchant for disdain needed to stop.

"It won't be the end of the world to spend an hour in my company," he snapped.

She twirled around and finally looked at him. It was on the edge of his tongue to say she'd not escape him now and certainly not again this evening, but something held him back. They were stuck with each other for an indeterminate amount of time. He had no plans to spend that time fighting.

Loose strands of wet hair ran over her temple and stuck to the sides of her cheeks. Her lips trembled from the cold and were tinged with a slight blue. She was shivering. Knowing she'd hesitate if he asked her to come closer, he walked toward her. Her eyebrows furrowed at his approach. He reached out and released the first few hidden eyelets on her bodice.

She smacked his hands away. "Stop that this instant."

"You won't do it yourself. You can take off your outer layers to keep from getting a chill."

He released a few more of the tiny hooks before she stepped away from him, her hand covering the swell of her bosom. He raised a brow and shrugged out of his jacket. Turning the wooden chair around, he draped the coat over the back and set it near the fire.

"Pass me your shawl." He held out his hand and waited for the scrap of material.

She didn't object, nor did her eyes meet his again. She stuck her arm out as far as she could—so she wouldn't have to come closer to him, he assumed.

He took the wet mass of lace and spread it out on top of his coat. Of course he didn't stop there. It wouldn't do for his wound to start festering beneath wet, cold layers of material. His vest came off next. His gaze locked with hers for a few seconds, daring her to tell him to stop. She pinched her lips together and gave him her back.

"You can't undress here." Her voice wavered with the statement.

"Why not? I'm not going to sit here soaking wet and cold for God knows how long. I'd rather be dry if you don't mind. It'll take less time to dry if you remove your clothes, too."

There was no mistaking his meaning. Yes, he wanted his wife naked. What sane man wouldn't? He was more than willing to do whatever necessary to warm her, as well. The less they talked, the less they'd argue. And there were a great many things they could do that didn't involve talking.

"Absolutely not!"

He untied his neckcloth. "Why not?"

"I'll not undress for you. To think you'd ask such a thing in the middle of the day when anyone can happen upon us."

"Have you never undressed for a lover during the day?" Stupid of him to ask. He didn't want to know the answer to that. The very idea of someone encroaching on his territory—on his wife—set his teeth on edge.

"How dare you assume such a thing! I have no lover, Richard. Nor have I ever had the need for one. Why do you speak so vulgarly to me?" She wasn't angry. She was upset. Damn it. "It shouldn't surprise me that you think so little of me."

How was it possible for anyone not to take a lover after twelve years? Hell, the rumor mill had made it all the way to the East with stories of his wife and the duke. There must be some truth to the whispers. Guilt for his many transgressions rose in his gut and put a bad taste in his mouth. No, she lied to save face. Lied to make him feel a cad for demanding access to her bed. Twelve years was too long to go without the touch of another.

He stepped forward, not sure what he wanted to do. Prove that he desired her as much as any other man might?

"It's natural to assume that you would find companionship with another after our separation. That is the usual course of things for many young ladies, I'm sure." Not that he'd had the acquaintance of many ladies. "Emma, you're shivering and your lips are turning blue. Come over by the fire. I have no ulterior motives."

Which was a lie, but he didn't want her to stand half a room away shivering. As if to prove a point, he shoved his hands into his pockets.

After a short hesitation, she walked over to the fire and basked in the heat. His desire to touch her won out over his promise of no ulterior motives. He wrapped his arms around her, his chest to her back, and he worked quickly at releasing each of the clasps on her shirt. Over her shoulder, he could see the creamy, white expanse of her chest. Gooseflesh rose over the exposed parts, the pink tips of her areolas showing through the wet chemise above the uppermost edge of the corset.

Good Lord, he wanted to taste her. He brushed the back of his hand over the swell of her bosom—they were as soft as they looked. He thought about holding her captive with her hands behind her back. Thought about raising his other hand to peel the damp chemise aside, free her breast, and fill his hand with its softness.

So very tempting to see what she'd do with his advances, but her posture was stiff, unwelcoming.

Forcing himself to take a step back so he wasn't tempted to do everything he was picturing to his half-naked wife, he dropped his hands to his sides.

Willing his erection to subside seemed a hopeless venture.

"I knew I shouldn't have come closer," she whispered over her shoulder.

Longing filled her voice. Almost like an invitation to continue his advances despite her rigidity, despite her words of not wanting him near.

"I will not have you catching cold."

He had to clear his throat; his voice seemed to have lowered with his heightened arousal. He left her by the fire and opened the door. Wringing out the shirt, he stood there, hoping the chilly wind would cool his rising passions. It was still black as night outdoors; the sky flashed periodically with lightning.

"You might as well take off your skirts. You're soaked right through."

"I'll be fine."

If she wasn't in danger of becoming ill from all the dampness, he'd have left her to her own devices. For God's sake, he was her husband. She needn't be modest in his presence.

"The weather isn't letting up any. Stop being stubborn, Emma, and take off your damned clothes."

Her mouth dropped open with his demand. Had she expected him to continue begging for something that was for her well-being?

With a sigh, he sat on the edge of the cot and pulled his boots off, then untucked his shirt. He didn't plan to wear all his clothes for much longer. He'd like to strip his shirt off, too, but he wasn't about to show his wife the raw wound on his side or the erection straining against his smalls. He released the ties on his trousers and had to peel them from his skin.

She'd given him her back as soon as he started removing articles of clothing. Bitterness made him want to laugh.

Her arms were crossed over her chest, her pale fingers curled over each shoulder. The scoop at the back of the white chemise revealed pale skin. He wanted to push the scrap of linen off her shoulders and see what lay hidden beneath.

"The door is locked, and I've a craving to be filled from last night."

Her fingers clutched tighter to her shoulders, the tips turning white with the pressure. He could see the outline of her sharp shoulder blades and was tempted to lick the droplet of water sliding down her spine. He found the ties at the back of her skirt that held the material around her waist. He worked them loose and let the heavy mass of pleated material fall to the floor. The ties for the second layer were easier to loosen, and that, too, fell to the floor.

When she didn't respond or step out of the mess, he boldly suggested, "Take off your corset."

If she obeyed, he knew he'd not be able to keep his hands off her. What did it matter? They were alone and he did not like to be denied by the one woman who belonged to him.